PATTERN
OF
DEATH

PETER GEORGE

The right of Peter George to be identified as the
Author of the Work has been asserted by him in accordance
with the Copyright, Designs and Patents Act 1988.

© Copyright 1954 Peter George

This edition of Pattern of Death edited by David George.
© Copyright 2016 David George

Published by
Candy Jar Books
Mackintosh House, 136 Newport Road
Cardiff Bay, CF24 1DJ
www.candyjarbooks.co.uk

A catalogue record of this book is available
from the British Library

First published 1954, T.V. Boardman, London
British Bloodhound No. 85
Printed and bound in the UK by 4edge Limited

All rights reserved.
No part of this publication may be reproduced, stored in
a retrieval system, or transmitted at any time or by any
Means, electronic, mechanical, photocopying, recording or
otherwise without the prior permission of the copyright
holder. This book is sold subject to the condition that it shall
not by way of trade or otherwise be circulated without the
publisher's prior consent in any form of binding or cover
other than that in which it is published.

FOR MY MOTHER

Introduction

1954 was a pivotal year for thirty-year-old Peter George, not only as a fledgling crime fiction author, but also for his future prospects in the RAF. The outbreak of the Korean War in 1951 had prompted George to abandon his final year of an English Literature degree course at the University of Exeter in order to join the RAF Volunteer Reserve.

By early 1952 he was back as a Flying Officer training night fighter crews on the De Havilland Mosquito, Armstrong Whitworth Meteor and Gloster Javelin aircraft before eventually being posted to 141 Squadron, a unit of Fighter Command based at RAF Coltishall in Norfolk. He undertook more than one h
undred night-fighter training flights in the Meteor between May 1952 and August 1953.

Since the early 1950s the military threat posed by the emergence of 'Red China' had led to the Ministry of Defence placing a greater emphasis on the need for Chinese language skills. The newly promoted Flight Lieutenant George leapt at the chance to pursue fresh opportunities and in October 1953 he enrolled on a Chinese language course at the School of Oriental Languages in Russell Square, London, travelling each day from RAF accommodation in Willesden.

On 5th May 1954, as he neared the end of his course, Peter George received a contract for his second crime novel, *Pattern of Death*, inspired in part by his time at RAF Coltishall. In September 1954 he was posted to Air Headquarters, Hong Kong, ostensibly to allow him to continue with his language training at the university, though there have been suggestions that it was in fact a cover for surveillance of Chinese military radio broadcasts.

In October 1954 George's mother Gwen died of cervical cancer in Romford, but he chose not to return to the UK for the funeral, remaining with his wife and children in Hong Kong.

Pattern of Death was published in November 1954. The book was dedicated to his mother.

Peter George's experiences whilst in Hong Kong, including a brush with death during the Kowloon Riots on 10th October 1956, would inspire his third novel, *Hong Kong Kill*.

Rhys Lloyd, 2016.

Prologue

It began in the cold heights over East Anglia. People on the ground pausing to look up in the brittle sunshine of a late spring afternoon were unable to distinguish the black speck of the aircraft. They saw only a white line, pencil-slim and vivid against the blue of the sky, probing swiftly forward like the head of a hunting snake.

And as the head moved further forward, so the white line swelled and thickened as the belly of a snake thickens, leaving rolled vertebrae of cloud where no cloud had been before.

The cloud became an intricate series of loops and whorls across the sky, a transient pattern in filigreed vapour chased boldly upon a pale blue backcloth.

The watchers on the ground heard the remote whisper of turbojet engines echoing faintly and yet triumphantly in the empty wastelands of the upper air. Then having watched for a while they hurried home for tea, perhaps bearing with them some consciousness of the shining beauty of the pattern.

They could not know that the pattern, already dispersing and spreading, was yet in some ways permanent.

No one knew that it was a preliminary design for a pattern of death.

1

To Winterley the pattern was neither a thing of beauty nor of death. Its curves and twists were merely a visible indication of the turning efficiency of the aircraft he was flying. He rolled the fighter smoothly out of a turn, flew back into the thickening condensation trail he had left behind him, watching the fibrous wisps slide past the clear perspex of his canopy.

His gaze flicked swiftly and with practiced efficiency round the banked instruments on the panel. The Machmeter was steady at 0.9 — nine tenths of the speed of sound.

Always, at these heights and speeds, it was to the Machmeter that the pilot looked first. No longer did one talk of speed in terms of miles or knots per hour. The reference was always to the speed of the aircraft in relation to the speed of sound at the particular height the aircraft was flying. The Machmeter automatically computed this for the pilot, expressing the answer as a decimal fraction of one. And of course when the Machmeter showed 1.0 it meant that the speed of sound had been reached.

Winterley had no doubt at all that the KB–12 would not only reach the speed of sound but considerably exceed it.

He pushed the throttles forward slightly, moved the

stick gently to the right. The movement was effortless, a mere caress of the fingertips — powerful servomotors operated the control surfaces of the fighter and they were instantly obedient to the touch of a hand on the stick. The starboard wing dropped quickly until he was looking past it straight down to the distant ground. He eased the stick back, pressing it toward him, watching the nose of the fighter whip round the haze of the horizon as the turn tightened.

The heaviness of centrifugal force began to crush him into his seat, forcing his chin down and draining the blood from behind his eyes, sliding a heavy veil of greyness in front of him. He pulled the stick back further, as far as it would go, his hands heavy as lead as the accelerometer passed the 6-G mark. The greyness darkened, shading steadily into black. He eased the stick forward and to the left, rolled the aircraft smoothly out of the turn.

He glanced at the Machmeter, saw it was still reading 0.9 and that the fighter had lost no speed in the turn.

Behind the clinging rubber of his oxygen mask he smiled. This was only the third flight the aircraft had made, the first time it had ever been to these altitudes. But already he knew. This one was good, really good.

He glanced again round the banked instruments in the cockpit, noting the normality of the instrument readings. The altimeter needle was steady at thirty-five thousand.

Suddenly he reached forward, pressed the transmitter button of his radio-telephone.

'Control, Bluebird One. Everything's just right, I'm going through.'

He released the transmitter button, waited anxiously for the dry crackle of the reply. After fifteen seconds it came. He recognised the voice of Fellows, the plane's chief designer.

Fellows simply said, 'Good Luck'.

Winterley glanced round, looking for the sprawled mass of the airfield's works and the white gash of the runway, saw them fifteen miles or so to starboard.

Pulling back the stick he climbed steeply, with the Machmeter steady at 0.7, until the altimeter showed forty-five thousand. There he levelled out, turned steeply to starboard to line up with the airfield, rolled out of the turn and eased forward into a twenty-degree dive.

He made a brief transmission to the ground, telling them that he was starting his run, then pushed the throttles slowly but firmly forward until they were fully open.

Ahead of him he could just distinguish the works and airfield buildings, an indistinct blur of grey and white through the smoky cloud of the lower atmosphere. Then he forgot them and gave all his attention to the Machmeter and the altimeter, transmitting readings continuously so that the tape recorders at the airfield would have a record of his readings.

The altimeter was unwinding rapidly as the acceleration of the aircraft pressed him back into his seat, and in the first five thousand feet of the dive his speed built up from 0.7 to 0.94.

Then at thirty-nine thousand and 0.97 Mach he felt the sudden impact of the shock wave as the speed of the air over the wing surfaces reached the speed of sound.

The whole airframe shook, vibrating and juddering

heavily as though it were being pounded by a vast hammer. He held the stick firmly forward, fighting a tendency of the port wing to snatch and drop, his body vibrating and shaking with the judder of the aircraft. And then, as suddenly as it had come, the vibration had gone.

The Machmeter had passed 1.0 — was still advancing — and the fighter was flying smoothly at a speed faster than sound.

Down to thirty-four thousand now and the needle creeping steadily round the dial. He kept the stick forward, letting the speed increase, watching the incredibly fast unwinding of the altimeter. At twenty-five thousand he had reached 1.15 Mach.

He pulled the throttles gently back, eased the stick toward him. The nose began to rise and he felt the force of gravity again, crushing him down momentarily and obscuring the horizon in a smudge of grey. Then the weight disappeared, the greyness dispersed, and the fighter was flying straight and level at eighteen thousand, losing speed rapidly.

As the needle dropped through 1.0 Mach the vibration came again, but less pronounced now and shorter lived, fading to nothing as the needle went down past 0.97.

Winterley sent a message to the ground that the run was finished and he was returning. Not until he had finished speaking and there was a heavy silence in the cockpit did he realise that his voice had been loud, almost a shout, and that he was soaking with sweat.

He selected air brakes out, hunching forward against his straps as the fighter lost speed. He left the air brakes out and descended at eight thousand feet per minute in a tight circle round the airfield. Within minutes he was flying downwind of the runway at fifteen hundred feet, working through the landing checks — air brakes back in, fuel levels and jet-pipe temperatures checked, undercarriage down with two hundred knots on the clock and a quarter flap as he turned into the base leg.

On the instrument panel three green lights winked on to tell him the undercarriage was down and locked. Seven hundred feet now, a hundred and sixty knots, and full flap going down as he turned on to the final approach. A brief transmission to the tower to tell them he was on finals. Then the runway slanting in front of him, a broad white slash across the green of the airfield. Past the high trees on the starboard of the approach, across the perimeter fence at a hundred and forty knots, the runway wide and straight before him. Over the end, ten feet up, chop the power off and check — check, hold the nose up.

Faintly at first, through the engines' roaring low noise, came the shrieking contact of rubber with concrete. Again the scream of rubber and the loud rumbling of the main wheels on the runway — hard, springy rumbling with the nose still up and the nose-wheel still clear.

The nose dropping now, slowly at first, then quickly in the final foot, hitting the concrete with a solid impact and a brief high-pitched squeal all of its own.

Touch of brake and let her run. Another touch, and another, hard braking until the speed was down to a comfortable level. Down now and safe. Let her run on easily to the end of the runway, turn off to starboard with a touch of the port throttle, taxi slowly on to the wide concrete apron in front of the hangar.

As the plane rolled along the smooth perimeter track Winterley released his straps and slid back the canopy. He let his oxygen mask flap clear of his face, savouring the exquisite coolness of a breeze over his damp skin. In front of the hangar, clustering on the concrete apron, he could see a crowd of people waiting for him, the men who had transmuted the lines on a blueprint into potent life.

When he drew nearer he saw that people were smiling, waving to him. He swung the fighter round on to the apron, taxied her up to the mechanic who was marshalling him in and braked her to a stop. He pressed down on the high pressure cocks and heard the blasting of the turbines die away into the near silent revolutions of the jet's air-intake blades.

Then Fellows was bending over the cockpit as Winterley half raised himself.

'Well done, Tommy. No trouble?'

Winterley grinned.

'Trouble? Not with this one, Bill. She went through like a dream. A little more power and she'll do it straight and level. Quite a lot of buffeting between nine seven and one. Get rid of that and she's the answer.'

'We'll get rid of it,' Fellows said, 'There are drinks waiting in the tower.'

'Don't think I couldn't use one.'

Winterley heaved himself out of the cockpit, dropped lightly to the ground.

'There are just one or two points, Bill...' he began talking as they passed through the crowd of technicians who were swarming round the fighter.

In the tower they discussed the fighter at length, their

drinks forgotten in the enthusiasm of the moment.

On the concrete apron the silver skin of the fighter was almost invisible beneath the number of technicians who were checking her over inch by inch. The KB–12 dominated the airfield and the factory. All interest was on her, all anxiety concentrated on her progress.

But interest was not confined to the factory. The fighter's development had been watched over with interest, and even more anxiety, in other quarters. In at least one of those quarters the interest was by no means friendly.

At a certain Embassy in London reports were received and duly transmitted to that strange semi-oriental city many hundreds of miles to the East.

There they were evaluated in the light of photographs that had been secured of the blueprints of the KB–12. Action was decided, and one of their best jet-fighter designers was sent to London to discuss the technical means of dispelling this new menace.

Rakiev travelled incognito and was whisked without ceremony straight from the airfield to the Embassy in a large, curtained limousine.

Two days after his arrival, Rakiev left the Embassy in the care of a contact-man named Kubin. He was told that his contact, *Nicholas* — no one at the Embassy knew him by any other name — never came near the Embassy. Meetings with him were only conducted at a rendezvous which Nicholas himself had selected.

It was four o'clock on a late June afternoon when Kubin and Rakiev went through the main entrance of a small apartment house in Kensington.

2

Rakiev, standing well back in the dimness of the small entrance hall, saw the girl first.

She paused for a moment, looking down at them from the top of the stairs. Then she began to come down, unhurried and graceful. She was very attractive, Rakiev thought. Above a crisp white blouse her face and throat were tanned to a warm golden brown. Her hair was sleekly blonde and her thighs full and exciting as they moved under the tightness of a fawn linen skirt.

He watched her pause momentarily as she came opposite Kubin, noticed the slight inclination of her head. Then she was gone through the door of the house, the clicking of high heels diminishing as she walked away. Rakiev followed Kubin up the stairs, obeying implicitly the instructions he had been given at the Embassy. Kubin was the expert at all this, the most experienced contact man on the staff. Rakiev's instructions had been simple. Just follow Kubin. Do exactly as he does. Do not speak unless absolutely necessary. Just follow.

They went up to the top floor of the house. There the stairs terminated in a small landing with a single door. Obviously the apartment occupied the entire top floor. Rakiev followed Kubin through a minute lobby into a large, well-furnished room that looked out on the sunny square. As he walked across the thick pile of grey carpet he noticed a dining alcove on the right, holding a table and four chairs. He walked straight to the window, stood gazing down through white gauze curtains on to the square.

Kubin placed two chairs facing the window, a yard or so from it and from each other. They sat down on the chairs, Kubin on the right and Rakiev on the left. It had been emphasised to Rakiev that he was not on any account to attempt to see the man he was meeting. Nicholas would arrive, they would talk, Nicholas would go. That was the pattern.

Rakiev glanced curiously to his right, saw that Kubin's face was rigid and set, that he was gazing fixedly at the window. He noticed that though he himself was suffering no discomfort from the warmth of the fine summer day Kubin, who should surely be acclimatised, was sweating freely. He wondered why it should be. Then, jerking his mind away from the unimportant detail of Kubin, he concentrated on the matter he would discuss with Nicholas. Kubin was merely the contact, the man who would introduce him to Nicholas. It was between himself and Nicholas that the real decision concerning the fighter would be worked out. He began to think about the fighter and the menace it represented.

Rakiev would have been surprised by Kubin's thoughts. There was really no reason why Kubin should have been hating him so bitterly. But Rakiev could not know that Kubin hated anyone who brought him into contact with Nicholas. He hated them because he hated Nicholas. And he hated Nicholas because he was very frightened of him.

*

Now, reaching for a handkerchief to dab his damp face, Kubin glanced sideways at Rakiev, saw that he was composed and untroubled. Blast him, Kubin thought wildly, blast him and the rest of them. It was easy for them, the people like Rakiev. There would be no sudden recall for them, no escort of big-shouldered men caring for them solicitously on the aircraft and whisking them away to some place of unimaginable horror. Some place where they would be left to wait, and wonder what had been reported about them.

The minutes dragged on in the thick stillness of the flat. Outside Kubin heard a clock chime, and then as the notes died away he heard the sound of the outer door of the flat closing. He became aware that the muscles along the backs of his hands were twitching uncontrollably, that a heavy sweat was breaking out on his face. He fought desperately for control, struggling against the accretion of fear that the long years of suspicion had left piled within him.

Rakiev, too, heard the soft click of the outer door. Then a rattle at the door of the room, a creak as it swung open. Tiny noises magnified in the silence of the flat. Out of the corner of his eye he saw Kubin stiffen perceptibly, his fists clenching as though he were a marionette and the noise of the door opening had operated a string which jerked him into rigidity. Rakiev heard the soft plump of footsteps on the carpet, the rustle of cloth as someone sat down. He waited for Nicholas to speak.

'Good afternoon, gentlemen. Not too bored waiting for me I hope. Ah, Kubin, and how are you? Still enjoying your stay in London?'

The voice was soft and smooth, in spite of the harshness of the Slavonic syllables. Kubin wondered whether he had not detected a shade of emphasis on the word 'still'.

Kubin coughed, spoke from behind his raised hand. 'Permit me to introduce Dr Rakiev.'

'Dr Rakiev, of course,' Nicholas said, 'I know you well by reputation, Doctor, please forgive the rather peculiar circumstances of this meeting. Perhaps we can meet more informally one day over there? How are things over there, by the way?'

Rakiev said, 'Very good indeed. Everything is going as satisfactorily as always.' His voice was slow and deliberate, not unpleasant.

'As always,' Nicholas murmured. 'Except for one little thing, I understand, Doctor. Is it not so?'

'The new British fighter,' Rakiev said. 'We are disturbed about it. The details of performance you sent are alarming. Naturally, it's only a question of time before we catch up, but at the moment…'

'Quite,' Nicholas said. 'At the moment. At the moment we have nothing that can touch it. Correct?'

Rakiev said, stiffly, 'Correct. We have worked very carefully through the photostats of the blueprints you were able to get for us. We believe we can suggest a course of action to deal with this aircraft.'

Nicholas said quickly, 'You do realise I can't do much to stop production, don't you, Doctor? Oh, a small stoppage here, a token delay there, but nothing significant. I hope you were informed of that.'

'Yes. We understand that. However, we are convinced that it is possible to interfere with production in another way, the best way of all. We feel that should certain things happen the machine would never go into production.'

Nicholas said, 'I don't follow you, Doctor. Perhaps you'll explain in detail?'

'Well, of course it's difficult for anyone who doesn't know the technical processes of aircraft production to understand, but we put ourselves in the position of the British and asked ourselves what we would do if certain things happened. You told us that there are two prototype models, one flying and one almost ready to fly.'

'As a matter of fact the second model is flying already.'

'So? Well then, we examined the position as it would be if the first model crashed, broke up in the air perhaps. These very high-speed aircraft sometimes do that you know. You will remember the de Havilland 110 incident at the Farnborough Show in 1952?'

'Most interesting,' Nicholas murmured. 'I saw it.'

'Indeed? Then you will know what I mean. Now, if the prototype of *this* fighter were to disintegrate in the air, we think that no one would be too alarmed. They would check through the design, fail to find a flaw and continue with the trials on the second machine. But suppose something happened to that one too. What would they do then?'

Nicholas said, 'I don't know. Build another I suppose.'

'Ah,' Rakiev said, 'but that is just what they *wouldn't* do. Especially if the second one broke up under roughly the same conditions as the first, and — this is the important part — after approximately the same number of flying hours. They would literally pull the design to pieces, analyse each part of it to find the basic flaw. But of one thing we are sure — they wouldn't dare gamble on putting the machine into production and committing their assembly lines until they had found that flaw and eliminated it. And now do you see? They will not find the flaw because there isn't one.'

There was silence in the flat for thirty seconds. Kubin, staring blankly at the window, was barely conscious of what was being said. As usual when he was near Nicholas he was dull and inert, too afraid of him and the people he represented to care about anything else.

Nicholas broke the silence at last. 'I see what you mean, Doctor Rakiev. The flaw will have been provided by us. I take it you have some means in mind which will leave no trace of interference?'

'Of course,' Rakiev said. 'I brought three technical devices with me which will do what we require. One for each aircraft and one spare. They are at the Embassy.'

'I see. Well, Doctor, I think I can help you. You understand that a thing like this will commit a large part of my resources. In two or three days I should be able to meet you again and let you know whether I am in a position to get results. We can discuss the technical aspects of the matter then. You are quite sure that if we succeed it will interfere with production?'

'Of course,' Rakiev said impatiently. 'Even if it doesn't mean the scrapping of the whole design another prototype would have to be built. Possibly you don't realise that that would delay final production for months, maybe years. We must have time to produce a fighter as good. We can do it — but I repeat we must have time.'

'All right, I'll let you know when we can meet again,

Doctor.' Nicholas paused. 'Anything else for me Kubin?'

'Nothing.' Kubin spoke stiffly, harshly, doing his utmost not to betray the fear that was inside him. 'Except the briefcase as usual.'

'Very well. Observe the usual delay before you leave. And make quite certain you take the customary precautions on the way back.' With his voice softer and more menacing, Nicholas added, 'Don't go making any silly mistakes will you, Kubin?'

Kubin swallowed. He felt a wave of sickness sweep through him.

'Certainly not. I won't make any mistakes.'

'Good. And now, Doctor, you must excuse me. I shall have a busy time ahead of me contacting people and arranging things. Two or three days, then.'

They heard Nicholas move quietly out of the room, the dull flat sound as the outer door closed.

For ten minutes they sat in complete silence. Then Kubin stirred, glanced at his wristwatch. 'Time to go.'

As they got up Rakiev looked at him curiously. Kubin was pale and drawn. His face was moist with sweat, and there was a hunted look in his eyes that was disturbing to Rakiev.

'He's one of *them*, of course?' Rakiev said slowly.

Kubin nodded, turned away abruptly to replace the two chairs at the table in the alcove. Lying on the table was a briefcase, but not the same briefcase as Kubin had placed there when he entered the flat. Nicholas had taken that with him, and Kubin would deliver Nicholas' case to the Embassy. The same procedure was repeated at every meeting for the passage of documents and information.

He touched Rakiev's arm, urged him out of the flat, down the stairs and out into the bright sunlight of the square. As they walked along they passed the girl whose flat they had been using. She walked briskly past them with no sign of recognition, her heels beating a quick tattoo on the pavement.

Kubin suddenly said, 'I was afraid you were going to say something in the flat. It's wired, you know.'

'Wired? Are you sure?'

'They always are when those people use them. Of course, you don't have to worry. They need you too badly. But me…?' he broke off abruptly, said flatly, 'Yes, it's wired all right.'

They walked on towards Kensington High Street.

Rakiev broke the short silence, 'Do you think he can do it?'

Kubin laughed, a short bitter laugh, completely mirthless. 'Of course he can do it, but not without permission from over there. He'll ask them formally, just for the record in case it ever crops up later.' He licked his lips nervously, feeling the warmth and dryness of his mouth. 'They have no mercy on anyone who slips up, not even one of their own people.'

'But surely,' Rakiev said, 'the authority I already have is sufficient. Surely the Ambassador can give the necessary instructions?'

'The Ambassador? Oh no, not the Ambassador. He takes his orders from the Secretariat. And they take theirs from the overseas division of those people, which means Nicholas since he's the chief over here. Don't rely on the Embassy, Doctor. It's just an anomaly now, a relic of the good old days before the Secret Police became the State.'

He stopped abruptly, looking at Rakiev with an expression in which anger was suddenly replaced by fear. For a short while the two men looked at each other. Then, as though actuated by a single master thought, they turned away, suddenly mutually suspicious.

Kubin was thinking, Have I said too much? What if he reports me when he gets back? Why was I such a fool? Why? Why?

Rakiev was thinking, He's scared. Just like the rest of them. All scared. Or is it just possible he was instructed to speak like that? To see what I would say? Better be safe.

'I'm sure the importance of the project will be recognised,' Rakiev said, his voice cold and impersonal.

Kubin responded, 'Yes, of course. I'm sure it will.'

He wondered, anxiously, whether the coldness in Rakiev's voice meant he would be reported. He thought probably not, but another little item of fear had been added to the many items that had frayed his nerves for the past few years.

The two men turned into the long arcade leading to Kensington High Street Station on the first part of their circuitous journey to the place where the Embassy car would pick them up. In their neat, dark, town suits they were quite inconspicuous among the jostling crowds. They did not speak again on the way back to the Embassy.

3

Kubin might well have been right when he assured Rakiev that Nicholas would make no move without consulting his superiors back home. It was a matter of policy, something about which junior officials like Kubin could only speculate. But whether Nicholas consulted his superiors or not, it later became clear that he began to act very soon after the meeting in the flat.

He issued instructions concerning two men. The first of these was called Williamson, the other Driscoll.

Williamson was a man of simple pleasures. He had led a full and active life, and it had not proved unprofitable. He was small, neat, unimpressive in appearance. But as he walked quickly down the steps of the Metropolitan Line at Baker Street he moved with a certain elasticity in his step which told of agility. Even now, when he had virtually retired, he kept in good physical trim, and that in spite of the simplest of his pleasures, which was the sampling of draught Bass at various of the bars which sold that particular beer.

He glanced at the indicator at the bottom of the steps, saw that the next train for North Harrow left from platform four. He frowned with annoyance as he saw that it was one of the old types, with faded, brown coaches divided into small compartments. He looked back at the indicator, saw that if he let this train go he would have to miss yet another before he got one on his line.

He looked at his watch. Ten past eleven. He shrugged, walked along the train looking for an occupied compartment. This did not indicate any sociability on his part. He did not care greatly for people, excepting always those kindred souls with whom he consumed his Bass at such widely dispersed taverns as the Cock and Woolpack in the City, the Imperial at Leicester Square, or the Chiltern Court just outside Baker Street itself. Yet he always travelled in the big, well lit, red coaches if possible, and on the rare occasions he took one of the older trains, he always travelled in the company of other people.

He paused at a suitable compartment, which already contained four other people. For only a second he hesitated before climbing in. But in that second he had assured himself that the people were harmless. Williamson was a man of great experience. He had an uncanny knack for self-protection.

In his long career — during which he had frequently committed such minor indiscretions as selling certain information to two interested parties, while assuring each that they were securing the exclusive rights — that knack had stood him in good stead. He never took unnecessary risks. And, to a man of his experience, travelling alone in a compartment on a suburban train was definitely an unnecessary risk.

Williamson took a seat in the far corner, opposite a lanky youth and his giggling, high-breasted companion. He opened an evening paper and devoted himself to a study of the racing results. Perhaps the amount of beer he had consumed was larger than usual. Perhaps the stuffiness of the dingy compartment was oppressive. Within a minute he was nodding in the corner, not asleep, but certainly not fully awake and alert. He was unaware of the two men who walked heavily past the door, and settled themselves further along the train.

Half an hour later, after Williamson had left the station and was walking home through streets empty and dark with the quiet indifference of a suburban midnight, he became aware of them. As the two shapes bulked out of darkness that was suddenly hostile, he knew that at last he had made a mistake.

As the arm went round his face he fought desperately against it, convinced that if he could only speak he would still be able to save himself. But the arm was strong, and he was small, and the man who wielded the knife was quick and expert.

It was over in a few seconds. There had been no sound, no commotion. The two men bent over Williamson, quickly collected everything from his pockets. They straightened up, satisfied that he was dead, and walked silently back along the road to a place where they could summon a car to meet them.

Williamson lay quite still where they had left him, the blood oozing thickly from the gash in his throat that gaped like a second mouth below his chin. He had been dead for nearly an hour when a policeman came upon his body and by that time the two men who had killed him were back in town.

The second man about whom Nicholas had given

instructions had already been forced into a large saloon-car that had lurked by a back street pub and was now being driven eastwards through London.

4

Driscoll leaned back into the corner of the big saloon car, relaxing against the softness of leather upholstery. His mouth was dry and sour. He ran a questing tongue round it, conscious of the thick whisky fuzz in his throat. He wondered where they were taking him, leaning back with closed eyes and wishing the thick mist in his mind would disperse.

The car rolled on, jerkily over the cobbles at Stratford, smoothly through Ilford Broadway, with the pavements becoming gradually emptier, the traffic lighter. Driscoll leaned forward, pushing his right hand deep in his jacket pocket in search of cigarettes. The man sitting beside him tensed. As the car flicked through brief pools of light thrown by successive street lamps Driscoll saw the dull glint of the gun push nearer to him. Outside the rain had increased from a drizzle to a heavy downpour.

Driscoll said, 'A cigarette, that's all. Just a cigarette.' His voice was deep, thick, a polyglot voice with no particular accent except for a faint background that might have been Canadian or American.

The man sitting beside the driver hunched big shoulders in silhouette against the windscreen. Without turning his head he said, 'Right, friend, a cigarette. Just that and nothing else. You with me, friend?'

'Yeah,' Driscoll said. He produced a crumpled packet,

conscious of the minute scrutiny of the man with the gun, selected a cigarette and lit it with a silver lighter. He inhaled deeply, dragging the welcome harshness of smoke into his lungs. He slipped the packet back into his pocket, kept the lighter in the palm of his right hand.

Romford market place slid by, bare and hostile in the rain, and a few minutes later the car crossed an arterial road, headed up a small hill, turned right twice.

Driscoll felt the speed of the car decrease, then the slight jar of brakes. He saw that they were stationary in a narrow lane between high hedges. Then the driver cut off the lights, and all was dark except for the small glow of his cigarette. He heard the door of the car open, a vague shuffling noise, the door closing. Then a hard white light hit his eyes, completely dazzling him.

The big man said, 'Just a talk is all, friend. A talk with Mr Smith here and we ride you back to town. All friendly and no trouble at all if you don't start any. You with me?'

Driscoll said, 'Believe it or not I am. But you've got the script a bit wrong. I don't talk with anyone while there's a light in my face. Even if his name is Smith.'

A new voice broke in. 'Let's assume that part, Driscoll. Keep the light on him.'

Smith paused, looking carefully at Driscoll, examining him minutely in the brilliant light of the torch. He saw a man who could have been anywhere between his early thirties and early forties, with a hard, tanned face that showed only a very slight puffiness beneath the eyes. The neck was thick and heavily muscled, and the shoulders spread widely beneath a material that had been very good when the suit was new. Smith thought that that would have been several years before. He looked at the face again, noticed that its innate ruthlessness was emphasised by a thin line of scar tissue running down from the corner of the right eye to just below the lobe of the right ear. Somehow the scar was not in the least disfiguring, possibly because it toned so well with Driscoll's generally hard appearance. Smith could imagine that women would find Driscoll very attractive.

Smith coughed, then spoke in a voice as cold and dry as a wind over a frozen lake. 'You've got it wrong, Driscoll. This is no social chat. There's a proposition to discuss. It pays off in cash. More cash than you've seen for a long time. If you're not interested say so now and don't waste our time. And the light stays on, because I'm not taking any chances with you. Maybe it hasn't occurred to you we could quite easily encourage you to talk, if we happened to feel that way.'

Driscoll drew hard on his cigarette, reached down for the ashtray he had seen on the door of the car, stubbed the cigarette out. 'Cash is a thing I'm always interested in. But not to the extent you think. An' stop trying to push muscle at me. If you don't put the light out I don't discuss anything. If you want to start something you can start it any time you like. But don't ever think you're going to scare me.'

Smith looked at him carefully again, wondering whether the things he had heard about Driscoll were true. Apart from the puffiness under the eyes he could see no sign of any disintegration. He thought for a moment, then he said, 'All right, Driscoll, I'll do it your way, just to show you we want to be friendly. I think I'm rather glad you're still as hard as you were. It makes you a better business proposition.' His voice was less cold and remote. As he finished speaking the light went out.

The brilliance in Driscoll's eyelids died away, the little red veins disappearing into blackness. His eyes hurt, but he kept them open, getting them accustomed to the dark as quickly as possible. 'All right, what's the proposition?'

Smith said, 'You have some particular talents we happen to need in the near future. We'd need about three weeks of your time, and we'd pay quite a lot of money for them. Interested?'

'I might be. Depends on three things — who you are, what you need done, how much money you'll pay. Let's discuss those little details.'

Smith said nastily, 'Don't be stupid, you know who we are. If it'll refresh your memory we approached you once before. Valparaiso in forty-eight. Incidentally, I understand you were very rude to our representative. But you had more money then, you weren't quite so pushed.'

'Maybe,' Driscoll said slowly. 'An' maybe I just didn't like his face. Now let's understand a bit more. The next thing's the job. Don't bother giving me the gab about party ethics because I've heard it before and it impresses me like a bag of birdseed. Keep it for your intellectual amateurs if they're still kicking around. The job and the price.'

The voice said, 'No go, Driscoll. Not the job anyway. I don't even know it myself. The money's all right. Five hundred, with half in advance, and a guarantee it won't take up more than three weeks of your time. You get the advance now, you're contacted when the job comes up, you pull it and collect the remainder. It's simple. Then you go somewhere you can get yourself in the chips again. Just too simple.'

'Yeah,' Driscoll said, 'but I'm not. Come around twenty years ago and I might be that simple. But not now — especially when I know who I'm dealing with. There are three words in my book simpler. Money in advance.'

'We don't write that kind of book. It might tempt people to take the cash and decide to go on holiday without doing the job. Not' — the voice got very edgy and cold — 'that anyone who tried it would get far. One of the advantages of a worldwide organisation if you see what I mean. Always someone handy to point out the error that's been made. I believe our proposition's quite fair. Think about it.'

'I don't need to think. The answer's no. Let me tell you how I see it. I'm an expert and you need an expert badly for something. So you'll pay. Real money, not the kind of peanuts you've been talking. Also, you'll pay in advance. Otherwise no deal. An' put that on the wire back east with my compliments.'

The man said, slowly, 'You're bargaining, Driscoll. You're broke and you're desperate, but you're still bargaining. Maybe we could push the price up just a little if we really felt we could trust you. You don't seem to realise we can be very reasonable with people we like. How much did you have in mind?'

'A thousand, paid in cash in advance. Also, I reserve the right to refund the money and turn the job down if I don't like it. An' brother, I'm not bargaining. If you need me badly you'll just have to pay to get me. It's the law of supply and demand — you know? I've got it, you want it, pay and you get it. That's the way I work.'

'So does a whore.'

Driscoll grinned. 'But on a smaller scale. Though I did once meet a blonde in Buenos Aires who…'

'All right,' the voice cut in coldly. 'I'll pass on what you've said. I don't think you'll get it. Maybe we could push the five hundred up a bit. Or again, maybe we could find someone else. I'll give you a card with two words on it. If you want to contact us insert it in the personals of the *Evening Standard*, with a number we can ring. Think it over, Driscoll. Five hundred would buy you a passage somewhere where they're not so fussy about the ways you make money as they are in England. It would buy you a new passport as well.'

'So you know about that too?' Driscoll's eyes were accustomed to the dark now. He edged the lighter forward in the palm of his right hand until he could feel the plunger with his thumb.

'We know everything about you. That's why I'm quite certain you'll decide to contact us. Here's the card.'

Driscoll heard the rustle of an arm reaching over the front seat, saw the vague white flicker of pasteboard. He reached forward, felt the card with his left hand, went past it to grab the man's wrist and jerk savagely. In the same movement he thrust his right hand forward, flicked the lighter into flame. He saw a wide face, the mouth open with surprise, a large and bushy moustache. Then he was pulled forward against the front seat and the lighter went out.

He released the wrist, swung the back edge of his left hand viciously in a chopping arc at Smith's neck. He felt it crunch on bone, but dully through cloth, so that he knew he had missed the neck and hit only the shoulder. At the same time he felt a dull pain impact on his right temple, spread instantly and sickeningly over his head. He swung again and missed completely, and again the dull powerful impact thudded on him. Then he was going backwards, suddenly somersaulting through a door open behind him, out of the car and tumbling backwards into the road.

Driscoll felt the roughness of gravel beneath his face, and then a violent jerking pain in his head as someone kicked it. This time the pain did not last but disappeared into a thick greyness through which a muffled voice at a great distance, said, *'That's all.'*

He was vaguely conscious of hands turning him over, and then a pool of inky blackness brimmed over its banks and flooded him, engulfing him in darkness.

Driscoll woke. He sat up in the lane, holding both hands to his head. It was an area of dull pain, with some crazy thing whirling madly inside it. The whirling thing dropped to his stomach, rose to his head, dropped to his stomach again. He leaned forward, retching in violent spasms. Afterwards he felt slightly better.

He struggled unsteadily to his feet. The car had gone and he was quite alone in the darkness of the lane. The rain was still falling, though more gently now, and his suit was soaking. He began to walk down the lane, looking for a way back to the main road and transport to town. After a while he reached the first of a series of street lights, knew he was getting near the main road.

He stopped under the light to feel through his pockets for money to take him back. He thumbed through them rapidly, finding no money. In his breast pocket was the lighter he had dropped in the car. And a piece of white pasteboard. In the hard glare of the electric light he could read the words: *Ready business*. Just that, nothing more.

Driscoll swore, cursing with easy fluency until he had exhausted himself. He lifted the card to tear it across, realised at exactly that moment that his shoes were letting in water and his feet were wet. He realised he was wearing his last good suit, that it was wet through and ruined. That he had no money with him for transport. That he had no money. Slowly and thoughtfully he looked at the two words, repeating them. Then he ripped the card into little pieces that he scattered as he went along. He moved off down the road following the lights, a big man moving easily and lightly in spite of the pain the earlier whiskies and the slugging had left in his head.

He came ultimately to the main road, and later on he picked up a lift into town from one of the lorries heading to London from the eastern counties.

5

Winterley came out through the arched station entrance, stood blinking in the early evening sunlight. After the grimy dimness of the terminus even the Euston Road seemed light and attractive.

He stood for a moment at the top of the steps, relishing the weekend before him away from flying and the incessant nagging whine of jet engines. It was good to contemplate a weekend in London. Not so good, perhaps, as Paris or Brussels, but still good. Brussels. He thought with a momentary regret of Brussels, and the little apartment near Cinquantanerre Park where he had spent his leaves with the long-legged showgirl from the Americaine. Then the regret vanished in the prospect of the weekend, and he descended the steps lightly, his bag swinging loosely from his right hand.

He turned right along the Euston Road, hailed a cruising taxi. The little man who had been standing on the corner watching him increased his pace. He strolled past in time to hear Winterley give the address of an hotel in Clarges Street. Then the taxi was pulling out and round, turning a full semicircle and merging with the stream of westbound traffic.

The little man walked on until he came to a telephone kiosk. He put his three pennies in the slot and dialled a Grosvenor number. At the other end he heard the high-pitched double buzz, then a voice repeating the number. He spoke rapidly for thirty seconds. When he had finished there was a click at the other end. The little man replaced the receiver, came out of the kiosk and crossed the road to the pub on the corner.

After the third pint he felt he had washed away most of the dust that had accumulated in his throat from a day spent on hot, dusty trains.

Winterley left his hotel a little after seven o'clock. He had shaved and changed into fawn gabardine slacks, a cream shirt with bright club tie, dark blue blazer and dark brown suede shoes. As he leaned back in the cool interior of a taxi heading for Knightsbridge he smoked a cigarette with enjoyment, catching occasional, intriguing glimpses of girls in light summer dresses walking along Piccadilly and in Green Park. He was quite unaware of the small black saloon that was following the taxi.

He decided The Scarlet Fish had changed very little. The cocktail bar had been redecorated but there were still the high red-leather stools round the semicircular bar. The mural was still the same exciting swirl of mermaids and strange fish picked out in red on a black background. He went to his favourite position at the far end of the bar, where he could see everyone in the room without turning his head.

He finished his first drink, nodded to the barman for a refill, watched the two measures of whisky plop slowly into the glass followed by the other half of a bottle of ginger and a glittering cube of ice. Over in the far corner of the room there were two girls, attractive girls. He looked at them carefully. But even as he took the first sip of his drink they were standing up, collecting their handbags, leaving the bar in a soft swirl of rustling taffeta. He thought it was a pity, but there was lots of time yet.

A man came in through the door of the bar. He was tall, well built, wearing a light grey suit with a white shirt and a dark blue tie. He took the stool next to Winterley, ordered a large whisky.

Winterley was vaguely annoyed. He raised his glass again, looked over the top of it in time to see a petite highly-coloured redhead walk trippingly through the door to a table. Winterley studied her closely, deciding she definitely had something. But not for him, he realised, as he saw a man walk up to her table and sit down while the redhead leaned toward him with a smile. He felt cheated, grimaced into his glass. Suddenly he became aware that the man next to him was watching closely and was now smiling at him. Winterley put his glass down.

'It's always the way, isn't it?' The man said.

Winterley looked at him. The man had brown hair, a wide, pleasant face, and a large brown moustache. He grinned. 'Not always, just most of the time. But there are exceptions.'

The man smiled. He turned to Winterley as though struck by a sudden thought. 'Look here, don't think I'm being rude but I've a feeling we've met before. In the service perhaps?'

Winterley looked at him, shook his head slowly. 'Can't place you,' he said.

He wondered just what was coming next. Sometimes it was a request for a small loan, sometimes the feeling of loneliness that a big city accentuated, and which made a man want to drink with another man rather than alone. Once it had even been… But this man didn't look that type.

Winterley went on, 'Can't place you I'm afraid, but that doesn't mean a thing. My memory's shocking. Where were you?'

'Oh, all over. But mainly the desert and Italy. Here, wait a minute that's it. Italy. You were in Italy weren't you?'

'That's right. Forty-three to forty-five.'

'I knew it. Never forget a face. You were with Desert Air Force at Forli — right?'

'Right again,' Winterley said. 'I was with a Spit squadron there. Can't place you, though. Who were you with?'

'Remember the Eighth Army, air liaison crowd?'

'Sure, just off the south end of the runway.'

'That's it. Well, I was their ops officer. Knew I'd seen you before. Probably went to parties together. Think I remember your name, too.'

'Do you?' Winterley asked. This was where they always failed. Maybe they had met you before, but they never remembered your name, just as you never remembered theirs. 'What is it then?'

'Well, don't hold it against me if I'm wrong, but I seem to remember your first name was Tommy.'

'You're right,' Winterley said. 'How about the rest?'

'Ah, now that's more difficult.' He twirled his glass on the bar. 'Don't forget we probably met at a party somewhere, and we'd have been introduced by first names. Incidentally, mine's Eric. Now let me think, Tommy, Tommy — I've got it Tommy Winters.' He beamed at Winterley.

'Not quite. But your memory's pretty good. As a matter of fact it's Winterley.'

'Winterley. Of *course*, Winterley. Look here, this really is splendid. What are you drinking, Tommy? My other name's Barnett incidentally.'

Winterley thought about it for a moment. The evening was still young. And there were still no interesting girls in the bar. 'Whisky and dry ginger, Eric. Long time since Forli. Pretty good there, eh?'

'Pretty damn good. Remember the marchesa's place in Bologna?' He laughed, paying the barman for the drinks, pushing back half a crown as a tip. 'Let's drink to it.'

They raised their glasses. Winterley let his drink go down in a smooth, continuous stream. It tasted even better than the previous ones. He put the empty glass on the bar, said, 'Let's have the other half. Still in the service Eric?'

Barnett sighed. 'Too old. Only bit of flying I get now is as a passenger. How about you?'

'No, but I'm still flying. I had an offer from one of the companies about four years ago. Been testing for them since then.'

Barnett said, 'How I'd like just one more trip in a really fast aircraft. You're testing jets I suppose?' There was undisguised envy in his voice.

Winterley felt the warm glow of whisky inside him expanding into a deep sympathy for Barnett. He could understand the feelings of ex-pilots who read about the fantastic performances of the latest machines. He noticed Barnett signalling to the barman, drained his glass and thumped it down on the bar.

'Yes, I fly jets. Jet fighters actually. They're not so very different, Eric. Except the really fast ones.' He lowered his voice, smiled at Barnett. 'And some of them are just that.'

'My God, some fellows really have it.' Barnett grinned a little wistfully, suddenly flicked back his left cuff to look at his watch. He went on, 'Look, I promised to phone a man. Business, you know. Don't go away, Tommy, I'll be right back.' He drank half of his glass, swung down from the stool, walked quickly across the room and out through the door.

Winterley picked up his fresh glass. He held it up to the light, savouring the warm amber glow, the momentary flashes as the slowly revolving ice cube caught the light. He lit another cigarette, smoked it slowly and with enjoyment as he sipped the drink. He thought Barnett was taking a long time with his phone call, and looked toward the door to see if he was coming back yet. And he saw her.

She was tall, very blonde, very beautiful. She was wearing a dress of heavy shot-silk, whose deep crimson colour toned exactly with her full lips. The dress was cut square at the shoulders, with a deeply slashed *décolletage* that showed a lot of her golden-brown throat and chest. Winterley thought she was something quite out of the ordinary. With a tightness in his throat and a surge of excitement he watched her move, the dress smoothly flowing, toward the only vacant stool at the bar, the one Barnett had left.

She slid gracefully on to the stool, noticed the half-full glass of whisky, turned to Winterley. 'I'm sorry,' she said,

'I didn't realise this was someone's place.' Her voice was rich and exciting, with a small, vibrant huskiness in it that was infinitely attractive.

Winterley smiled quickly at her. He said casually, 'Not to worry. He's gone to telephone a man or something. Anyway, it's yours — he can have mine when he comes back.' He emphasised the 'he' very slightly, looking carefully at the girl to see if she noticed it. He was quite sure she did. He moved the glass further along the bar, called the barman over and said, 'Will you please ask the lady what she drinks.'

The blonde looked at him coolly, raising her eyebrows very slightly, a hint of amusement in blue eyes that were delicately flecked with green. She said, 'A little quick, don't you think? Or am I wrong?'

Winterley said, 'Dead wrong. Completely wrong. You spoke to me first. That gives me the right to ask you to have a drink.'

The blonde looked straight at him, half smiled, nodded. 'A gin and French then. Large and cold, but no lemon peel.'

Winterley pushed his own glass forward. He considered buying one for Barnett, decided against it. He paid for the drinks, lifted his glass toward the girl.

'Happy days. I'm Tommy Winterley.'

'Janine Maxwell.' She sipped her drink, still looking at him over the rim of the glass. 'Very cold, very good. In fact, just right. Did you know that it takes a really good barman to mix the simple drinks to perfection? This one is very good.'

'I'm glad. The whisky and ginger is good too.'

He looked at her, noting every little detail of her

appearance. Including the fact that there was no ring of any kind on the third finger of her left hand. He decided she was every bit as good as the girl in Brussels had been. Better. He felt he had been right about this weekend, that it was going to start with an evening when everything went just as it should.

He took out his cigarette case, flicked it open, held it out to the girl. She leaned forward to take a cigarette, and over her shoulder he saw Barnett coming back along the bar toward them.

6

Barnett came to a stop behind Winterley and the girl. He looked down at her with undisguised admiration. 'Well, well,' he said, 'so this is the one that didn't get away.'

Winterley said, 'Janine, like you to meet an old friend of mine. Eric Barnett, Janine Maxwell. I knew Eric in Italy during the war.'

Barnett leaned over, lifted his glass from the bar. 'So there we are. Now, what are we all having?'

Winterley held his half-full glass to the light, swirled the amber liquid casually. 'Not for me, Eric. You know how it is — too fast, too early.' He smiled. 'You understand, don't you?'

'Of course,' Barnett said. His voice was a little stiff. He turned to Janine. 'But the lovely lady will certainly have one. Yes?'

Janine looked at him coolly. 'No,' she said. 'Not just now if you don't mind.'

She put the cigarette Winterley had given her between her lips, waited for Winterley to lean across and light it for her. He snapped the lighter shut, held it in front of her for just a shade after the cigarette had been lit.

'Well, maybe it's time I was pushing on,' Barnett said.

He stood there uncertainly behind them, his empty glass in his hand, looking as though he wanted them to protest, to ask him to stay and drink with them. Janine blew smoke in a long jet across the bar. Winterley stared at his glass. Neither of them said anything.

Barnett placed his glass quietly on the bar. 'All right, all right, it was a nice half hour.' He grinned at Winterley. 'Happy landings, Tommy.'

Winterley smiled. 'You bet. See you around, Eric.'

'Wish I was still young enough to travel really fast,' Barnett said as he winked delicately at Winterley over Janine's shoulder. 'Not just in jets either.' Then he turned abruptly on his heel, walked out of the bar.

Janine looked at Winterley, her eyes slightly troubled. 'Perhaps you shouldn't have done that,' she said. 'He knew you before I did, and I think he was rather upset.'

Winterley leaned over, put his head close to hers, said softly, 'I don't really mind if he was. After all, he could see how it is. Don't you feel it too? You know, the feeling this is going to be one of those evenings, the kind you dream about but never get around to having. Would you like to hear the rest? It's a very good line.'

Janine smiled. 'But not original. Let's not bother with anything that's not original. Let's go on to something else.' She finished her drink, placed the glass delicately on the bar. Her eyes were very warm in the smooth tan of her face.

'OK, then how about this?' He pushed their glasses forward, signalled to the barman. 'We have one more here, then we move on and celebrate this inspired meeting. Any place you like. I'm quite sure you know lots of places where we could stage a really good celebration.'

Janine said, 'Well, I can think of one or two you might

find amusing. One of them has a very good coloured band. Very much New Orleans, if you know what I mean, and good enough so they don't have to bother with the commercial stuff. We could begin there, if you liked.'

She took her fresh drink, sipped it, looking at him over the rim. She decided he was definitely attractive to women, though perhaps not quite so attractive as he thought. She shrugged, sipped her drink again, said, 'Mmm, very good. Just as good as the first.' She drained her glass, quickly and gracefully. 'Shall we go?'

'Sure,' Winterley said. 'You disposed of that one very neatly. I'll do the same.'

He raised his glass, gulped the whisky, swung down from the stool. As he followed the exciting tick-tock of her hips out of The Scarlet Fish and into a taxi he realised he was weaving slightly. Then, as he felt the cool night air on him, he knew that he had done just what he'd told Barnett he wouldn't do. Drunk a little too fast, too early. He wondered whether it was the whisky, or Janine, or a mixture of the two. Then he thought that it didn't matter anyway. Nothing mattered except the evening ahead of him.

And the evening went. It went in a whirl of high notes from a muted trumpet, ice tinkling in tall glasses, the breath of exciting perfume from Janine. It went on a stamp-sized dance floor, pressing her close to him as they slowly circled to the dragging, aching rhythm of a slow blues. Feeling her vital body close to his. Savouring the rippling glow her nearness sent through him, a glow that was as fast, and smooth, and warm, as the glow of strong bunched cocktails.

Then it was dark, and a chase from one place to the

next for the last drink, the last dance. Cold air blowing over a dark, deserted pavement. A taxi and an unwilling taxi driver, afraid of him perhaps because he staggered and fell as he climbed in.

Then, somehow with no transition, a room. A big room, well furnished and softly lit. Winterley looked at the walls, watched them recede and advance again as he looked. He laughed, finding their movement infinitely amusing. He looked round for Janine.

Suddenly she was with him, standing above the settee on which he was sprawling. With difficulty he focused on her, seeing she had changed into a long, tight-fitting housecoat in deep blue satin. She was holding a glass in each hand. Winterley, seeing the curves of her figure smoothly outlined in the clinging satin, thought she was wonderful.

'Here you are, Tommy, but it's the last. You really mustn't have any more after this one. You've had far too much already, you know.' She stood looking down at him, her expression troubled.

Winterley grinned a loose, lopsided grin. He raised the glass, gulped at the whisky, spilling some in tiny golden driblets down his chin. 'Don't worry, Janine. Never worry. Old Tommy here's all right, all right? *All right.*'

He looked at her, screwing up the corners of his eyes in an effort to see her better, reached out to pull her down on the settee with him. She did not resist, and the next moment she was sitting beside him, leaning back against his arm. He kissed her, hard, pressing his lips on hers, feeling the soft warmth of her body tight against him.

For a moment she resisted. Then her lips were soft

and open and hungry, moving fiercely against his. Suddenly she stiffened, pulled away from him. She was breathing heavily with a deep movement of her taut breasts under the cling of the satin. Winterley thought she was the most desirable woman he had ever known. He bent toward her, saw that something was wrong, perceived with sudden surprise that she was crying.

He reached out clumsily and uncertainly, tried to turn her to face him. She was sobbing now, as though it were something really important that had upset her.

She said, in a voice muffled by the deep sobbing in her throat, 'It's no use, Tommy, I just can't do it. I just can't let myself go when I'm worried about you like this.'

Winterley shook his head, bemused. 'Listen, Janine, wha's d'trouble, OK? You tell me, huh?'

His voice was slurred and inexact but he did not notice it, would not have cared if he had. Then he started forward struck by one of those blinding flashes of intuition that only drunks and children ever have.

'Janine, lemme tell you somethin', huh? You've fallen for me. Yes you have, you have. Tha's d'trouble, right? OK.' He gazed at her with satisfaction, knowing he was right, knowing his intuition was infallible.

'All right,' Janine said, in a small, soft voice. 'It's no use my trying to deny it. You're right, Tommy. I suppose it was just one of those things, I felt it as soon as we met tonight. I wouldn't care otherwise, but now I'm worried because you're drinking so much. How will you be able to fly those awful fast things on Monday if you're going to drink like this?'

She leaned forward, nuzzling her head on his chest. The smooth burnish of her blonde hair, the warm perfume rising from her, were like drugs to him. He put his open hand on her back, pressing gently on the firmness of her flesh.

'Listen, Janine. Tell you somethin'. Never fly Mondays. Never, never, never. So no need to worry.'

Janine pressed closer to his chest. Her voice was muffled.

'Tommy, don't you see it isn't just I don't want you to drink. If you weren't in the job you are I wouldn't care at all. But how do you think I'll feel when you go back, when you might be drinking like this the night before you fly?'

Winterley put his hands beneath her armpits, gently lifted her from his chest, held her with difficulty so he was looking right at her. Her face swam mistily before him. He spoke with an effort, trying not to stumble over the words.

'Look, you just don't understand, Janine.' He paused, groping uncertainly for the phrases he wanted. 'I don't do anything special. Not at all.' He grinned. 'Tell you all about it, that's it. Then you won't worry. Tha's d'answer.'

Janine brought her face very close to his. She slipped a smooth brown arm round his neck, pulled him to her. She kissed him with a fierce urgency that sent a rippling thrill down his spine. Then she pulled her mouth away from his, said, 'All right, Tommy, maybe I'm silly. Tell me about it if you want to darling.'

Winterley looked at her, wondering why she had moved away, reached out for her again. She resisted gently, then bent forward to nuzzle her head on his chest again. She stretched her legs, swinging them up on the settee, and the housecoat fell away from one of them, revealing a long slimness of silky brown limb.

'No,' she said, as he moved again, 'no, please, Tommy. Tell me about it first. Then I won't be worried, darling.' She brought her right hand up, smoothed it down his cheek.

Winterley said, 'Nothing to it. Jus' routine. Nothing to it.'

'Tell me,' Janine breathed. She snuggled a little closer to him, squirming like a nestling cat. 'Tell me darling.'

'Nothing to it.' Winterley said. 'All I do is this…' He began to talk.

Twenty minutes later Janine slid delicately from the settee.

She moved with the easy grace of a prowling panther, her body rippling under the smooth satin. Winterley was snoring softly. With an effort she lifted his legs from the floor, stretched them out on the settee. Her face was quite expressionless except for her eyes. They were still moist from the tears she had shed — as soft as rain-washed concrete.

She removed his wallet from his jacket, sifted through its contents. Then, very carefully, she went through his pockets. She looked at him again. He was breathing heavily through his nose, out to the world. She decided that the sedative that had gone into his last drink had been quite unnecessary.

Having finished searching him she walked across the room, passed through a door into her bedroom. She sat on the bed, lifted the bedside phone, dialled a Grosvenor number. She heard the click at the other end of the line, the voice repeating the number.

'I got it. He's asleep now,' she said, 'there are some

things might interest you. Nothing much, but it might be worth looking at them.' She listened while the voice at the other end spoke, then responded, 'All right, I'll wait for you... No, he'll never be able to find his way here, I'm quite sure. If you drop him near his hotel someone will pick him up... no, I'm quite sure he won't wake. He was very drunk, you know, and he's had a double dose of sedative.' She listened to the reply. 'All right, ten minutes then. Goodbye.'

She replaced the receiver, kicked her shoes off, stretched out on the divan bed and reached over to the cigarette box on the bedside table next to the telephone and selected a cigarette. Then she lay back, smoking slowly and with enjoyment, waiting for Eric Barnett to arrive.

7

Driscoll waded straight in, 'All right I'm here in person. You haven't changed a bit and neither have I so let's skip that. Why did you send for me?'

The man sitting on the other side of the heavy mahogany desk looked at him carefully. He noted the shabbiness of Driscoll's suit, the slight puffiness under his eyes. He thought things were not so good for Driscoll, but that he was not desperate yet.

'Take it easy, Johnny. Have a cigarette and remember I get orders too.' His voice was quiet and cultured, with a trace of a lowland Scottish accent.

Driscoll took a cigarette from the silver box and saw it was a Perfectos just as it had always been. He wondered as he lit it whether Davidson knew everything he'd been up to in the past six years. He looked at him seeing that the old man had not aged at all, that he still looked the same as the last time and the time before that. Davidson was not the type to age. His smoothly brushed silver hair with thin tanned face and impatiently drumming slender fingers were just the same as ever.

'Let's skip the stuff about orders,' Driscoll replied, 'why did you send for me?'

Davidson sighed. He rose from behind the desk, walked over to the window. He was very tall and thin, dressed in a perfectly fitting dark blue suit.

'You see, Johnny, it was just one of those things. I know how things were between you and Patti. I knew when Moller killed her that you'd risk anything to get him. But I couldn't let you, not just then. That's why I told you to wait. And what do you do? You go to Switzerland off your own bat, get to Moller and fix him up, and just beat the Swiss police to the frontier. What you didn't know was that you were seen with one of my contacts. I was afraid of that, you were too well known. That's why I didn't let you go in the first place. You got to Moller all right, but someone else got to my contact. He died, and the man he was watching — a big one I really wanted — got out to South America. You see why I was a little annoyed?'

Driscoll said, 'All right, I was wrong. Once, in six years, I was wrong. I admit it but I don't feel sorry for it. Who got out?'

'Kolnrich, but that isn't the point. You put a personal thing before the organisation. I had to let you go. They were cutting down anyway and you'd trodden on too many people's feet. You never were very popular, Johnny, not with some of the high-up people.'

'Yeah, I know. But I got results.'

'They admitted that. They didn't like the way you got them. I wanted to keep you, even after the Moller business. I just couldn't swing it.'

'All right,' Driscoll said, 'you couldn't swing it. And now?'

Davidson said, quietly, 'It depends on you. Things haven't been too good lately, have they?'

'It's a buyer's market. I'm getting by. An' don't kid me you don't know every little thing I've been doing.

Why not have the file in and I'll fill in the missing bits.' He ground his cigarette savagely in the tray.

Davidson smiled. He walked back to his desk, pressed the bell-push. 'That's a good idea, Johnny, have another cigarette.'

Driscoll took a cigarette, tapped it thoughtfully on the desk. He heard the noise of the door and a girl walked in past him, placed a slim folder on the desk. Driscoll looked her over thoroughly. He saw that Davidson still picked them for quiet good looks, the kind of girls who well repaid a second glance if you were smart enough to see that they deserved one.

'I like your new office. And the fixtures,' Driscoll said.

Davidson smiled again. 'Ann, this is Johnny Driscoll. You've heard me talk about him.'

The girl looked at Driscoll, examining him carefully and quite impersonally, as though he were a laboratory specimen.

'Frankly, I'm rather disappointed,' she said. 'Was that all, Mr Davidson?'

'That's all, Ann.'

The girl walked past Driscoll without another glance. He heard the door shut behind her. He blew a smoke cloud in the air, grinned through it at Davidson.

'So the children scream when they see me coming. So I'm a real bad boy an' I'm getting the treatment. What else?'

Davidson said, 'I was going to go through your record, but why worry? You know it and I know most of it. There's nothing very big there.'

Driscoll shrugged. 'The market's dead, you know that as well as I do. Except of course in the one place.'

'You couldn't do it, Johnny.'

'Don't be too sure. Remember what you once told me, when I was just starting out with you? Never be certain about anything. Never. Even something you think *must* be true. Anyway, I haven't worked for them yet.'

'I know.' Davidson said. He walked across to the window again, stood looking out into the street. 'And you won't have to. I've made my mind up about you. I'm asking you to come back. How do you like it?'

Driscoll said, simply, 'I like it.'

'I'm glad. We might need you any moment now. But there's a snag. It's provisional — I'm hiring you just for the one thing. Do a good job and you're back on a permanent basis. The other thing you'd better know is about *my* backing. I ran into a lot of opposition when I wanted you back in. They made it a condition that you're on your own.'

'I've been on my own before.' Driscoll said.

'If you run into trouble with the police or the security people you may be out on a limb. I'll do what I can, but I can't promise anything. You see, there isn't a war any more.' He grinned wryly. 'Not an official one anyway. How do you feel about it Johnny?'

'That'll work out, provided the price allows for it of course.' He crushed his second cigarette in the massive glass ashtray, took another. 'Let's talk about the price, shall we?'

'Why not? Fifty a week as long as it lasts with a guarantee of two fifty. Plus the usual bonus and the standard things like a flat and clothes.' He broke off, smiled at Driscoll. 'I imagine you'll do well out of the clothes, Johnny. You need rather a lot at the moment don't you?'

'Maybe not as badly as that. And the job?'

Davidson swung round abruptly, faced into the room. 'I just don't know. I'm playing a hunch. I don't need to tell you there's a certain group doing their utmost to slow up rearmament, nor who they represent. So far their success hasn't been worth a damn, but I've a feeling they're preparing to pull something any time. Something big. Look, I'll give you some isolated facts and you can judge for yourself. First, an aircraft works in East Anglia was broken into about ten months ago and some blueprints photographed. They were the plans of a very secret fighter, the hottest ever designed, it's been flying some while now from the works' airfield and it's really good. Make no mistake, if all our squadrons are equipped with them this country's pretty safe — or at least very much safer than without them. It's called the KB–12, and if all goes well with the tests it will go into production next month. Clear so far?'

'Clear. Carry on.'

'We never found out who took the photographs. But a fortnight ago a man called Williamson was found stabbed in one of the northwest suburbs, quite near his house. His pockets were empty, and the police assumed it was a killing for gain. Recognise the name?'

'No. Should I?'

'I don't know. Perhaps you knew him as Smythe, or Grattan, or Penny. He used all those names at some time. The point is he was an acknowledged expert at getting into places and getting photographs. I used him quite a lot myself at one time, but then he dropped out of sight. I had his house thoroughly searched — unofficially of course — but we drew a blank. You see where it's heading?'

'Yeah.' Driscoll said. 'What else?'

'Three days before Williamson was murdered, a visitor arrived here by air. His name is Rakiev and he's their top aircraft designer. A specialist in jet fighters. We don't know where he went or what he did while he was here. It's quite impossible for us to trace everyone who leaves their Embassy in a closed car and they know it as well as we do. As a matter of fact we didn't even know he was here until after he'd left. Couple those things with the fact that the KB–12 is simply vital to the defence of this country, and what have you got?'

Driscoll said, slowly, 'It depends. But if Williamson took those photographs you've got trouble. It's too much of a coincidence for him to be knocked off just after Rakiev gets here. It looks to me that if there's anything cooking it's in the oven.'

'That's the way I feel too, Johnny. Now, I can't tell you where you'll fit, not until something breaks. When it does — and if it does — you can start in from there. Until then you're on the payroll anyway, provided you'll accept those terms. How about it?'

Driscoll said, 'It sounds fair. I'm in.'

'Good. I'm glad you're with us again. Now relax for a few minutes. There are some points I want to cover with you about the general set-up. Drink?' He looked directly at Driscoll, smiling slightly.

'Not right now,' Driscoll said lazily. He smiled, too.

'As you like. Things have changed a little since you left us, Johnny. That stuff about there being no official war is quite a handicap, you know. However, we still manage to get some useful things done. My organisation is just about where it always has been. Each member is directly responsible to me.' He paused, selected another cigarette.

'And you,' Driscoll murmured, 'you're still responsible to the big man himself. Right?'

'Right. He's very good you know. Just as good as he was during the war. I get on very well with him, provided my people don't give too many openings for embarrassing questions to be asked. Of course, money's a little tighter than it was, but I get a big enough allocation from the Secret Estimates to do more or less as I like. Unfortunately that doesn't altogether apply to my right to hire anyone I wish. Some of the Intelligence people have a say in that. That's why I got opposition. I didn't think it was worth troubling the old man about it.'

'Do you work in with the Intelligence people more than you used to?' Driscoll asked.

'Not altogether. But of course I make use of them quite a lot when I need information. Their organisation has changed a great deal. Are you in the picture on that?'

'Not really. Maybe it's just as well. I won't know whose feet I may be treading on.' He reached forward and took another cigarette, grinned at Davidson as he lit it.

'I hope your tread isn't as heavy as it used to be. There are one or two more things. I've arranged for someone to work with you. Not *for* you Johnny but *with* you,' Davidson smiled as he emphasised the point, 'he will be a contact for you with the Intelligence people. His name's Landford, and he's rather high in the security set-up. As a matter of fact he's one of the three people who spend most of their time looking for traitors in our own security forces. Naturally the security people themselves don't know he exists, I expect he'll tell you about it.'

'Where do I contact him?'

'You don't. He'll contact you. In addition to Landford I've got someone else for you. She's one of my people, nothing to do with the Intelligence crowd. As far as I know neither they nor anyone else know anything about her. That should make her quite useful. Before I bring her in to meet you there's just one more little thing.'

Davidson looked very serious, the half smile that usually hovered on his lean face suddenly disappearing.

'Yes?' Driscoll said softly. He thought he knew exactly what Davidson was going to say.

'One of the reasons I ran into opposition when I wanted you back was because there's been some talk about your drinking. It's been suggested that you can't control it any more, that it's been getting steadily worse ever since Patti was killed. I told them they were wrong. How about it, Johnny?'

'I drink because I like it,' Driscoll said slowly and deliberately, 'I've done a lot of drinking in the past, and I propose to do a lot in the future.' He looked straight at Davidson. 'It doesn't have to worry you at all. I'm quite OK.'

Davidson sighed, relaxed, the little smile back on his face. 'So we'll forget it. Now I'll bring the girl in to meet you. Her name is Marian Courtney. I picked her for you myself. Took a lot of trouble over it.' He grinned mischievously and leaned forward to press the bell-push.

Driscoll got up from his chair, wandered over to the window, turned as he heard the door open. He saw the girl, and for a moment his jaw sagged, as though he were horrified by what he had seen. Then his head jerked round to Davidson, a hard expression on his face as the girl shook hands with the old man. He took in every little detail of her appearance, conscious that while Davidson was shaking hands with the girl he was looking past her at him.

The girl was about five feet five inches, with a lithe, graceful figure attractively displayed in the classic lines of a cool grey linen suit. She was wearing dark green court shoes, and a broad striped silk scarf in two shades of green that filled the vee between her jacket lapels. Driscoll took all that in at a glance, but it was at her hair he looked, and her eyes. Her hair was the warm, vital red of glowing coals, brilliant with living fire. Her eyes, set wide beneath her smooth forehead, were the distant blue of smoke on the horizon of a warm day. She was very lovely.

Driscoll looked past her at Davidson, spoke with a cold savagery in his voice that made the girl open her eyes very wide. 'I hope to Christ you don't think you're being funny, Davidson.'

Davidson shook his head slowly. For a moment he looked very old and wise and tired.

'Not that, Johnny,' Davidson said softly, 'you know me better than that. You can guess if you think hard enough.'

The girl glanced from one to the other, puzzled and a little alarmed at the tension that filled the room with its tangible presence.

Then Driscoll laughed. It was a peculiar, rasping laugh, which ended as abruptly as it had begun. 'All right, Davidson you old fox, you had to make one final check. Just to see how I'd react. And I hope you're satisfied.'

Driscoll turned to the girl. 'You probably think this is very peculiar. The point is you look very much like another girl I once knew. Davidson was wondering about the stories he's been hearing about me. Wondering whether I'm enough of a lush to have lost control when I saw you. Whether I'd do something foolish. Whether my mind still works quickly enough to spot why he did it. When you get to know him better you'll know he's full of laughing little tricks like that.'

Driscoll turned back to Davidson, looked at him with a gaze in which affection and anger were strangely mingled. 'Satisfied now?'

'Satisfied,' Davidson said. 'Forgive me, Johnny. I simply had to know. Marian my dear, this is Johnny Driscoll. You'll be taking instructions from him for a while.'

'Yes,' the girl said. Her voice was low and pleasant, a voice that could bubble with vitality, a warm voice. 'Tell me Mr Driscoll, this other girl, was she very much like me? I mean, in what points did we differ?'

She opened the smoke-blue eyes, looked dreamily at him. She thought that Driscoll was a little shabby, possibly a little dissipated, but that he still had a great deal. She liked the ruthless lines of his face, the thickness of his black hair. She thought he could be very amusing if he were handled properly. She was not the first woman to think that about Driscoll, but of course she had no way of knowing that. Neither did she know that only one woman had ever come near handling Driscoll the way she wanted. The rest generally found that after a short while it was very much the other way round.

Driscoll looked into the innocence of the blue eyes, saw behind them and realised that here was a girl who had heard all the usual questions, remembered the really useful answers. He decided that she could be very intriguing indeed, once she had been provoked a little.

He said carefully, 'It's a little difficult to say. Patti was maybe a little taller, possibly a little browner. I can't pick out any particular feature where you differ too much, it's just the general aura you might say.' He paused, looked at her with an innocence that matched her own.

'Oh, I wonder how our auras differed?'

'Well,' Driscoll said slowly, 'perhaps I'm being a little unfair to make the comparison. After all, Patti'd been around a lot, had a lot of chances to learn how to make the very most of herself. I don't think she was any better looking than you. It was just… I suppose I haven't made myself very clear?'

Davidson, watching Driscoll closely, thought that the expression of frankness and integrity on his face was a masterpiece.

'Oh yes,' the girl said, 'very clear indeed. You know, Mr Davidson, I don't know that I'm going to like working with Driscoll very much.' She paused, as though struck by a sudden thought and flashed white teeth in a delighted smile. 'But of course I forgot. He's working now, isn't he, and he'll be able to buy a new suit. I'm sure that will make all the difference.'

She sat down in the chair, crossed one leg over the other, smiled sweetly at Driscoll. She was very angry to find that he was laughing, even angrier when Davidson joined in. She decided, coldly furious, that Mr Driscoll would have plenty more to laugh about before he finished.

Davidson said, 'All right children, I can see you'll get along well. Johnny will put you in the picture, Marian. He'll contact you at your flat when he wants you. You run along now. Maybe,' — he grinned wickedly at Driscoll — 'you'd like to escort Marian home. I'd like to think you were getting acquainted. It helps when you have to work together.'

'Sure,' Driscoll said. 'And maybe I can remember just what it was about Patti I was trying to say.'

Marian stood up. She said, 'I'm afraid I must decline Mr Driscoll's charming offer. I have a date.' She turned on her heel, walked swiftly to the door, opened it and turned to them. 'With a man.' She finished sweetly, stepping through the door and closing it behind her.

Driscoll smiled at Davidson. 'You could always pick them,' he said. 'I've got a feeling this one's going to be really good. I suppose Ann has the money and the rest for me?'

'Money, expenses on account, the key to a flat. Also Marian's telephone number and address. You know how to contact me if you want to.'

'Sure,' Driscoll said. 'Incidentally, you know Kolnrich was killed in South America four years ago. So it didn't matter too much.'

'Yes, I knew. They fished his body out of the Plate just inland from Montevideo didn't they?'

'Yeah,' Driscoll said. 'I put it there. I never did like him.'

Davidson chuckled softly, sat down in his big leather armchair behind the desk. 'I knew that too, Johnny. That was one of the things that made me want you back again. Surprised?'

'Not particularly. Well, so long. And thanks for the girl. She should be most useful. Also amusing.'

'Take it easy with her will you, Driscoll? For a start.'

'You know me.' Driscoll waved his hand casually, disappeared through the door into the outer office.

Davidson tapped a cigarette on the desk, smoked it slowly without noticing he was smoking it.

'I wonder if I do Johnny,' he murmured, 'I wonder if I do.'

For at least ten minutes he sat quite still at his desk, smoking and staring down at his blotter. He thought about Driscoll the whole of the time.

8

Winterley walked slowly across the wide concrete apron in front of the main hangar. In his white flying overalls he looked younger than he was, and competent. An old squadron badge was sewn on the breast pocket of his overalls, clipped to his right thigh was the pad on which he would record data from the engine and other instruments during the test flight.

The KB–12 stood alone at the edge of the concrete apron. Not for the first time Winterley thought that on the ground she was nothing like as beautiful as in the air. The tricycle undercarriage was short and squat, and the aeroplane seemed to crouch on the ground, its long, ferocious nose reaching forward as viciously as a striking snake. The swept back wings began half way along the fuselage, and their tips were swept even further until they were running parallel with the length of the body. The fighter was sleek and brilliant in polished aluminium.

Winterley looked up and grinned as the second model of the KB–12 flashed overhead with a whining yelp of sound that was loudest after it had already passed. He walked slowly round his fighter, checking that the locks had been removed from the control surfaces, and that all panels were safely secured. A panel breaking open in flight would be a major hazard, allowing a wind of supersonic speed to rip into the structure of the machine.

At last, satisfied with his external inspection, he hoisted himself into the deep cavity of the cockpit. For the next five minutes he busied himself with the various details of strapping in and connecting his services. First he removed the safety locks from the ejector seat mechanism. Then he clipped on his dinghy, inflated his anti-G suit, fastened and locked his parachute harness.

Next, a mechanic held the safety harness straps over his shoulders for him to grasp. He pulled them down, clipped them into a quick-release junction box, tightened them. Then he pulled on his white helmet and checked his oxygen supply was connected and working. Then he checked his radio-telephone lead was plugged into his socket and that the controls moved easily and smoothly as he pulled on the control column. Only then did he signal the mechanic that he was ready to start.

As the mechanic pressed the contact button on the trolley accumulator that had been wheeled up and connected to the aircraft, Winterley pressed his own starter buttons. He felt the slight vibration as the turbine blades began to revolve, lifted the high-pressure cocks to feed fuel to the engines. The vibration increased, then died away into a steady throbbing as the two massive turbines, first port, then starboard, came to life. On each side of the fuselage, just behind the cockpit, the gaping orifices greedily sucked air into the blasting turbines behind them. Behind the fighter the twin jets of heated air bounced shimmering off the white concrete, scorching and darkening it with their heat.

Winterley waved to the mechanic in front of the aircraft, received his answering thumbs up to show the trolley accumulator had been disconnected and wheeled away. Then he released the brakes, swung the aircraft round, and began to taxi across the concrete apron to the perimeter track of the airfield.

As he moved, the noise of the engines reached a shrill intensity which made the small cluster of onlookers grimace with the pain in their eardrums. But to Winterley, in his sealed, insulated cockpit, the noise was little more than a harsh buzz, to which he had long grown accustomed.

As he taxied fast to the downwind end of the runway, he went through some of the take-off checks. He selected air brakes out, heard the hiss as they extended in the wings, checked they were fully out, and then watched them retract as he selected the in position.

As he followed the smooth curves of the perimeter track he finished the checks, ran through in his mind the programme for the flight. It was a normal test for the stage of testing that the KB–12 had arrived at.

First there would be the climb to height — fifty thousand feet — which he would time. Then a check on Mach numbers at selected throttle settings followed by a few aerobatics at speeds below the speed of sound. Then would come the break through the sound barrier over the nearby North Sea, with notes taken of any unusual characteristics. Finally a maximum speed run, straight and level, followed by a rapid descent at low power.

Just before turning on to the runway he brought the KB–12 to a standstill, performed the last few take-off checks. He satisfied himself that fuel and oxygen were feeding satisfactorily, that his bubble canopy was sealed and locked. He gave a final check to the tightness of his safety harness and then he called the control tower for permission to line up on the runway.

In his earphones he heard the dry crackle of the controller telling him he was clear to line up after the aircraft coming in on final approach had landed.

Winterley turned his head to the right, watched the second of the KB–12 series approach the runway. She came in low and fast, a beautifully judged approach that put her main wheels on to the runway only twenty yards from its beginning. Even above the noise of his turbines he heard the faint scream of rubber as the main wheels took the strain of twelve tons of aeroplane contacting the concrete at a hundred and thirty knots. He watched the fighter run along, losing speed until the nose wheel dropped and the machine ran smoothly on its tricycle undercarriage. When it was six hundred yards along the runway he pressed the transmitter button on his control column, said, 'Bluebird One, lining up and holding.'

Without waiting for acknowledgment he swung the KB–12 on to the smooth flatness of the runway, allowed her to run fifty yards along the centre line to centralise the nose wheel. He saw the other fighter turn off half way along the two-mile runway, then he pressed his transmitter button again, said, 'Bluebird One, permission to take off. Over.'

He released the transmitter button, heard the dry crackle in his earphones as the controller replied, 'Bluebird One, clear take off. Over.'

Winterley pressed the button again, said, 'Roger, scrambling now.' With his left hand he pushed the throttles forward, smoothly and gently, watched the turbine revolutions build up on the dials in front of him. When both indicated nine thousand revolutions per minute he released the brakes, felt the fighter start to roll forward, continued pushing the throttles forward until they were fully open. The aircraft was accelerating fiercely now. He could feel the pressure against his back as the forward speed rose swiftly.

He corrected a slight swing to port, positioned the nose firmly on the black line that stretched like a finely stitched thread down the middle of the ribbon of white concrete. He gazed straight ahead of him down the runway, glimpsing occasionally, in quick glances, the needle of his air speed indicator. When it showed one hundred and twenty knots he eased back very gently on the stick, saw the nose rise slightly as the nose wheel left the ground. He held the fighter in that position, with the speed rising ever more rapidly until, at a hundred and thirty five knots, he felt the sudden transition from bumpiness to smoothness that told him he was clear of the ground.

He held the control column steady, reached down with his left hand to operate the undercarriage retraction lever. He heard the hiss of hydraulics, the bump as the undercarriage doors folded into place over the retracted wheels. He applied a touch of brake to stop the wheels spinning round in their retracted position, and held the fighter level at eighty feet, letting the speed build up to three hundred knots before he banked in a tight turn to fly back over the airfield.

Once more he pressed the transmitter button, said, 'Hello, tower. Bluebird One. Airborne, over to B-Baker.' He heard the acknowledgment from the controller, then pressed button B on his radio set to select the radio frequency on which the test flights were carried out.

He reduced his throttle settings slightly, straightened out of the turn, and flashed toward the airfield to make a low run before climbing away to test height. As he came over the boundary fence his speed was just on five hundred knots. He screamed across the airfield parallel to the runway at two hundred feet, catching brief glimpses of the red fire-tenders and crash wagons, the grey sandstone of the control tower, the brilliant silver of the second KB–12 model on the concrete apron. As he crossed the far boundary of the airfield he pulled the stick hard back into his stomach, held it there until the aircraft was climbing almost vertically and settled back to time the climb.

At twenty thousand he burst through the last layer of thin altostratus cloud, and at twenty-nine thousand the last delicate wisps of white cirrus undulated swiftly past his canopy. With the Machmeter steady at 0.7 — seven tenths of the speed of sound — the KB–12 bored and blasted her way up through the thinning air to the icy wastelands of the sub-stratosphere.

At fifty thousand he levelled out, reduced the engine revolutions to economical cruising settings. He noted on his pad that the climb to fifty thousand had taken only three minutes and twelve seconds.

He settled himself comfortably in his cockpit, snugly warm in the heated, pressurised cabin. Below him he could catch occasional, distant glimpses of the ground through breaks in the veils of cloud, and he felt, as he always did, that it bore no relation to him. Twenty thousand feet below him the wisps of high cirrus marked the boundary between earth and sky. Around him and above was the dark blue of the great heights, a blue so dark as to be almost black, and yet so bright that the sky seemed to hang over him in a tangible, polished bowl.

Here, in the wastes of the stratosphere, the temperature was about minus-seventy in degrees centigrade — almost two hundred degrees of frost in the Fahrenheit scale. The air was thin and refined, free of the gross impurities that poisoned the lower atmosphere. That was the cause of the darkness, of course. Without impurities to reflect light the rays of the sun passed unhindered through this air, as they had passed unhindered through millions of miles of space, and the upper air lived always in semi-darkness, in which no human vision could detect another aircraft at more than three or four miles, even on the brightest day.

Winterley glanced quickly round the cockpit then commenced his tests with steep turns and aerobatics with the Machmeter steady at 0.95. He threw the KB–12 around the sky, revelling in the amazing manoeuvrability in air so thin that standard fighters found difficulty in sustaining even the gentlest of turns. He grinned as he thought how staggered the boys on the fighter squadrons would be when she started rolling from the production lines.

He finished with two steep turns to left and right, turning full circles, holding the turn as tight as the fighter would go. Even the KB–12 would not turn as viciously at this altitude as in the thicker air nearer the ground, but he was quite satisfied that she could easily out-turn any aircraft flying in the world.

Then, four minutes after reaching height, he prepared for the drive through the barrier, but in straight and level flight, not diving through.

The KB–12 was the first aircraft in the world to be capable of breaking through the barrier in level flight. Every other aircraft had to be dived through, simply not having enough power to thrust through the shock wave and burst into the calmer supersonic regions. But the KB–12 had done it time after time. Indeed, so routine had the procedure become that the test pilots no longer transmitted continuously as they went through, merely notifying base before and after the start of each run.

Winterley did this now, passing a brief message, receiving an equally laconic message of acknowledgment.

Once more the practised flick of his eyes round the instruments, seeking any abnormality however small, failing to find it. Smoothly and steadily he pushed the throttles open, at the same time putting in the air brakes which he had been using to check his speed down to 0.8.

The acceleration was moderate at first, then progressively faster as the increased thrust from the turbines took effect. The speed built up rapidly to 0.95, continued through to 0.97 where the heavy buffeting and judder began. But the acceleration was rapid now, and after only seconds the needle was sliding past 0.99 and the judder was diminishing, dying away, suddenly gone.

The KB–12 continued to accelerate through the supersonic belt, until at 1.3, with speed still in hand, Winterley reduced the throttle settings slightly. Another and even more hazardous barrier lay ahead — the thermal barrier, and for the time being the aircraft was cleared only to 1.3 Mach.

No one yet knew very much about the thermal barrier. It was known only that at these speeds the heat generated by the friction of air on the skin of the aircraft was terrific and could not be dispersed. If Winterley had been able to reach out and touch the silver skin of the KB–12 he would have found it hot enough to burn off his hand. Indeed, though the cockpit was insulated and refrigerated — as well as electrically heated when necessary — already the temperature was rising unpleasantly, and Winterley was sweating heavily.

He reduced throttle settings again, letting the speed fall off slowly, thinking that the sonic barrier presented little in the way of a problem to the KB–12.

The second model of the KB–12, which had modified wing surfaces, was even better. Though it still juddered quite noticeably at 0.98 it was steady enough, even at the most critical point, to be a good gun platform. And that was something designers had striven after, and failed to achieve, since supersonic flight first became more than a theoretical possibility.

Winterley watched the needle come down to 1.15, glanced at his watch and saw he had been at altitude for six minutes. He checked his fuel, found he had approximately thirty minutes of flying time to go. He was just stretching his left hand out to the airbrake lever when it happened.

There was a very small, very faint noise somewhere in front of him in the nose section where the radar was housed. As he jerked his gaze down toward the nose cone he saw it was rising, instinctively he pressed forward on the stick. Then, in an infinitely small part of a second, he realised that the nose was rising because it was splitting away from the aircraft.

The nose cone shell hurtled past his cockpit, and

instantly he heard the terrible ripping blast of the airstream as it sent an eight-hundred mile an hour wind tearing into the gaping mouth that had opened up in the front of the fighter.

Before he could even move his hand to jettison the canopy the aircraft had begun to disintegrate. The perspex canopy cracked, split, then burst explosively outwards as the pressurised air within forced its way into the thin air of the stratosphere.

Within half a second of the noise occurring, before any human brain could possibly register what was happening and act to save itself, Winterley was dead. He was killed instantly, his body ripped to pieces by the shattering fury of the air-blast and the disintegrating components of the fighter.

Only a cloudy puff of vaporising fuel, sprayed from burst tanks, remained to mark the passage of the aircraft through the air. A puff of vapour, and shattered, minute pieces of aircraft that fluttered down into the sea over an area of twenty square miles.

9

Driscoll turned the key in the door, walked into the living room of his new apartment. He thought it was a considerable improvement on the room he had been using before Davidson sent for him. He tossed his hat on a chair, walked across to open a window.

Someone behind him said, 'Hello, Driscoll.'

He spun round. For a big man it was surprising just how fast and easily he turned. His hands dropped to his hips, the fingers lightly clenched. Then he relaxed, letting tension fade from poised muscles.

The man who had spoken was standing in the open doorway between the living room and bedroom. He was small, round faced, with smoothly brushed sparse dark hair, and sleepy eyes that were staring at Driscoll from beneath drooping eyelids.

'Come right in,' Driscoll said, 'Since you know my name I suppose you know this is my apartment. Funnily enough I like it kept as my apartment. Or am I pushing it too much?'

The man smiled. His plump cheeks were rosy with blood near the skin.

'I have a way with locks.' He waved his right hand deprecatingly in the air. 'This one was nothing,' he murmured. 'A very easy one. Incidentally, it needs a little fine oil. Just a little and very fine.' He beamed at Driscoll.

Driscoll walked over to the occasional table by the empty fireplace, opened a packet of Players, lit one. He inhaled deeply then spoke as he exhaled, 'Any old locks or just mine?'

The little man raised a plump, well-manicured hand, coughed delicately behind it. 'Excuse me, my chest, I smoke too much. Yes, any old locks, you know... You've been told about me, I'm Landford.'

'I see.' Driscoll said. He examined Landford carefully, probing at the bland exterior of the man, seeking some little flaw in the carefully harmless appearance. He didn't find it. 'Yeah sure, I've been told about you. Ten days ago.'

'By Davidson, of course.'

'That's right. My other name's Johnny. As I expect you know.'

'Of course. Really, I know quite a lot about you. From what I know I'm sure we're going to get on well together. I'd better mention that my name's Willy.' He smiled, contrived to look almost coy. 'For some peculiar reason everyone thinks it's very amusing to call me Little Willy.'

'OK, Willy,' Driscoll grinned, 'I'm glad to know you. I'm quite sure we'll do all right when we start working together.'

'Yes,' Landford said. 'Which is right at this moment. The KB–12 broke up in the air yesterday and the test pilot was killed.'

'That's not too clever is it, any details?'

'Details? No, not really. It happened over the North Sea, about fifteen miles off Cromer. A few pieces have been recovered, and the technical people are working on them. They don't think they'll be able to tell anything much. Judging by the time he'd been airborne the fighter would have been doing anything between eight hundred and a thousand miles an hour. Apparently if something goes wrong at that speed there's usually very little left of anything, including the pilot.'

'Who was he?'

'Chap called Winterley. A very good one. I've brought a report on him. Also some other papers for you to look at.'

'All right, where do we start?' Driscoll asked.

'It's not so easy, Johnny. Maybe it was just an accident. He could have wrenched the wings off turning too fast, run out of oxygen, hit trouble going through the barrier. Anything. But the people who designed and built the plane don't think so.'

'And you? What do you think?'

'I agree with them,' Landford said softly, 'I'm not a technical expert but I've got a hunch. I've got a hunch the KB–12 was made to break up. And I think we might work on that. What harm can it do?'

Driscoll, watching him closely, decided he had found the flaw in Landford's gentleness and smooth amiability. The man had shed that manner as easily as an unrequired coat. His voice was still soft, but with the throaty softness of a jaguar's growl. His face was still calm, but his eyes were glowing and savage.

'No harm at all, and maybe a lot of good,' Driscoll said. 'How much has been done?'

'Quite a lot. I'll sit down if I may. I've been on it continuously for the last twenty-four hours.'

'Feel like a drink?'

'I think a drink would be very nice.'

He followed Driscoll with his eyes as Driscoll walked across to the sideboard, swung down a shelf to reveal a small cocktail cabinet. Driscoll carried a bottle of whisky across to the fireplace, poured a long drink, handed it to Landford. Landford took the glass, poured the liquor down in one long swallow, smiled.

'More?' Driscoll asked.

'No thanks.' He fished in an inner pocket, brought out a bundle of papers, tossed them across. 'Here it is. I think there might be something among this lot.'

Driscoll examined the bundle. There were several foolscap sheets of a security report on a man called Glazey. The papers dealt with the routine of test flights, then a security report on the dead pilot, a plan of the airfield and then a diagrammatic representation of the plane's reported track on the day of the crash. There was also a small brown notebook with Winterley's name scrawled on the flysheet.

'All right, I can go through these later,' Driscoll said. 'Is this all?'

'That's all. I've got some doubts about the man Glazey. I suddenly came across something in his screening report that made me wonder. Incidentally, I'm working on something else there, something that may tie in with all this. Glazey — he's a departmental head in a large radar development company by the way — seems to have gone to some trouble to check on the aircraft radar before its last flight. Normally the job's done by a fitter. This time Glazey did it himself, which is unusual at least. That, plus the irregularity I saw in his screening, made me wonder about him.'

'Has he been questioned?'

'Not yet. But…' Landford paused, added grimly, 'he will be. I'm going in on that one personally. It's too important to leave to the security people. And I think I'll take you up on that second drink.'

Driscoll brought the bottle across, poured another long drink into Landford's glass. 'Water?' he asked.

'For washing only,' Landford grinned. He lifted the glass, drank half the whisky, sighed with satisfaction. 'I think I'd better put you in the picture about my set-up. I don't think it existed when you left Davidson.'

'No, it didn't. There wasn't any particular need for it.'

'Right. But things have changed, Johnny. We pretty well had tabs on all the people who sympathised with the Nazis. This lot are different. We're not just concerned with the professionals any more. Now we have to worry about people in all walks of life, people you'd never dream were helping them. When they get a man they usually hold him. They turn him into a fanatic, someone quite incapable of seeing anything but the party line. Someone capable of anything, even murder, if it's represented to him as a step forward for the party.'

Driscoll nodded to Landford to continue.

'So far we're just scratching at the edge of the problem. God only knows how many of them we don't suspect. The only time we get to know is when it's too late. Look at Fuchs, May, Pontecorvo. We found them too late. And why? Simply because however well you can check a man's antecedents, you just can't see into his mind. Especially when his mind is set in that peculiar twist that slants everything into an argument for the party. The sort of mind that thinks of the village grocer as a vile capitalist and condemns the trade unions as enemies of the working class. You see the problem?'

Driscoll said, 'Yeah. Don't forget I've run across them once or twice. Though most of the contacts I've had have been with the professionals, mostly with their overseas police division. So what are you doing about it?'

'There are three of us who have a floating job. We like to think none of the security or intelligence people know exactly what we're doing. As a matter of fact I don't think they do. But primarily our job is to check on the people who do the security screening. Just suppose, for example, that one of the security people clearing scientists for work at an atomic plant were really one of *them*.' He spat out the word with concentrated venom. 'You see what he could do? Why, he'd be worth an army corps. And you'll be surprised to know we've caught two or three already. All minor ones, you know, no one really important yet. But it goes to show.'

Driscoll took another cigarette, lit it and blew smoke in a long, thoughtful jet toward the ceiling.

'So you run the checkers who check on the checkers? Pretty complicated, Willy.'

'It's all pretty complicated. Nothing straightforward any more. Not when an ex-public schoolboy with an impeccable record, plenty of money, a lovely home, can be one of them — and no one even begins to suspect it until he's been over there for about three weeks thumbing his nose at us after delivering God knows how many secret documents to them. You're damn right it's complicated, Johnny. And I don't run them. Colonel Browne does that. Clifton and I come under him. You know Browne?'

'I don't think so. Army?'

'Honorary rank. A very good man, Johnny. His anti-fascist record was pretty spectacular. He's one of those slow-moving people with a face like a horse and a brain that's always about three thoughts ahead of anyone else. You'll like him.'

'OK, so I know where you fit. Where does Davidson tie in now? Things seem to have changed.'

'They have. But I think Davidson's more or less where he always has been, on the end of a direct line to Downing Street. Anything he decides usually happens. He seems to be able to swing practically anything he wants to.'

Driscoll smiled. 'In that case things haven't changed too much. Will you leave this stuff with me?'

Landford raised his glass, finished the whisky. He stood up, stretched. 'That's what I brought it for. Read that and you know as much as I do. I'm going to bed for a few hours. Then I'm going to see Glazey. I'll keep in touch.'

'OK. Where can I contact you, Willy?'

'You'll find my telephone number among those papers. There's just one more thing I might mention.'

'Yes?'

'You can reach me anytime you want. Don't forget the same goes in reverse.'

His voice was very soft, and Driscoll caught the implicit menace in it, wondered what it meant.

'OK, Willy, so you can reach me. So what?'

'Don't get me wrong, Johnny. You remember Hamilton?'

'Vaguely. He was carved in an alley off the Rue d'Isly one night.'

'Right. He made the old mistake of trying to play both ends at once. He'd done it before and got away with it, but that time he was foolish. You see, I was on one of the ends, and I found it necessary to go all the way to Algiers to point it out to him. It was a nuisance. But I'm sure you won't be a nuisance, will you?'

Driscoll said, quietly, 'You should know me better, Willy. I never play both ends at once. Except,' he grinned at Landford, 'when I'm in the middle myself. So don't let it worry you, Willy.'

'No,' Landford said. 'I don't think it will *worry* me. Really, I never let things develop far enough for that.'

He walked across the room to the door. Driscoll noticed that he moved easily and lightly, with the delicately precise foot placings of a man who would be catlike in his agility.

At the door Landford paused, said, 'So long, Johnny. Be good.'

'So long,' Driscoll said.

He watched the little man open the door, slide unobtrusively through it, close it behind him. He looked at the bottle of whisky, realised he needed a drink badly. He walked across, stood frowning down at the bottle. He reached out for it and picked it up, turned abruptly and walked across to the sideboard, replaced the half-full bottle and slid the shelf up with a bang. He still needed a drink.

He lit a cigarette, began to think about Landford. He thought that Landford was a very tough proposition. The sort of person one should always work with rather than against. Which, he reflected, a fair number of people had discovered about himself at one time or another.

He wondered what Landford would think if he knew about the message he had inserted in the *Evening Standard* two days back. And the fact that they had telephoned him the next day telling him to be at the Mandolin tonight. He glanced at his watch, saw it was just past eight. He thought there was plenty of time to go through the stuff Landford had brought before he changed.

Having quickly examined the papers he decided there was very little there apart from Glazey. He paid most attention to Winterley's notebook, memorising the telephone numbers that were dotted through the pages. The report on Winterley had already told him that the test pilot had been quite a boy for women. He went carefully through the numbers, discarding the obviously foreign ones, storing the others away in his mind.

He wondered whether anyone but the professionals realised that the difference between a good agent and a brilliant one was often merely the possession of a trained and selective memory. Just the ability to draw from the mind when required some little fact that had lain dormant there for years. The little fact that explained everything when it was fitted into the jigsaw.

He put the papers away in a drawer of the sideboard, picked up the telephone and dialled a Flaxman number. After a while he heard Marian Courtney's voice.

'Driscoll.' He said, 'Feel like some work?'

'I think that would be a good idea. I take it you mean official work?' Marian said.

Driscoll grinned. 'You can take it any way you like. I'll be round to your flat some time after midnight. You'll have to go away for a few days.'

He stopped talking, listened to her for a moment, then

said, 'No I can't make it before midnight. In fact it may be quite a long time after midnight. It all depends.'

Marian snapped, 'Depends on what?'

Driscoll thought her voice was very attractive when she was annoyed.

'Not that it's any of your business but I have a date,' he said, 'You know how it is with a date, especially with someone you're taking out for the first time. It may be over quickly, it may last a very long time indeed. Some time after midnight. An' make sure you've got some strong black coffee ready. I'll probably need it.'

He slammed the receiver down. He thought that Marian was a most interesting girl, that she should prove very entertaining when she started trying to trip him up.

He walked into the bedroom, wondered idly what the girl they were sending to contact him at the Mandolin would be like. As he changed, he thought that things might become very interesting. There was Landford to consider, and there was the question of how much money they were prepared to offer. There was the girl he was going to meet, and the possibility of lots of things happening when they found he was willing to play.

And of course, there was Marian.

He whistled to himself as he changed, thinking that things looked quite promising. He wondered what Landford had thought of the flat, was absolutely sure the little man had searched it very thoroughly.

10

Driscoll walked across to the bar entrance of the Mandolin Club, his feet plumping noiselessly on the soft luxuriousness of a deep pile carpet. He checked his hat at the little glass kiosk to the right of the bar entrance, placed a half crown in the plate on the glass counter. The check girl smiled. It was a mechanically inviting smile, a smile with years of practice behind it. She had long black hair, finely tapering legs, and eyes as distant as half-forgotten sins, and a cockney accent as raucous as an Aldgate Saturday night.

He pushed open the heavy swing door of the bar, stood a moment at the door to select a stool that would give him a view of the whole club. He crossed to it and leaned on the bar, watching the white coated barman serving drinks to several customers. He saw the barman flick money from two orders into the till, palm the money from the third. It was neat and fast. A smooth professional job. Driscoll grinned. The barman moved down toward him.

He said, quietly, 'A large whisky. Straight.' He grinned again. 'Tell me, how do they lift you out at night? With a crane?'

The barman looked at Driscoll carefully. He shuffled back one step, reached behind him for a bottle and a glass, set it in front of Driscoll without once taking his eyes from him. He tilted the bottle, poured a little whisky into the glass, said, 'So?' His tone was pleasantly conversational.

'So I could be HPA.'

'In this dump? Don't make me laugh. Again, so?'

'So who cares? Except if they're thirsty.'

The barman arched his eyebrows delicately. He cocked his head slightly on one side, looked straight at Driscoll and nodded slowly.

'The gentleman has a point,' he said.

He tilted the bottle again, poured whisky until the glass was half-full. He carefully placed the bottle, unstoppered, on the bar close to Driscoll, moved away to serve drinks to a plump, white-haired man and his young, sleekly lacquered companion.

Driscoll topped his glass with water, sipped the drink. It was good, really good. He thought that not for years had whisky tasted so good. Perhaps, he thought, the last ten days had been worth it. He swung his stool round, looked down over the scrolled metal railings that separated the bar from the main floor of the club.

He decided that both the club and most of the women present had seen better days. In the soft lighting they could get by. But in daylight the brittle elegance would look just what it was — a little gaudy, a little cheap, a little too striving after the real thing.

He sipped again at his drink as the lights dimmed and the first of the two singers who were advertised as the main floorshow appeared in the spotlight.

She was a handsome blonde, tall and beautifully proportioned, and with no voice at all.

He turned back to the bar, half hearing the succession of short point-numbers, looking around him and seeing that there was no one at the bar yet who seemed to be interested in him. He pushed a cigarette between his lips, felt for his lighter, saw flame in front of him as the barman struck a match. He dragged smoke into his lungs, said, 'Thanks. Do you have to listen to this every night?'

The barman spoke softly. 'Twice a night. For the last six weeks. Me, I'm tired of her. The customers are tired of her. The band's tired of her. So they've just signed her up for another six weeks.'

Driscoll said, 'Who's they?'

'The boss. He isn't at all tired of her. He takes her wrestling.'

'Maybe if she stuck to wrestling she'd make a good act.'

'Not the kind of act you could put on here though,' the barman said, 'strictly in private it would have to be.'

He moved away down the bar, turned, came back and added as an afterthought, 'The boss is a slob. Help yourself to whisky.' He moved away again.

Driscoll laughed softly to himself. He thought the barman was doing a lot to make his evening. He poured himself a small whisky, added a lot of water.

The blonde finished her act and swayed off the floor to a weak spatter of applause. The lights came up for a while as the band took a break, and then gradually dimmed again. Through the darkened room Driscoll saw a tall woman he hadn't noticed before, but then suddenly over his head an amber beam sliced through smoke-laden air to impact in a tight, hard circle on the floor. He heard the band slide into a slow blues, then a voice that made him jerk round in time to see the second singer step slowly into the circle of light.

He drew his breath in as he looked at her. She was tall, slender, a sinuous high yellow. She was a picture in her white silk dress, taut over her rhythmically swaying thighs, smooth sepia tones seemingly brushed lightly on bare shoulders and arms, hair as black and brilliant as polished ebony. She moved slowly in the bright amber of the light, singing of something old and distant and unhappy in a voice like crimson velvet.

For a few minutes he forgot the Mandolin, and London, lost himself in something that was out of time and place.

He remembered a steaming, walk-up club, three floors above the Loop in the roaring heat of a Chicago August — musicians with under-vests soaking in sweat, and the bitter smell of hemp in the air. And a girl just like this girl, only better. And a song that was just a song and didn't matter except that once you heard it, it stayed with you and became a part of you, and was unhappy when you were.

When he went back to Chicago ten years later it was the place he had tried to find again and couldn't. The place he had told Patti about, promised to take her to. The place which was only a dream now, maybe had never existed.

Then it was over, and the girl was bowing to applause that broke in thick waves round the room. Behind her the bandleader broke into the spot, his fat, pallid face bobbing grotesquely over her shoulder as he got in on the applause — the pale monstrosity of his pudgy hand, white and hairless as a plate, flung carelessly round her smooth brown shoulder.

Then the girl walked quickly off the floor and through

a door marked *Private*. The bandleader turned back to the musicians, started them on a slow number.

Driscoll, back in the present again, was briefly grateful for the memory of the murdered past. When he turned back to the bar he saw that the woman he had spotted earlier had taken the stool next to him.

She was tall, very blonde, dressed in a plain, black velvet gown that fitted her like a sheath. Her golden throat was encircled with a single strand of very large, very red stones. Her eyes were bright with the reflected fire of the necklace, and alive with a steady blue flame that was all their own. She looked straight at him, smiled.

Driscoll smiled back, said, 'It couldn't possibly be. Or could it?'

'If you're ready for business it could,' she replied softly. Her voice was rich and warm, with a small part of vibrant huskiness.

Driscoll laughed. 'Let's not make it too dramatic. Obviously I'm the person you were told to meet. You must have seen me while I was watching the girl who sang.'

'Two girls sang.'

'One. One girl sang, the other wrestles. Drink?' Driscoll offered.

'Wrestles? I don't understand… a gin and French, please. Very cold, no lemon peel.'

'You don't have to.'

He ordered a small drink for himself, a large one for her. This time the barman took money. His face was quite impassive. Driscoll handed the girl her drink.

'I thought it might be better if we went somewhere from here,' Driscoll said, 'you know, somewhere we could talk a little, maybe drink a little too. How does it strike you?'

The girl sipped her drink, said, 'Very cold, very good. Why not? I have a flat with whisky, gin, French, even a refrigerator. Of course, I'd like to feel before we went there that it would be an agreeable talk.'

'So would I. As I see it, it can't help being agreeable from my point of view.' He grinned at her. 'After all, you're obviously going to offer me something... I feel already I'm going to be interested.'

'I'm glad you feel that. Everyone will be very pleased. My name's Janine Maxwell, by the way. I know yours already.'

She raised her glass, finished her drink, said, 'Yes. Definitely very cold and very good.' She set the glass down on the bar. 'Shall we go?'

Driscoll nodded. He let her precede him out of the bar, leaned over and said to the barman, 'Very cold, very good. No?'

The barman smiled. He said softly, 'Very cold? No. Very good? Who knows?'

'Who indeed,' Driscoll said.

He winked at the barman, walked swiftly out of the bar, took his hat from the check girl.

Janine was waiting for him by the main doors of the club. He took her arm, helped her into a taxi summoned by the commissionaire. She gave the driver an address in Kensington. Neither of them spoke during the journey. When they arrived Driscoll paid off the taxi, followed Janine up to the top floor of the house.

He noted that her flat occupied the entire floor. There

would, he supposed, be a flat exactly similar on each floor beneath hers. She opened the door with a Yale key, led him through a small lobby into a large, well-furnished room overlooking the square.

Over to the left a deep and comfortable lounge chair faced a long settee, an occasional table between them. To the right a dining alcove held a light oak table, four matching chairs. Near the door a cream telephone sat on a high pedestal. The floor was covered with a thick carpet in plain grey.

Janine said, 'Have a seat while I fix the drinks. Whisky?'

'Whisky. A small one with lots of water while we talk business. Nice flat.'

Driscoll wandered over to the window, looked down on the quietly lit square. Out of the corner of his eye he saw Janine walk through a swing door next to the dining alcove. He heard her moving in the kitchen, the tinkle of glasses. He looked carefully round the room. To the right of the window a grilled ventilator set high in the wall was painted an attractive shade of cream that toned exactly with the decorative scheme of the room. He lifted one of the dining chairs, swung it beneath the ventilator. From the kitchen came the sudden plop of the whisky bottle's cork leaving the bottle.

He stepped up on the chair, peered through the grill of the ventilator. Tucked well back from the bars in the recess of the airshaft, he could just see the dark outline of a small microphone. He stepped down from the chair, replaced it silently at the table and was staring out of the window as Janine came back with the drinks. He wondered whether she knew that the flat was wired.

He watched her cross the room, thinking the small sway of her hips was most attractive. It was not conspicuous, yet it drew just sufficient attention to make one very conscious of the lithe body under the smooth sheath of the black velvet. He took the glass she held out to him, sipped it. It was very strong.

'Not a small whisky,' Driscoll said, 'not much water either. So you'll pardon me if I don't drink any more of it until we've talked business.'

He sat down in the lounge chair, found it as comfortable as it looked.

Janine sat at the far end of the settee. She said, 'Of course, provided we *are* going to talk business. Perhaps you'd like to get straight on to it.'

Driscoll lit a cigarette, inhaled deeply. He said, 'Let's put it this way. I feel I'd like to have an idea of the kind of business I'll be talking. I've already made it clear that I'm not interested in any deal for the kind of money I was offered. I'm still not interested.'

'So I understand. But the people who asked me to meet you feel that you would be interested in one thousand pounds. How do you feel about that?'

'It interests me more than the five hundred I was offered before. If I knew what the job was I could even say definitely whether it interested me enough to go ahead.'

Janine opened a small black cigarette case, selected a cigarette, lit it carefully.

'I also have to pay you five hundred pounds in advance. Provided, of course, that you agree to follow instructions.'

'I still don't know the job.' Driscoll said.

'And neither do I. But I was told to tell you it's something you should find quite easy. Someone seems to have a pretty high opinion of your ability. Look Driscoll, to show our good faith we're prepared to make you an advance payment of five hundred. All we want from you is a promise you'll obey instructions when you get them. Surely that's fair?'

'Maybe. Let's put it this way. If I take the advance I want to feel I can hand it back if I decide the job's not for me. Also, I'd like to feel that I wouldn't be kept waiting for the money. No post-dated cheques if you see what I mean.'

Janine smiled at him. 'All right, no one would object to that. And if you'll say the word, you can have the five hundred within thirty seconds, maybe.'

'Cash?'

'Used pound notes. Are you in?'

Driscoll looked straight at her. Suddenly he grinned.

'Cash is a word I'm very fond of,' he said. 'Yeah, I'm in. Let's see the money.'

11

For a moment there was silence in the room. Then Janine smiled, her teeth very white against the red of her full lips. She stood up, walked gracefully past Driscoll to the door that led to her bedroom, stood there looking at him. She was thinking that Driscoll was a very peculiar man. She was thinking that without trying to be attractive he was very attractive indeed. Maybe because he so obviously didn't give a damn for anyone or anything. She decided that she was very pleased Driscoll was coming in with them.

'I'll get the money right now, help yourself to a drink in the kitchen if you want one.'

She went into the bedroom, closed the door behind her.

Driscoll rose to his feet, wandered round the flat with his glass in his hand. He paused by the telephone, his eyes narrowing slightly as he noticed the number. He frowned, picked the telephone up and examined it closely. He saw the additional lead that had been braided carefully into the other leads, so carefully that it would have been indistinguishable to anyone unless they were deliberately looking for it.

He heard a slight noise at the bedroom door, walked casually across the room to examine one of the Degas prints on the far wall.

Behind him Janine said, 'I like that one. It's only a print, of course. The original would cost even more than I've got for you here.'

Driscoll turned, saying, 'This is the kind of business I like. Cash business.'

He paused, looking at her. The black velvet gown had gone. She had changed into a long, white silk robe, held together at the waist by a casually knotted black silk belt-tie.

Driscoll said softly, 'Yeah, good business.' He thought that this girl had a shape to make any man feel it was spring. Also that she knew it, and knew just how to use it. And that it wouldn't be too hard to play along and see what happened.

He moved forward to her, stretched his left hand out for the packet of money she was holding in her right hand. He felt the packet, twitched it out of her fingers without looking down, tossed it aside on the settee. She smiled, lazily, her lips parting very slightly, the tip of a pink tongue just protruding between her teeth. He put his right arm round her waist, pulled her slowly and deliberately into him, bent forward and kissed her. Her head went back, and her body pressed against his.

He pulled his mouth away, pushed her slowly to arm's length. She was flushed, and a little blue vein was beating heavily in the delicate skin of her temple. Driscoll thought she was as lovely as a beautiful, golden snake. And probably as dangerous.

'You're quite something, Janine.' Driscoll said slowly.

She smiled, twitched her shoulders. Her voice was husky as she said, 'They were so keen to hire you I knew you must be something special.'

She walked quickly across the room, pulled open a drawer in the oak table, turned to him with a little, nervous laugh. 'I think you'd better sign the receipt before anything else happens.'

She came slowly back to him, a piece of paper in her hand.

Driscoll, watching her, thought she was a hell of a woman. With all his experience he couldn't quite decide whether she was genuine or a very fine actress. Probably some of both, he thought, the actress first and then the woman taking over as the control slipped.

'Receipt?'

Janine turned to the settee, picked up her glass, and swallowed what was left of her drink. She took up the bundle of notes from the settee.

'For this.' She tossed the bundle to him. 'I wouldn't want anyone to think I'd spent it on myself.'

Driscoll looked at the bundle, saw five small packets held together by a sealed wrapper. 'All right.'

He separated one of the smaller packets after breaking the outer seal, slipped off the rubber band. He riffled rapidly through the notes, counting roughly, noting the absence of sequence in the numbers. He did the same with the other four packets, examining notes at random. Then, satisfied, he put three of the small packets in his hip pocket, the other two in the inside pocket of his tuxedo.

'OK. Let's have the receipt.'

She passed him the slip of paper. On it was typed: *Received from J.M. the sum of five hundred pounds sterling.*

He took out a ballpoint pen, scrawled his signature and the date underneath the typed words, handed the signed receipt back to her. She folded it, tucked it away in a small pocket of the robe behind a lace handkerchief.

'That's fine, Johnny. I suppose it's all right to call you Johnny now we know each other isn't it? How about another drink?'

'Not now,' Driscoll murmured. 'I made an appointment before I knew I was meeting you and I'm an hour late already. What happens next?'

'Someone will contact you in the next day or so. Just sit tight until they do.' She walked with him to the door of the flat, came close to him as he opened it. 'I bet that appointment's with a woman,' she said softly.

Driscoll looked at her with the sincere, honest expression he always assumed when he wanted to lie convincingly.

'No. Matter of fact I arranged to play poker with some fellows. They're into me for quite a bit. I've got a feeling I'm getting it back tonight.'

'All right, I believe you. But don't lose the money I've just given you.'

Driscoll laughed. 'No chance. They won't even know I've got it. It's going straight in a safe-deposit box tomorrow morning.'

'I'm glad,' Janine murmured.

She slipped one silk-clad arm round his neck, pulled his head down to hers, fastened her mouth on his. It lasted thirty seconds and thirty years. Then he broke away, held her gently away from him.

Driscoll looked down at her and marvelled again at her beauty. Then he eased quickly through the door, pulled it shut behind him before she could move.

Janine heard the sound of his steps on the stairs. She leaned back against the wall near the door, her eyes closed, a dreamy smile puckering her lips. She thought that Driscoll was going to be a lot of fun, not least because she could sense the hard ruthlessness that was part of him.

She shivered slightly, moved back into the kitchen and poured another drink, wondering what the woman he was meeting was like. She smiled maliciously at the thought that Driscoll might find her quite insipid after her own embraces.

She finished her drink, left the glass by the sink and went back to the living room. She sat on the settee, crossing one long smooth leg over the other, not sure now that she wanted Eric Barnett to come. She began to hope that he would merely telephone to find out about Driscoll. She lit a cigarette, sat smoking quietly, kept thinking about Driscoll and the woman he was meeting.

Driscoll closed the door of the house behind him, walked slowly along one side of the quiet square. He was thinking about the microphone concealed in the ventilator shaft, the extra lead that showed the telephone was tapped. Thinking about Winterley, who had obviously been to the flat since the number of the telephone was the same as one of the numbers in his brown notebook.

He wondered about Janine herself, whether she knew the microphone and wiretap were there.

He smiled, thinking that right now Janine was wondering just what sort of a woman he was going to meet. He knew quite well that she hadn't believed him, that his story of the poker game had only convinced her he was going to meet a woman. He thought that Janine was probably busy wondering what the other woman had got that she hadn't. Or else convincing herself that after her he'd find the other woman disappointing. All that and then of course notifying someone that he'd taken the money and signed the receipt.

He thought that Janine was very nice work indeed, the kind of girl who could have twisted Winterley round her finger with the utmost ease. He wondered how long she would last, decided that she would be very amusing while she did.

Aimlessly he turned left at the end of the square, walked north in the direction of Gloucester Road. He heard one o'clock boom flatly over the rooftops, and the sound broke in on his thoughts, reminding him of Marian. He thought that Marian would be simmering quietly by now. The idea pleased him very much.

He glanced casually back over his shoulder in the hope of spotting a taxi, just caught the dark blur of a shadow moving into the darkness of an entrance. He walked on slowly, took the next turning on the right, straining his ears for the sound of footsteps. At last, very faintly, he heard the soft plump of rubber-soled shoes on the pavement.

He walked another fifty yards, stopped deliberately and took out a packet of cigarettes. He put one in his mouth, lifted his lighter, glanced quickly down the street before he flicked the lighter into flame. The street was deserted, badly lit. But Driscoll's experienced eye noticed a faint ripple of movement as someone pressed closely against the deep shadowed darkness of a wall. He lit his cigarette, walked slowly on. He thought things were beginning to roll.

On the other side of the street, fifty yards away, he saw the lighted windows of a telephone kiosk. He started toward it, walking diagonally across the deserted road. Again, very faintly, he caught the soft plump of moving feet. He entered the kiosk, lifted the receiver, put three pennies in the slot and dialled Marian's number.

As the bell rang at the other end of the line he turned, glanced casually down the street, turned again. The brief glimpse had shown him the street bare and deserted, the man who was tailing him quite indistinguishable in the darkness.

He heard Marian's voice, said, 'Driscoll. Listen carefully and don't interrupt.' He paused for a moment as she spoke, cut in on her and said, 'All right, keep it till you see me. But just listen for the next few moments. I'm not coming to your flat. There's someone tailing me an' I can't risk leading him there. Here's what I want you to do. Get a taxi to the Curzon Street entrance of Shepherd's Market. You know, the one with the archway and the suggestive advertisements... All right, all right, I didn't say you did... Go down through the archway, and walk along until you come to Number 87. Ring the bell and when someone answers tell them I told you to meet me there. They'll take you in to wait for me. Got it?'

'Yes, but...'

'But nothing, Marian. I'll join you there when I've shaken this tail. If I can. If not I'll call you there. Now repeat the instructions.' He listened while she repeated them, 'OK. You've got it. Get round there as soon as you can, but don't leave until I get there or telephone you. Oh, and one more thing.'

'Yes?'

Driscoll smiled nastily. 'You can take off whatever pretty thing you put on for my benefit and wear something plain. No one's going to worry what you wear at that place, an' you'll be less conspicuous in something like a quiet two-piece. Pity really after you've been to so much trouble, but there you are.'

'You conceited ape, if you think…'

Marian's voice tailed off as she realised she was talking into a dead phone. She looked down at the immaculate lines of the hostess gown she had bought in Paris a few months ago, had carefully kept for a special occasion. She stormed into the tiny kitchen of her flat, turned off the hotplate under the coffeepot. She called Driscoll a lot of very bad names. It was surprising just how many she knew and how bad they were. Then she went into the bedroom to change. She wondered how Driscoll knew she was wearing something special. Finally she decided it was just a lucky guess, or merely the flippancy she had come to expect from him. The thought made her feel much better.

12

Driscoll replaced the receiver, stood looking at it for a moment. He took a wallet from his inside pocket, pulled out a piece of paper, made a few meaningless marks on it with a pen. Then he pushed the door open, came out putting the wallet and the pen back in his pocket. It looked quite natural.

He walked back slowly along the street, looking neither to left nor right, whistling softly through closed lips. When he came to the intersection of streets he paused at the corner, looked at his wristwatch, turned as though on a sudden impulse and walked along the pavement of the street on the right. Five yards past the corner he saw what he wanted, a deep recessed doorway leading to the entrance of a block of flats. He walked past it for fifteen yards or so, then turned and went quickly back, placing his feet very lightly, making no noise at all. He pressed back into the darkness of the recess, breathing very quietly through his nose, listening for the sound of footsteps.

He heard them, very faintly, as they approached the corner where he had looked at his watch. Driscoll imagined the man looking carefully round the corner. He tensed himself, held his breath. The footsteps came on. Driscoll saw the dark shape move past the doorway, moved forward himself, fast and silently. The man's head jerked round with the sudden surprise of someone detecting a quick movement in the corner of their eye.

Driscoll flicked out his left arm, caught him by the throat to stifle any noise, ducked under the round swing of a left arm as he turned. He moved in half a pace, smashed his right hand into the man's stomach, just below the solar plexus, felt his fist sink in with the whole weight of his heavy shoulders behind it. The man groaned faintly through his constricted throat, started to bend forward. Driscoll let him bend, caught him with a short right hook on the side of the chin, a vicious punch that jarred his hand as he felt the jawbone crack.

The man slumped, his knees collapsing under him. Driscoll took his left hand from his throat, bustled him back into the recess, let him slump unconscious to the ground. He looked down at him, saw a man of middle size and build, wearing plain, dark clothes. He had brown hair, a small brown moustache, neatly clipped. Driscoll kneeled beside him, ran his hand along the side of the face, realised that he also had a broken jaw. He grinned, thinking that next time he would be a much more efficient tail, would never make the elementary mistake of keeping right against the wall.

He straightened up, walked quietly to the corner, looked round it cautiously. A hundred and fifty yards away he saw a light bobbing, watched for a few seconds while the light came nearer, flashing into doorways and shop entrances as the policeman walked slowly along. Driscoll cursed, ducked back into the doorway.

He reckoned he had two minutes at the most. Certainly not enough time to wait for the man to recover consciousness and question him. He kneeled down beside him. Quickly and expertly he went through the clothes, found nothing at all except for some loose silver in the trousers. He straightened up, went out of the doorway and peered round the corner again. The policeman was only fifty or sixty yards away. He turned, walked swiftly up the street, turned left and then right into Gloucester Road. Pretty soon he flagged a passing taxi, told the driver to take him to Shepherd's Market.

He relaxed in the dim interior of the taxi, lit a cigarette. He wondered just who was tailing him and why. Then he wondered if they were really smart, if they'd put two tails on him and not one. One to be rather obvious and spotted. The other to take over when the first one had been detected and the person being tailed would think he was clear. He turned in his seat, looked back through the small window. There was very little traffic now, and none of it following the taxi.

He decided to take no chances, leaned forward and told the driver to drop him in Park Lane. He paid the taxi off, walked briskly along the familiar streets to Shepherd's Market. Five minutes after leaving the taxi he was ringing the bell of Number 87.

Number 87 was a place Driscoll had used quite a lot from time to time. From the outside it was just a large house. Once inside it was a twisted maze of little passages with rooms branching off them, the passages leading ultimately to a large room, rather badly ventilated, where the crowd who habitually used the house could sit all night taking their pleasure. All kinds of pleasure, since the management was very broad-minded indeed. Provided, of course, that the customers were known. And provided, even more importantly, that they could afford to pay, and pay in cash. Credit was a word that was quite unknown here.

Certain of the elder *habitués* did dimly remember a golden age when a new management — on the average there was a new management every six months, though there were certain grounds for supposing that the ownership of Number 87 never changed — had, in its ignorance, allowed credit to the customers. It had even in a sublime act of folly cashed cheques.

That particular management had lasted only a week, just sufficient time for the cheques that were gratefully showered upon it to return promptly and unfailingly from banks all over the country bearing such unkind stamped messages as 'No Account' and 'Refer to Drawer'. But the older *habitués* still talked lovingly of that week, during which all their pleasures had been sweeter than ever in the warming knowledge that they were not being paid for.

The present management, a swarthy gentleman of Mediterranean origin and Soho upbringing, escorted Driscoll through the passages to the main room, and instructed the waiter to make sure that Driscoll was served with the same whisky the staff drank, not the potent but killing fluid that was served to less favoured customers.

The current management was fond of Driscoll, and also a little afraid of him. People who depended on Number 87 for their pleasure — whether it was the harsh weed or the white powder, the discreet loan of a private room or a hypo — were easy to control. One had merely to cut off their particular pleasure. People like Driscoll were different.

The main room of the house was long and T shaped, the entrance being at the base of the T. At the junction of the upright and crossbar four pallid musicians, dressed in rather dirty frilled white blouses and tight black trousers, beat out lethargic and depressing samba music. It was punctuated by occasional shouts of *Olé!* from the maestros, that being the only Spanish they knew.

Wreaths of smoke, not all of it from tobacco, hung in spiralled layers near the ceiling, and the dim light helped to hide the unattractive complexions of the customers. Most of them spent all night in places like Number 87, crawling into their beds only when dawn came and daylight, which they hated, threatened to catch them in view.

Driscoll looked down the room, saw Marian at once. She was sitting in one of the small booths which ran down the left wall, pointedly ignoring glances which a middle-aged person of indeterminate sex, but dressed in female clothing, was directing at her from the other side of the room. Driscoll grinned. The female customers at the place tended to divide into two well-defined and mutually exclusive types. She looked up, saw him, raised her hand. He began to walk toward her table.

Marian was very annoyed with Driscoll. She objected to being driven out of her flat at this time of the night. She objected even more to being left to wait for him in a place like this, Number 87.

She had never seen anywhere like it before, was not particularly anxious to see anything like it again. She watched Driscoll striding toward her, caught herself thinking that he looked very good in evening clothes. His big shoulders fitted snugly under a well-tailored tuxedo, and his tanned face was attractively dark over the white of his shirt.

He stopped at the table, slid into the seat opposite her. 'Sorry to keep you waiting. Something came up.' He thought she looked very nice indeed in a plain, dark grey suit and a soft white cotton sweater with a high neck.

'Don't bother to apologise,' Marian snapped back, 'just tell me what you want so I can get back to the flat. I don't think a great deal of your haunts.'

Driscoll grinned. 'All right, if that's how you want it. Personally I'd have welcomed the experience. Drink?'

'I don't want a drink.'

'No? Well I do.' He called the waiter over, ordered two whiskies, called the waiter back and said, 'By the way, I mean whisky. Not the stuff you've got at the bar. Catch?'

The waiter smiled, screwed his face into an ugly grimace that was possibly his interpretation of a knowing wink, hurried away.

Marian tapped her fingers impatiently on the table. 'If you think I'm going to drink anything they serve in here you're mistaken.'

Driscoll looked at her carefully. He said, casually, 'Look, let's get one thing straight. I don't give a good goddam what you think or what you want, so long as you do what I tell you. If you don't want the drink, leave it. An' stop behaving like a child. You don't really need to'.

Marian took a deep breath, started to say something, thought better of it.

Driscoll looked at her with amusement, said, 'That's

better. Now we're coming on. An' I meant it when I apologised for keeping you waiting. The point is I had no option about bringing you here. I had to see you tonight and it might not have been very good for you in the long run if I'd been tailed to your flat.'

'I can take care of myself.' There were two spots of high red in her cheeks, and her eyes were sparkling and angry.

Driscoll laughed. He said, 'In a pig's eye you could. Listen, Marian, You're a nice kid. But I've been around this business longer than you have. If I tell you to do something, do it. Be angry if you like, call me nasty names if you like, but *do it*.'

He paused, then spoke again, but more softly now, leaning forward and smiling pleasantly.

'You know why Davidson gave you to me for this job, Marian?'

'No,' she replied.

Her voice was calmer now, the small spots of red dying away from her cheeks. She thought Driscoll was doing his best to be nice, felt the strange charm that he could turn on and off like a tap.

'Because he knew I'd look after you,' Driscoll said, 'you'll be fine at the stuff I'm going to give you, but you're not ready for the really tough stuff yet. You can play a thing like this lots of ways, but I'm playing it so there's no connection between us that can be traced, that way I know you'll be all right. And just as important I'll know that your flat will be all right if I need a place to duck into and lie up. That's why you're here, because it's safe here. Did Davidson give you the outline of what's happening?'

'Yes. I saw him the day before yesterday. Funnily enough he told me almost the same thing you've just told me.'

She stopped talking as the waiter returned with the drinks.

Driscoll paid for the drinks, sniffed at his glass. 'It's quite all right to drink it. Special bottle.' He smiled at her, poured water into her glass, raised his own. 'Good luck. Let's start from now, shall we?'

Marian nodded, sipped her drink, was surprised to find that the whisky tasted very good. She thought that she had misjudged Driscoll, that he was really very well intentioned, that the hard exterior was not really typical of the man at all. She did not quite know whether that made him more attractive or not.

Driscoll said, 'All right. Here it is. I'm not going to give you too much, because I want you to start on it with a fresh mind. The jet-fighter we're concerned with crashed yesterday.' He leaned forward, spoke very softly. 'This is what I want you to do. Go to the plane's works.' He named a town in Norfolk. 'The airfield and the works factory, where they're making the prototype jets, is about two miles out of town. On the airfield side of the works there's a pub called the Roebuck. It's a good pub, with accommodation, you'll be comfortable there. Register in any name you like except your own. Clear?'

'Clear.'

'Right. Now the Roebuck is the pub where a lot of the pilots and engineers from the airfield hang out. I'm told it's pretty lively there on a Friday and Saturday, so you should just be in time. I want you to pretend you're an old girl friend of Winterley's — that's the pilot who was killed flying the fighter yesterday. I want you to find out all you can about him, including the names of his current girlfriends. I'll leave it to you how you do it.'

He grinned at her.

'You shouldn't have *too* much difficulty getting friendly with people. Naturally you won't know Winterley's dead until they tell you. But since you're just an old girl friend of his you won't be too worried. It won't stop you drinking with whoever you meet an' having a good time, if you see what I mean. It's the last six months I'm particularly interested in. Can you do that?'

'I like pilots,' Marian said, 'they're generally very dashing. And very interesting too, when you get to know them well.'

Driscoll grinned. 'Don't have too good a time,' he said. 'An' don't forget those boys are used to moving pretty quickly. Another drink?'

Marian put her empty glass on the table, said, 'I can move quickly myself. Where am I supposed to have met Winterley?'

Driscoll took a long slim envelope from the inside pocket of his tuxedo, passed it over to her. 'Don't open it here. You'll find a photograph of him there, also his personal details. Pick any one of the places he's been to in the last four years. Preferably a place he was at about three years ago. That would account for you not knowing much about his present life. Did you say another drink?'

'No thank you. I think I'd rather like to go now. This atmosphere is a little hard on the throat.'

Driscoll said, 'OK.' He smiled at her. 'How long would it take to get the coffee hot again in your flat?'

'About five minutes, it's all ready. But…'

'But what?'

Marian looked at him. She thought he was very attractive indeed. And very clever. She thought it would be much better for her to return to her flat alone. She didn't want Driscoll too near her until she had decided exactly what she felt about him. She knew instinctively that things might start to happen very quickly if he was too near.

'Would you mind awfully if you didn't come back tonight? I feel very tired,' she said quickly, before she could change her mind.

Driscoll looked straight at her.

She saw a little half-smile give a cynical and infuriating twist to his lips.

'The Chinese have a proverb,' he said, 'it goes: *Pu tao ho pien pu t'o hsieh*.' Driscoll stood up, moved sideways out from the table.

Marian picked up her handbag, stood up. 'And what does it mean?'

'*Don't take your shoes off until you reach the river*,' Driscoll said softly. 'I'll arrange a taxi for you.'

He turned, walked up to the waiter, talked to him. Marian realised, suddenly, that he had never intended to come with her. She felt very annoyed, but with herself not Driscoll. He beckoned to her and she followed him through the passages into the street. The management had produced a taxi with surprising speed.

Driscoll slammed the door behind her, said, 'Call me as soon as you get back. It shouldn't take too long. You have my number?'

'Yes. Goodbye.'

She leaned forward, gave the driver her address. As

the taxi moved off she suddenly felt very sorry that she had left Driscoll behind. She wished she could have thought of a snappy retort to the Chinese proverb he had quoted. She spent the whole of the ride thinking about it.

Driscoll went straight back to his flat. He slid aside the picture over the mantelpiece revealing a small safe. He opened the safe, put most of the money inside. Then he slid the picture back, checked that it was fully home. Two little spots, one on the wall, one on the picture, stood exactly opposite each other to confirm it. They were very small spots, not noticeable unless one looked for them specially. Driscoll grinned, thinking that even an expert like Landford had not noticed them. After Landford had been in the flat he had discovered that the two spots were not quite opposite each other, showing that Landford had slid back the picture and looked at the safe.

Driscoll wondered if Landford had opened it. He thought the little man was probably thorough enough even for that. But if so he would have found nothing. It was the first occasion that any safe of Driscoll's had held money for a long time.

13

'Look,' Fellows said, 'I built the aeroplane and I know. Damn and blast it all, *I know*. If I could I'd gamble my own life on it but I can't. That's why I'm asking you to gamble yours. You see that Gordon, don't you?'

Gordon Bellamy looked at Fellows, saw the restless twitching of his fingers, the nervous way he tapped a cigarette repeatedly on the desk before he lit it.

'Take it easy, Bill,' Bellamy said, 'I get paid for that sort of gamble, so let me worry about it. I've already flown her a good few hours and I know she's been checked and counterchecked all that's possible. Now leave it to me.' His voice was slow and deep, his whole attitude calm and solid.

Bellamy was that sort of a person, very slow and deliberate in all he did. Looking at his short, powerful body, his thick neck and calm brown eyes, it was difficult to imagine him at the controls of a supersonic fighter. Yet those spatulate fingers were capable of an amazing delicacy of touch when they caressed the controls — that seemingly slow brain capable of the split second decisions that meant the difference between life and death.

Fellows inhaled a deep lungful of smoke, felt that it was a great comfort to have someone like Bellamy available to step straight up into Winterley's shoes as the senior test pilot. His face clouded momentarily as he thought of Winterley. Then he forgot him in his intense concern over the testing of the second fighter.

'All right, Gordon. Take her up and prove me wrong. Break her if you can. She's done fifteen hours less flying than the first model. *If* anything's going to happen it'll happen in the next twenty hours. Get through that and I think we'll have it licked.' He paused, leaned forward and stubbed his cigarette in the ashtray with little, jerking movements. 'But you won't break her. I know that, Gordon. She'll stand all you can do and more. She's all ready for you now.'

Bellamy stood up. 'See you in an hour or so, Bill. Going to listen in the tower?'

Fellows nodded. He watched Bellamy walk to the door, said quietly, 'It would be silly to say be careful. Just good luck. She won't break, I know it.'

Bellamy paused, said, 'I know it too. And if she does *I'll* never know it so it's all right either way.' He smiled, went out through the door.

Fellows lit another cigarette, walked slowly across to the tower. From there he watched the brilliant silver of the fighter flash along the runway then rocket up into the grey stratus that hung like a pall over the airfield. As the plane disappeared into the cloud he went and sat by the receiver to wait for Bellamy's transmissions to begin.

At forty-five thousand Bellamy leaned forward, pressed his transmitter.

'Bluebird Two. At height, ready to start. Receiving? Over.'

His earphones vibrated with the crackle of the ground controller's voice coming through, 'Strength five.

Standing by. Over.'

Bellamy pressed the transmitter button again, clicked in an override switch that kept the button continuously depressed so he could transmit all the time.

'OK, stall and spin first.'

He moved the throttles slowly back, reducing the turbine revolutions to five thousand. Then he pulled back on the stick, held the fighter in a steep climb, watched the airspeed falling off as she climbed, talking quietly into the transmitter and giving the airspeed readings as the needle slipped back.

He used knots to call the speed now, not Mach number. The stalling speed of an aircraft was always measured in knots, for the airspeed in knots was exactly the same at the stall point whether the aircraft was at fifty thousand or five.

He watched the speed drop past one-fifty, felt the increasing sloppiness of the controls as the fighter approached the stall. At one-thirty he felt the roughness as the airflow started breaking up over the wings, and at one-twenty-five the fighter's nose suddenly dropped, the left wing flicking down. He pressed gently on the left rudder, helped the fighter into a left hand spin, looking straight down at high cirrus wisps that spun giddily beneath him. He tightened the spin with more rudder, then at thirty-five thousand pushed the stick forward, at the same time pressing gently on the right rudder bar. The spin eased, stopped, leaving the aircraft still pointing down in a steep dive, the airspeed building up rapidly now. As it reached three hundred he eased the stick back, opening the throttles, pulled the fighter up into a steep climb.

'OK,' he reported, 'that one came about one-twenty-five. The left wing dropped quite fast. Recovery normal. Climbing to forty-five again.'

He whistled tunelessly between his teeth as he held the fighter in the climb, levelled off at the top and let the speed build up to 0.95 Mach.

Then he said, 'Maximum rate turns now, port first.'

He continued transmitting as he rolled the fighter smoothly into a steep port turn. The greyness began to come down on him at four-and-a-half G, and he pulled the stick harder back into his stomach, opening the throttles firmly as he did.

He looked only at the accelerometer now, calling the readings as light faded from the greyness, and the curtain of black descended.

On the ground they heard his voice calling, 'Six, six and a half, seven, half, eigh…' and then the silence that showed he was out.

Pressed down in his seat, unable to lift his hand or to talk, Bellamy felt, through a muffling black veil, the sudden surge and release as the fighter flicked viciously out of the turn and fell away. The blackness turned to grey again as the blood began to flow back behind his eyes and he eased the stick gently forward, pulling the throttles back to prevent the speed building up too quickly. Again he found himself in a steep dive, but a spiral one this time, with just enough G to press him into his seat and make his hand difficult to move.

He pulled her out and up, climbing back to forty-five again, saying, 'She was past eight when she flicked. Starboard now.'

He went through the same procedure, turning to

starboard this time, again flicking out of the turn when he blacked out.

'All right, Bill, if you're there listening, I'm going through in a dive, trimming back, pulling her out at one point four. Listen for the bang.'

Fellows, sitting tensely by the transmitter, looked across to Jack Armstrong, the works manager. He said to him, tonelessly, 'If she'll take this she'll take anything. He's going to dive through, then trim back. Trim right back, so that if he let her go she'd climb steeply. But he isn't just going to let go. He's going to pull hard back at one point four. You know how much G that will put on the aircraft?'

'Eight or nine?'

Fellows laughed shortly. 'About twelve. It'll knock him cold of course. He'll only come round when she's steady in the climb.'

'If the wings don't come off,' Armstrong said.

'The bloody wings *won't* come off.'

Fellows' voice was loud, almost a shout. He was trembling. He reached into his pocket for a cigarette, mumbled without looking up.

'Sorry, Jack. One of those things.'

'It's all right, Bill. I know just how you feel. Listen, he's starting the dive through.'

Fellows bent forward, his head close to the receiver.

Bellamy's voice crackled out, 'Point eight five. Diving now.'

In the aircraft Bellamy glanced at the inclinometer, saw he was diving at seventy degrees. The throttles were fully open, the speed building up rapidly.

At 0.97 Mach the judder began, heavy enough but not

nearly so noticeable as it had been on the first model. It lasted only six seconds as he shot through the barrier, and the Machmeter flicked steadily on past 1.0, 1.1, 1.2.

As it passed 1.2 he reached down with his left hand, felt the fore and aft trimming lever. He moved it slowly back, at the same time increasing his pressure on the stick to hold it forward. With the trimmer three quarters of the way back he could hardly hold the stick forward as the trimming tabs tried to push the elevators down and bring the nose of the aircraft up. He pushed forward on the stick with all his strength, holding it there as the altimeter sped past thirty thousand, with the speed up to 1.35. Then as the needle, moving slower now, crept round to 1.4 he said, 'Twenty-five, one point four, pulling out now.'

They heard his voice tail off into complete silence as he released his forward pressure, pulled the stick toward him. The nose began to rise with a speed that startled him, and he was literally smashed down as the centrifugal force built up rapidly. No warning curtain of grey this time, just a solid wall of black before his eyes, an awful weight on him, his head slumping forward and down. And then nothing.

On the ground they heard the banging through the radio as the airframe of the fighter shivered and shuddered under the awful strain. It continued for fifteen seconds, heavy and menacing, surely more than the airframe could possibly endure. Then, slowly, it died away to a soft shudder, was gone completely, they waited, absolutely silent, for Bellamy to speak. They heard first a gulp, then the heavy panting of his breath.

And then it came, loud and clearly, getting stronger as he spoke, 'All right, she stood it, Bill. Can't see any damage anywhere. Feel a bit tired. Coming back in now.'

Fellows acknowledged Bellamy's transmission then turned abruptly away and stood quite motionless for a moment, looking out of the window, before turning back to Armstrong.

'OK, Jack. Let's have a team on her right away. I'm willing to bet you won't find her stressed beyond the limit anywhere.'

His voice was quite different now, though a faint tremor was still discernible in it. He felt in his pocket for another cigarette, realised with a start that he had one in his mouth already, hadn't lit it in the strain of listening to Bellamy.

He grinned, chiding himself for his foolishness, promptly forgot to light it again as he watched anxiously from the control tower for the fighter to land.

14

Driscoll walked slowly across Bloomsbury Square, following the instructions Landford had given him on getting to the section.

He wondered just what the conference was about, thought that he was looking forward to meeting Browne. He remembered hearing about Browne during the war when Browne was one of the key links in the French set up. Browne had got himself a very big reputation out of his activities there. From what Driscoll remembered of them he thoroughly deserved it.

It would be pleasant to meet Mike Clifton again too. He and Driscoll had worked together often during the war. Driscoll grinned as he thought of the times they had almost dropped themselves into something very deep. But it was always just almost. One or the other of them had always produced something at the last moment to get them out of trouble.

Driscoll wondered if Clifton would be different at all. He remembered that he had been a very changeable sort of person, always going off on some tangent or other, changing his opinions to suit new theories, about every five minutes.

He came to the address Landford had given him on the telephone, saw that the bottom floor was occupied by a furniture shop. The windows were full of broken down furniture that looked as if it might once have been expensive. Driscoll thought the whole neighbourhood was very much like that. He went along to the side entrance, found himself facing a flight of uncarpeted stairs. A small brass wall plate said: *Tasmanian Import Export Co. Ltd.* To the right of the plate an arrow pointed up the stairs.

Driscoll went up two flights of stairs to the top floor, found himself on a small, uncarpeted landing. A door stood facing the top of the stairs, carrying a plate exactly similar to the one at the entrance. Below the plate was a brass bell-push and a notice which said: *Please Ring.*

Driscoll leaned on the bell. He heard it ringing inside, then the door swung open and Landford's plump face appeared in the doorway.

'Come on in, Johnny. We're ready to start.'

He held the door wide for Driscoll to enter, waved him to a door on the far side of the room.

Driscoll looked round the room as he walked across it. It was plainly furnished, looked almost bare. Two office desks faced each other in opposite corners. A large brown cupboard stood near the door. The floor was thinly covered with two large and well-worn rugs.

Landford came past Driscoll, waved an airy hand round the room, said, 'Clifton and I.' He smiled. 'Where the real work's done. But don't tell Browne I said so.' He reached out, opened the door, waved Driscoll into the next room.

Driscoll walked across the threshold, saw that the room was the same size as the other but slightly better furnished. In the corner opposite the door a large executive desk stood diagonally facing out into the room.

There were two steel filing cabinets, a large cupboard, a long wall bookcase. The floor was covered with a carpet not much newer than the ones in the next room. Driscoll smiled as he looked round, thinking things were much the same. Everything done as cheaply as possible, so that the limited allocation of money could be stretched to the utmost.

Driscoll walked across to the desk, saw the man who had been sitting behind it rise to greet him. He was a tall man, sparely built, with dreamy blue eyes and a very long, mournful face.

Driscoll remembered Landford saying, 'Face like a horse,' found himself mentally agreeing with the little man's description.

He took the Colonel's outstretched hand, gripped it firmly. He looked at the dreaminess of the blue eyes, found them surveying him very carefully.

'I'm glad you're with us in this Driscoll,' Browne said, 'let me introduce Maclaren, he's the managing director of the firm that builds the KB–12.'

Browne turned and indicated a short heavily built man who was sitting in a chair to the right of the desk.

Driscoll nodded, 'Glad to know you.' Then he went back a couple of paces, sat down in the chair that the Colonel pointed to.

Browne passed round a packet of cigarettes, spoke while he was lighting his. 'Reason I asked you to come in, Driscoll, was because Maclaren's come down to tell us what they think happened to the aircraft, leaving aside the possibility of interference. Would you like to examine a few of the possibilities, Maclaren?' Browne smiled, 'in non-technical language of course. We're none of us experts, are we?' He looked inquiringly at Driscoll.

Driscoll grinned, puffed smoke from his cigarette. 'They have wings and an engine, and they fly. That's about my limit.'

'This one has two engines. Or rather turbines,' Maclaren said. He rolled the '*r*' sounds, his voice harsh and with the hard emphasis of a Glasgow Scot.

He stood up, spread out a large blue sheet he had brought with him. 'There they are.' He pointed at the jet's turbines on the blueprint. 'I brought this because I thought it would explain things more clearly. Now, you see where these arrows are pointing. Those are the points where our engineers think a breaking stress might have been imposed. Those are the points, shall we say, where we'd naturally look for anything first. In this case they're not much help because as far as we can tell complete disintegration occurred. But you can rule out some possibilities. We do not consider the aircraft was caused to disintegrate by anything the pilot did. Anoxia — lack of oxygen that is — is unlikely. And Winterley was far too experienced to do anything really drastic to the aircraft without notifying the ground first. We are quite sure that whatever caused the disintegration the pilot was not aware of it.' He paused, looking round at them.

Browne nodded, said quietly, 'Go on, Maclaren.'

'Very well. Now, the engineers consider that if there was a structural failure it is ten chances to one it would have occurred at one of the points I've shown with arrows on this blueprint. Oh, it's true the aircraft might have blown up, ripped apart for some reason we can't possibly fathom. But ten chances to one that's where it happened. All right, now we can go slightly further. If the failure occurred at one of these points it is almost certain that it was due to one of two things. Either metal fatigue or some stress imposed by the design that has been totally overlooked. Am I making myself clear, Colonel?'

Browne nodded. 'What about those two things. Which is more likely?'

'They are interdependent. You probably know that any metal will become fatigued and weaken in time. And remember, the metal in this aircraft has to stand fantastic extremes of temperature, and stresses that are quite unbelievable.'

'But what if there was a basic flaw in the design?' Browne asked.

'Ah, now that's where it gets difficult. Because that could mean that one of those vital points was being subjected to stresses greater than the metal has been planned to withstand. And that, gentlemen, will mean that it becomes fatigued far more quickly than it should. So after a certain number of hours it reaches breaking point. But of course we can't suspect that because the design has made no allowances for it. That's the problem.'

Browne said, 'But can't you check the design, work through all the calculations and mumbo jumbo you chaps specialise in. That would cut out that possibility.'

Maclaren looked straight at him. 'Aye,' he said quietly. 'We can do that. It will take about a year.'

'A year? But surely you can do it quicker than that.'

'Aye, indeed we can. Provided we can borrow every aircraft designer in the country and electronic calculators from all the research centres. Then it would only take about three months.' He leaned back in his chair, his thumbs tucked into the armpits of his waistcoat.

'Well, so what do you propose to do?' Browne asked.

'I'm not proposing anything. I've left it to the designer and the test pilot. They've decided to fly the second model to breaking point if they can. Incidentally, it's stressed a little differently from the first, but that shouldn't matter. If any part's going to go they'll make it go. If the aircraft can stand what they're going to do, it's all right.'

Landford said softly, 'And how long will that take?'

'Three or four days,' Maclaren said. 'Here's the point. We're as sure as we can be that leaving out sabotage the fault lies where I've just said. Now, the first model had flown for forty-three hours when it broke up. The second one's done about twenty-eight. If anything goes wrong it's going to be after roughly the same period of hours. So you can say that from now on, with the extra stresses they'll be putting on the second model by flying it deliberately to breaking point, the amount of metal fatigue at the vital points will be the same as the first.'

Browne said, 'Not very nice for the pilot, is it?'

'No, but if the second model can pass the total of the first by three or four hours we'll be satisfied it's OK. The metals used are exactly the same, and the engineers are certain that this one will stand roughly the same as the other. If it comes through the next three days, then I'll be quite sure it was sabotage. If not — well, I'm afraid that's it.'

Browne said slowly, 'Thank you, Maclaren.'

Maclaren shrugged. 'Not nice for the pilot, agreed, but he's got faith in it. They all have. Including myself. Would you like to keep this print?'

Browne stood up. 'I suppose we might as well,' he said, 'it could be useful. And thank you again for coming along.'

'Not at all, I suppose you'll be looking after the security end?' Maclaren asked.

'Don't worry about that side of it. We'll cover everything possible of course.'

Maclaren heaved himself ponderously to his feet. 'Anything I can do to cooperate, just let me know.'

He shook hands with Browne, nodded to Driscoll and Landford, went out of the room.

Browne lit another cigarette, said, 'Well, there we are. You in the picture, Driscoll?'

'Yeah.'

'Landford?'

'Indeed. So we have to sweat it out for two or three days. I'd like to go on to Glazey.'

'Yes,' Browne said.

Landford swung his chair round a little, talked toward Driscoll.

'Glazey,' he said thoughtfully. 'Now there's a man. Clever. But unfortunately nothing to do with the crash. I questioned him for nearly six hours. When I got tired one of the security people took over. Then I went back again. Nothing. I'm quite convinced he did nothing to the aircraft.'

Driscoll said, 'Not very good. That looked like the best lead. He's been taken off anything to do with the aircraft I suppose?'

Landford said slowly, 'No need, Johnny. He's dead. Suicide. Funnily enough, that helps to prove he was innocent. You see, we've found that though he had nothing to do with this crash, he was being groomed for something else. We don't know what. But we're working on something quite important there. The Colonel's taken that part over.'

Browne said, 'This is absolutely confidential, of course. Just between the three of us. I'm afraid we may have turned up something nasty with Glazey. I don't want to say any more at the moment. But it may mean some very important things. Incidentally, higher authority is very concerned about this fighter. We've been given absolute priority on anything we need. That's why I've been brought into it as well as Landford. Contact me if you need anything.'

Driscoll said, 'Right. Anything else?'

Browne looked at him. 'No, I don't think so. What are you working on?' His eyes were very dreamy, his voice casual.

Driscoll said carefully, 'As a matter of fact I might have a lead. I can't be sure yet, so if you don't mind I won't say too much about it. Naturally, I'll let you know if anything develops.'

'Yes, do that,' Browne murmured. 'It's very important to keep in touch. But of course you know that. You've had a great deal of experience at this sort of thing haven't you?'

'A fair amount,' Driscoll said. 'I'll keep in touch.'

'All right. Willy will go out with you.' Browne smiled, settled down at his desk, reached out for paper and a pen.

Driscoll turned, went to the door with Landford, and through into the next room. He was thinking that Browne was probably very good. The dreaminess of the eyes, the casual manner, did not deceive him in the slightest.

The room they passed into was no longer empty. A tall, well-built man with thick, sandy hair was standing looking out of one of the windows. He turned as he heard the door, smiled as he saw Driscoll.

Driscoll said, 'This is the end — when they use dugouts like you, Mike.' He grinned, shook Clifton's hand.

Clifton said, 'And you? Boy, you must need the money badly. I suppose you're broke again. Nice to see you, Johnny.'

Landford said, 'Of course, I forgot you two knew each other. Mike does most of the actual screening.'

'Right.' Clifton said, 'I can smell 'em out. I'm worth twice what they pay me. But then, that's always the way.' He looked straight at Driscoll, grinned, went on softly, 'They never pay you what you're worth. If I died tomorrow there'd only be a little money. A very small amount of money indeed. You remember the old place, Johnny?'

'Do I? Those were good days, Mike.'

'You're right, they were. Still, now you're with us again there'll be more of them. We might even take Willy out and show him how to drink.' He laughed.

Landford said, 'Maybe I'll take you up on that. I've got a feeling I could put either of you under the table. Let's try it when all this fuss about the fighter is sorted out.'

Driscoll said, 'Why not?' He moved toward the door. 'See you around, Mike.'

'Sure. Be good, Johnny.'

Driscoll grinned at Landford and Clifton, said, 'I'm always good these days. No one tempts me any more.

But I'm working an inside angle on this one that may be very entertaining.' He waved his hand, opened the door and went out.

Landford turned to Clifton, said, 'He's quite a card isn't he, Mike?'

Clifton smiled, said softly, 'quite a card.' He turned away abruptly and walked over to his desk.

Landford stood watching him for a moment. There was a smile on his face. Then he turned, walked back into Browne's office.

15

If there had not been an unpredictable series of events that day it is probable that Kubin would never have taken the fatal step. Each of the events was, in fact, quite unconnected. But to Kubin they seemed to form a significant whole.

As the big limousine swept out of the Embassy yard, Kubin sat nervously on the edge of the rear seat. He was clutching, with fingers that trembled slightly, the briefcase that he was to deliver to Nicholas. He was profoundly disturbed by the way in which the first secretary at the Embassy had spoken to him, when ordering him to deliver the briefcase at a rendezvous he had never visited before.

There had been a distant, cold look in the first secretary's eyes, a clipped and impersonal tone in his voice that had sent shivers of fear through Kubin's body. He had not looked at Kubin, but straight through him, as though Kubin no longer existed as a living person. As though he were merely a parcel being despatched in accordance with instructions.

Kubin strove vainly to discover some reason for the first secretary's attitude. He clutched the briefcase tighter, thinking that this was the first time he had left the Embassy since he took Rakiev to meet Nicholas. Nicholas. Abruptly his mind, which had been disturbed all the time by the subconscious thought of Nicholas, focused sharply on the name now that it had been thrust into the forefront of his consciousness.

He became aware that the palms of his hands were sweating and that the leather of the briefcase was becoming sweaty and greasy. He flung it from him into the far corner of the rear seat, noticing for the first time that it was lighter than it had ever been before. He wondered if that were significant on its own — what its significance was when coupled with the fact that he was being sent to a strange rendezvous. And above all when coupled with the first secretary's remote detachment.

His mind whirled, refusing to accept what he suddenly felt must be the truth. Then, even as the car slowed to a stop, the explanation for it all was momentarily quite clear. He was condemned, under suspicion. He saw nothing peculiar in regarding the two states as one and the same.

The first secretary's remoteness could mean only that. And of course the briefcase was light because there was nothing in it. This time he was not delivering documents to Nicholas, he was delivering himself.

At the next red traffic light he fumbled for the door handle, pushed open the door and quickly stepped out, hurried away from the car along the busy pavement.

He walked fast, stepping round women with shopping baskets, conscious only that he must keep walking, must try to find some other explanation. In his haste he walked straight into a stout woman, knocked her basket from her hand, hurried on without noticing her shouted invective. And then, as his mind cast desperately around, he realised that he had made the big mistake. The mistake that would surely condemn him. He realised he had left the briefcase in the car.

He stepped to the edge of the pavement, hoping against hope that the driver had noticed it, was following him. The big car was nowhere in sight. Kubin swayed, feeling a wave of purely physical nausea sweep over him, turning his knees into weak things incapable of sustaining his weight. And with the shock of the forgotten briefcase came another, greater shock. He realised with absolute certainty that he had completely forgotten the address of the new rendezvous.

Perhaps it was not altogether his fault. The human mind can take only so much, and Kubin had lived for many years in an atmosphere of fear and suspicion, a world where one false word, one careless sentence, could deliver the speaker into the hands of the merciless ones who were the real power in the State.

Kubin could not know that the briefcase was thin because Nicholas didn't want to be bothered with the normal flow of Embassy information. Nor that the rendezvous had been altered because the usual rendezvous was not available and that the first secretary's remoteness was because he was himself under suspicion and had received orders to return home.

Kubin's mind, weakened and tormented by years of hidden worry, could stand no more. It assumed control of his actions as though he were a puppet, urging him on away from the spot where the car had dropped him. He walked fast and jerkily, all hope gone, seeking now only some means of self-destruction before they could catch him. The one secret he had managed to preserve through the long years was all that mattered to him now. He knew that he was finished. But he knew also that he must die before they caught him, or else the girl and the little boy would suffer.

The thought of the girl and the little boy gave him a sudden, sane strength. He examined the matter carefully. He was quite sure that no one knew of any connection between Ladia and little Vitu and himself.

Originally the association had been kept secret to protect him. Ladia's family were politically undesirable, and though he knew of no words that had been breathed against her, one never knew. If it were somehow known she were associating with a young man destined for employment overseas it might have spelled trouble for them both.

And so the association had been secret. Miraculously, it had remained so. The only evidence was the small photograph he carried, wrapped in clear cellophane and taped under his armpit. He decided that must be destroyed before he killed himself. He would need to go to a place where he could destroy it in privacy.

He had often noticed the substantially built conveniences for gentlemen that dotted the streets of London. He thought, with sudden savage humour, that in his own land such places would be instantly condemned. They represented a possibility of privacy, and the State would far sooner risk insanitary conditions than have some place where its citizens might be able to attain a degree of privacy.

He stepped to the edge of the pavement, looking up and down the street. In the same direction he had been going the street forked into two. Experience told him that the sort of place he wanted was often to be found in such a position.

He glanced back again, and suddenly he saw them. They were fifty yards away, on the opposite side of the road, two tall, heavily built men in dark suits. Even as he looked they stepped off the pavement and began to cross the road toward him, walking in step and with regular, implacable strides.

Kubin knew it was hopeless now. He knew they were after him, would run him down wherever he went, he walked fast along the pavement, willing his body to move away from them, putting off as long as possible the inevitable moment.

The last hope for Ladia and Vitu had gone. It would not take them long to wring that out of him.

He walked on automatically and hopelessly, looking back every thirty yards or so, noticing that they were maintaining their distance behind him, content to wait until he reached a place where they could summon up one of their cars to take him away.

He was almost at the crossing now, walking without purpose, staring dully at the shops as he passed. And then there occurred the last of the little incidents that were to decide matters for him.

At the fork two newsvendors were standing by their posters and their piles of papers. Kubin stared uninterestedly at the posters, blinked, looked again.

Suddenly, incredibly, there was yet hope for him. And if there were hope for him, then there was hope that Ladia and Vitu would never be traced. He glanced across the road, saw a square blue box standing at the edge of the pavement. Above it, illuminated letters said: POLICE.

And outside it stood a sergeant and a constable.

Kubin hesitated only long enough to estimate the distance between himself and the two men who were following him. Then, without any heed for the traffic, he plunged across the road, ran rather than walked the last few steps toward the two policemen.

In a queer, constricted voice, he said to the sergeant, 'Please. There are two men. They will kill me.' He stretched his hand out, pawed vaguely at the sergeant's chest.

The sergeant frowned at the constable, who was grinning widely.

'Now sir,' the sergeant said, his voice round, large, and very reassuring, 'we mustn't carry on like this, must we? Perhaps you're feeling ill. Can I call you a taxi?'

Kubin looked up at him. Safety was very near if only he could say the right words. He struggled with his English, trying desperately to convey his fear.

'I am not English,' he said. 'I work at the Embassy. I have information. I demand political…'

He stopped, seeking vainly for the word he wanted, knowing that he would not be able to find it.

The sergeant looked at him. He was an experienced officer, with long years of service in tough districts. He knew fear when he saw it. And he saw that this man was truly afraid.

'Do you mean political asylum, sir?'

'Yes, yes,' Kubin sobbed. His voice was almost inarticulate now. 'Asylum. Please. The two men over there will kill me.' He jerked his head back, indicating the other side of the road.

The sergeant looked carefully, could not see any two

men there. But he had already made his decision about Kubin.

He turned to the constable. 'Get on the blower for a car, Evans. I'm taking him in.'

The constable picked up the phone, had hardly replaced it before a wireless car was sliding to a stop beside them.

Kubin looked from the policemen to the car, the realisation came to him that he was safe. Suddenly the buildings whirled in front of his eyes, the pavement slid away from his feet. The sergeant caught him as he fell, motioned the constable to help lift him into the car, the sergeant climbed in after him and slammed the door. The car moved away.

The constable stood at the corner, rocking slowly back and forward on his heels with his hands clasped lightly behind his back. He watched the car disappear toward the station, savoured in retrospect the incident that had relieved the tedium of a dull afternoon. He glanced across at the newsvendors, noticed the posters they were displaying.

'I wonder,' he said to himself very softly, 'I wonder.'

The posters read: PETROV: AUSTRALIA REFUSES SOVIET DEMAND.

16

Driscoll thumbed the top bell-push on the little brass plate, held his thumb there for several seconds listening for the sound of the bell ringing in Janine's flat. He heard nothing.

He removed his thumb, turned and began to climb the stairs. He was thinking just how he was going to handle Janine. After the news about Glazey he had to have another angle. He thought Janine could provide it. She was a smart girl, but not nearly smart enough. He wondered if she would be alone, would merely act as the relay for the instructions he was sure were waiting for him. He decided that he would start something about Winterley, work on that line. If it got him nowhere, at least the people behind her would know he'd questioned her, might decide they had better start something too. Then the situation would be nice and open. Driscoll was very fond of nice, open situations. They were always interesting, and often profitable.

The outer door of Janine's flat was ajar, he pushed through it, shut it behind him, took two steps through the small cloakroom and tapped firmly on the inner door. After a few seconds it swung slowly open.

A man stood on the threshold. He was tall, heavily built, with a wide, pleasant face and a bushy, dark moustache. Two rows of strong, even, slightly nicotine-stained teeth smiled at Driscoll, 'Come on in. Nice to see you again.'

Driscoll said, 'Thanks.' Following him into the living-room, he said casually, 'You know, I've been promising myself the next time I saw you I was going to bust you one. Just to make things even. How do you feel about that?' He smiled unpleasantly.

'Forget it, Driscoll,' the man said softly, 'it was just one of those things. You shouldn't have tried it. The boys were very upset. Really, you should be grateful I stopped them when I did, otherwise they'd have been very rough.'

Driscoll said, 'All right, I'm grateful. But don't ever make the mistake of trying it again or you'll think you've been through a mincer.' His voice was very hard, and he was watching the man closely, his hands hanging loosely by his sides, the fists slightly clenched. Then he relaxed, said, 'So let's leave it at that. An' who am I being grateful to? Besides Smith, I mean.'

'My name's Barnett. Eric Barnett. Nice, don't you think? I picked it specially for the sound. It's such an Anglo-Saxon sort of name, isn't it?'

'Yeah, an' there are a few other Anglo-Saxon names I was calling you the other night, but they weren't Barnett or Smith. Like to hear them?' He smiled at Barnett.

Barnett smiled too, but with his mouth only. His eyes were as soft and happy as a dentist's drill.

'Oh, let's not go into all that Driscoll. We understand each other better now. Have a drink on it?'

'Why not.'

Driscoll watched him walk across to the table between the settee and the lounge chair, followed him across. He was conscious of a vaguely disturbing smell, and he wondered whether it was imaginary or not. He put it away from him, concentrated on Barnett. He thought Barnett must be someone important in the set-up. Also that he was quite a hard specimen.

Barnett waved a hand casually at the table, indicating the bottle of whisky, the two glasses, the plain water jug. 'Help yourself. Pour one for me as well, if you don't mind.'

Driscoll bent forward, poured an inch or so of whisky into each glass. He filled his glass to the brim with water, swallowed some of the weak mixture.

Barnett watched him, making no effort to take his drink. 'Would you like to tell Janine we're ready. She's telephoning in her bedroom.' He waved his hand. 'That door over there.'

Driscoll looked at him. Barnett's eyes were very bright and hard, like fine cut diamonds. He wrinkled his nostrils as the vague smell irked them again, but this time more definitely, forcing itself upon him. Somewhere deep inside himself he felt a small trip-hammer start, pounding insistently against the walls of his stomach. A tiny warning voice was whispering to him, cautioning him.

He took infinite pains to make his voice quite natural as he said, 'I'll get her.' He walked across to the bedroom door, tapped on it, waited. He tapped again, louder this time.

'Go right in,' Barnett said, 'she won't mind.'

Driscoll turned the handle, pushed the door open. As he stepped into the room the smell was fresher and stronger. It was no longer vague but definite, with a strongly mixed tang.

Janine was lying across the bed. It was a big, wide divan. She was lying diagonally from corner to corner, half on her back and half on her side. She was wearing a black silk slip that had rucked up so that her long, golden legs were showing. She was very still.

He moved along the bed until he was looking down at her face. The smell of cordite was harsh. Janine was looking at the ceiling with large, vacant, unseeing eyes. They were still blue, still flecked here and there with green, but the colour was muddied, lustreless, and the sparkle had gone.

He bent over, looked at her right temple. There, where he had seen the little vein pulsing, was a small, neat, round hole. The inside of the hole was a thick, slowly welling red, and for half an inch all round it the delicate brown skin was blackened and scorched. A thin line of bright red dropped vertically, like a clean slash from a razor, to disappear in the cold blonde of her hair. Beneath the golden skin was a faint, pallid tinge, as though white paper had been slid beneath thick brown cellophane. She was very dead.

Driscoll gently raised her right hand from her breast, the fingers still warm and drooping limply as he sniffed at the palm. He let the hand fall back, flicked his eyes round to look for the gun, knew as he did so that it would not be there. He cursed himself for not bringing a gun with him, turned slowly round.

Barnett was leaning against the open door, smiling at him. There was nothing but viciousness in the smile.

Driscoll took a pace forward, his face tight and hard, stopped as he saw Barnett flick up his right hand, point the small automatic at him. He noticed the gun looked like a .32 Beretta, just the right size to have made the hole in Janine's temple. He noticed, too, that Barnett had put on a pair of tan, hog-skin gloves.

Barnett said, slowly and clearly, 'The end of the line, Driscoll. Sit down while you still can.' He moved the muzzle of the gun slowly, indicating the bed with it.

Driscoll looked at his hand, saw the steadiness of it, registered the ominous tightness of leather glove knuckled round the trigger. He sat down on the bed, carefully avoiding Janine's body.

'It's a pity about Janine,' Barnett said, 'great little girl that. I'm very sorry about her. You, on the other hand, will be no loss to anybody.' His voice was dry and cold, the tone exactly similar to the way it had been when Driscoll had first heard it that night in the car.

Driscoll found with surprise that his brain was working smoothly and easily. Not for several years had he found himself in this position, but the time interval didn't seem to have made too much difference.

The basic problem was still the same — how to get the man with the gun before the gun went off. And the answer was the old classic. Stall, stall for time, stall with all the desperation of a human being very close to death. Act as if it didn't matter, as if the problem were unimportant. But above all — *stall*...

'Killing me just doesn't make sense, Barnett. For that matter killing her doesn't. Don't be a sucker to think you can get away with it. Why kill her anyway?' His voice was calm and steady.

'I didn't. She killed herself, with this gun.' Barnett tapped the side of the blued steel barrel with his free hand. 'Of course, she had no alternative really after killing you. But they won't be able to touch her for that now, will they?'

Driscoll said, 'Oh nuts. You think they'll fall for that one? Never in your life boy, never.' He drawled the words lazily, impersonally, as though the whole thing was a faintly ridiculous show put on for his benefit.

Without seeming to, he was watching the space between himself and Barnett, estimating the exact amount of spring that would have to go into his movement the instant the gun barrel wavered.

'You're not so smart, Driscoll. This one's been worked out to the last little detail. She killed you, then herself. Maybe a quarrel between two lovers. Why not anyway?' He sniggered unpleasantly. 'She's dressed right for love.' He pushed the gun a little further forward. 'That's the way it'll look and it'll stick that way. There's nothing to tell them different.'

Driscoll grinned at him, a lopsided, cynical, infuriating grin. 'The trouble with you boys is you never grow up. You plan it to the last detail — you think. You cover every angle — you think. An' that's where you hit your big trouble.'

'Where?'

'Thinking,' Driscoll said unpleasantly. 'Just that — you think. You get subtle and complicated and finish up by tying a nice tight knot round yourselves. You amateurs make me sick. I could pick half a dozen holes in it right now. That's why you'll find it much, much smarter not to kill me.'

'Don't push it too far, Driscoll. It's not getting you anywhere but out of here on a stretcher under a blanket. It'll stick all right, and I'll tell you why. Janine got it just after you rang the outer bell. You're going to get it very shortly. When they find you — and it probably won't be for days — they'll never be able to tell which of you died first. So when they've snooped around a bit, seen how things are, they'll just naturally assume she shot you, then killed herself.'

'For god's sake grow up,' Driscoll said, 'that one won't fool a kid of two.' He laughed shortly. A nice laugh, he thought, pitched just right. He hoped frantically that Barnett would not see he was bluffing, would not discern the tightening of his stomach as Barnett's gun remained as steady as ever.

'No? Listen, Driscoll, and listen carefully, because I haven't much more time to waste on you. I'll tell you how it's going to look. You've seen the powder burns on her face. They prove she was shot close up, about the right distance for a suicide. And in just the right place if she used her right hand. So with you shot by the same gun everything will point to murder and suicide. They'll find her prints on the gun. Just hers, no others. They'll use the paraffin test to check on nitrates in her hand and they'll prove from that she's fired a gun recently. You know that part will stick — I saw you sniffing at her hand just now. And that's not all. They'll find your prints on the bottle, the glass, the jug. I didn't touch my glass. It's got her prints on it. They'll find a receipt for five hundred pounds, signed by you, in her bag. See how it's shaping? Then they'll go to your flat, find the money in your safe. So everything ties in nicely. Still want to pick a few holes in it?'

Driscoll grinned. He hoped the grin was more cheerful than he felt. 'Easy,' he said, 'If you bent her hand round the gun when you shot her they'll find slight bruising under the skin. They always look for that. Then they'll proof-fire the gun, check the nitrate deposit. They'll find the amount deposited on her palm would come from one shot only, not two. Unless you're going to do something really subtle like putting the gun in her hand again to kill me. How about that? Why don't you try it that way?'

He finished speaking, continued to watch Barnett very carefully out of half open eyes, straining to detect the smallest sign of concern, the smallest movement of the gun barrel. The iron band pressed in on him, tightening its grip as he realised Barnett wasn't worried at all, that the barrel was very straight and steady.

'I'll tell you again, Driscoll. You're not so smart. I've covered all that. Janine and I carried out a little experiment about ten minutes before you arrived. I really am sorry to lose her you know, she was so perfectly disciplined. That's what made it so easy for me to get her in the right position to shoot her. You know what we did? We filled the bath with water, soaked a sponge and let it rest on the bottom, a foot of water over it. Then I showed Janine how to fire a gun. This gun. She was quite thrilled, because it was the first time she'd ever used one. She fired it twice. Do you see what I'm getting at?'

'Yeah,' Driscoll said. He was beginning to feel really worried now. This looked like one that he wasn't going to beat.

'She really couldn't miss the sponge, even though it was the first time. The water slowed the slugs down so much they didn't even penetrate the sponge, certainly didn't mark the bath at all. I dug them out straight away to show her. They're in my pocket now with the two used cases.'

Driscoll could see Barnett's smug enjoyment as he explained how smart he'd been.

'Then, of course, I had to show her how to clean the gun. We went into her bedroom for that, so she could change while we cleaned it. I'd just finished when you rang. Naturally, I put on gloves while I was doing it, so that my hands wouldn't be dirtied. That means her prints are still on it and mine aren't. So, with regret, as soon as I heard the bell I shot her. And now I'm going to shoot you. And the prints will be right, and the nitrate test will be right. And how would *you* like to take it now?'

Driscoll looked directly at him, opening his eyes very wide. The gun was still steady, still pointing directly at him. Barnett was smiling, pleased with himself. Driscoll decided that at the last moment, when he saw the knuckles really tighten, he'd go for him anyway. Deep down, something told him it wouldn't be any good, he'd never make it. The distance was too great, Barnett obviously too good. But he'd still go to meet death, not wait passively for it to come to him.

He tried the last possible stall, as it registered on his mind that Barnett thought he was pretty good. Flattery. Just possible. Good for a small delay anyway, and even seconds might help.

'OK, I'll admit it's pretty good,' Driscoll said, 'it looks like you've thought of everything and it's the end of the road. Just one more thing before I go, Barnett. Why? It can't hurt you to tell me now.'

Barnett grinned. 'All right, Driscoll, here's why. I think you were going to sell us out. I think you were going to do it through Janine. She was good, but not really very smart. You might have found out quite a lot about us through Janine, and we don't like anyone doing that. She thought she concealed it, that I didn't suspect it, but I knew quite well she'd fallen for you. You shouldn't have that effect on women, Driscoll. It's going to plant you. It's so neat to do it like this, don't you think? Both at once and accounting for each other. You realise that she *had* fallen for you of course?'

'No. And you're killing me just for that?'

Barnett laughed again. 'Not altogether. Let's say your purpose has been fulfilled. The thing we had in mind for you isn't necessary any more. Have a last laugh on that one. I wanted you for one particular reason, and then suddenly the reason just didn't exist any more. No need for us to bother at all. I needn't have approached you, and I needn't ever have used Janine on it. Funny, isn't it?'

Driscoll looked at him, watched the gun push forward very slightly. He sought desperately for one last stall, one last chance to bluff.

Behind Barnett his straining senses picked up a small sound, automatically rejected it as immaterial to the immediate problem. He saw the expression in Barnett's eyes change perceptibly as something slid across them. Driscoll knew exactly what it was. He had seen it before, and it was a thing no one would ever forget. Always, just before they killed, something came into their eyes. It was a blank, impenetrable curtain that stripped them for a time of all humanity, let hell itself peer directly out from their eyes.

He knew he had only three or four seconds left, began to tense his muscles for the last, desperate, useless spring, his eyes fixing on the bulging hog-skin finger round the trigger of the gun.

Then, born of desperation, it came to him. He spoke in a sneering tone that was quite instinctive, a tone of cold, weary contempt that was the only tone which could penetrate the grey curtain that the imminence of killing had lowered round Barnett's mind.

'You stupid bastard, Barnett, they can tell from the rifling marks exactly which slug was fired first. Didn't you even know the rifling changes slightly with each shot? So they'll know she was killed first, me second. An' that'll tell them there was a third person here, because I'd have to have fired that shot into her otherwise, and the second shot, the one that kills me, will be fired from a distance, not close up.'

He looked at Barnett's face. It was working slightly, the lips trembling just a little. It had jolted him, held him for a moment. But the killer look was still there in his eyes.

Again he heard a noise behind Barnett, but this time his brain accepted it, welcomed the possible distraction it offered. He realised there was something or somebody behind Barnett, hoped desperately that Barnett would hear the noise, that it would distract him for just the tenth part of a second.

He saw that Barnett's face was still again, and mask-like, that the eyes were glazed, filled only with the thought of killing. He saw the fingers tightening on the trigger, watched the knuckles swelling out the hog-skin glove.

He willed himself to dive, but even before the message from his mind had galvanised his muscles into action someone said, very loudly, 'Don't move,' and

Barnett was jerking round towards the voice.

Driscoll was completely forgotten as Barnett whipped round. Frozen into stillness on the bed, Driscoll caught a fleeting glimpse of Landford's face, a glimpse that printed the image of his tight, savage expression indelibly on his mind.

Then the sound of a gun crashed out in the flat, echoing from the walls. He saw Barnett staggering backwards, his gun dropping from nerveless fingers as Landford's big Luger crashed twice more, the slugs ripping audibly into Barnett's body, spinning him round and driving him against the wall.

Barnett hit the wall, checked, slid slowly down it, finishing in a loose, untidy bulk on the floor where he lay as quiet and motionless as a heap of poured concrete.

Driscoll reached into his pocket for a cigarette. He was surprised to see that his fingers were shaking only a very little.

17

Driscoll sucked smoke into his lungs, felt the deeply satisfying bite of it. He looked at Landford. The little man was standing by the door, a curious half smile on his face. Driscoll watched him slip the Luger back into a shoulder holster, pat his jacket into place over the gun. The savage expression had disappeared. Landford looked as casual, as harmless as ever.

'I owe you one for that, Willy. Half a second later would have been too late.' His voice was quite steady.

Landford smiled. He walked past Driscoll, stopped over the slumped heap of Barnett's body. Delicately, like a cat turning over a dead mouse, he put the toe of his small shoe under Barnett's shoulder, flipped with his leg until the body was turned over on it's side. Then he looked carefully at Barnett's face.

Driscoll, sitting on the bed, looked too. It was not a very pretty sight. One of the slugs had caught Barnett just under the chin, bored upwards into his brain. In the process it had smashed most of his facial structure. The other two slugs had ripped into his chest, not making much mess, merely leaving blood flecked holes in his jacket. Landford flicked the jacket open with his foot. Barnett's white shirt showed corresponding holes, each with a much bigger area of dark crimson blood.

'That was nice shooting, Willy. Very nice shooting

indeed.'

Landford turned his head, looked at him. 'You think so?' he asked. 'Not as nice as it could have been. Another half second I could just have been in the right place to get him through the arm. Then we'd have had him alive. That would have been much more interesting.' He shrugged, smiled at Driscoll. 'I wonder just what he'd have told us.' His tone was cold and impersonal.

'He might not have said anything,' Driscoll said. 'Some of these boys are pretty good you know.'

Landford laughed, an unpleasant high laugh. 'He'd have said something. He'd definitely have said something. The only question would have been how long it took.'

Driscoll stood up, walked over to the window. It was shut. He looked down into the street, not going too close to the glass as he did so. The square was quiet and sunlit. No one seemed to be taking any interest in the house at all. He swung round, 'No one seems to be worried about the noise. Who was he, anyway?'

'I can't place him at the moment. I'm fairly sure I've seen a picture of him somewhere,' Landford said. 'I think you'd better tell me about it, Johnny.'

'Sure,' Driscoll said. 'I told you I was trying to get on the inside. I had a phone message this morning from the girl. She told me to be here at three o'clock, that I'd find the outer door open. I came in, found Barnett. That's the name he's using, by the way. He got me in the bedroom where I saw the girl on the bed. He shot her when he heard me ringing from downstairs. He'd got her to fire the gun earlier on, so her dabs were on it. He wore gloves to shoot her, and he shot her close up so it would look like suicide. Then all he had to do was give it to me with the same gun, leave us both here for someone to find us. It would have looked a perfect murder and suicide.' He paused, looking very thoughtful. 'I think he'd have got away with it. He'd thought of just about everything.'

'I got in here in time to hear something about the rifling marks on the bullet,' Landford said, 'actually, without you saying that, I don't think I'd have been in time. I didn't think they could tell as finely as that.'

'They can't,' Driscoll grinned, 'but I banked that Barnett didn't know that. I figured it might give me a little more delay. It did, but was I ever glad to see you.'

Landford smiled. 'I was glad to see you, as well. To be quite honest, I didn't trust you at all until now. Even when you told me you were working an inside angle. You were very vague about it, you know. Let's go over what he said to you. There might be something.'

'OK, Willy. I don't quite understand *why* he was going to bump me. After all, I'd never been told anything about the project they wanted me for. Incidentally that girl,' he waved a hand casually at Janine, 'knew Winterley, the number of her telephone corresponds with one of the numbers in the notebook you gave me. That might have been the reason for bumping her off, but I can't see where I came in, unless they figured I was going to start work on her and break her down.'

Landford said, slowly, 'It doesn't make sense.'

'You're telling me. The other thing he told me was that I wasn't going to be needed anyway. Apparently they thought they were going to need me for something, and then the need disappeared.' Driscoll paused, rubbed his chin, took out another cigarette. 'There's just one idea seems to fit the facts.'

'What is it, Johnny? Tell me about it, convince me.'

'OK. Let's assume they wanted me to get at the KB–12,' Driscoll replied slowly, 'I can't be sure of that, but it seems the most likely thing. OK, what do they need altogether? They'd need to know everything about the aircraft, everything about how the tests were carried out. Right, we know that Janine had been in contact with Winterley. Maybe she got it out of him. You can see from the report on him that he was a bit of a sucker for women. And this one was good, believe me.'

Landford walked round the bed, looked down at Janine. Until then he had paid her very little attention. He pursed his lips, nodded. He said, 'Go on, Johnny. You're making sense so far.'

'Right, they have all the technical data they need. Now they've got to get at the aircraft itself. We know Rakiev was over here, so we can assume that he instructed them just how to fix things so they could destroy the aircraft and still make it look like an accident. Probably he designed something that would do the job for them, *if* they could get at the aircraft. That's where Glazey and I came in.'

'Why Glazey and you,' Landford asked, 'why not just Glazey?'

'This is why. Suppose Glazey gets at the first aircraft. He fixes it and it crashes. They're bound to check everyone who ever went near the thing. Remember Willy, you were suspicious of him immediately. Let's assume that he's questioned. All right, there's no evidence, and they have to let him go. But what happens then? You can be damned sure they're not going to let Mr Glazey anywhere near the second aircraft. An' you can be double damned sure they'll put the tightest security curtain you ever saw round the second model. Am I still making sense?'

Landford said quietly, 'Go on.'

'All right.' He leaned forward, wagged his cigarette in emphasis. 'Now get this. People like Glazey are all right so long as the heat isn't on. As soon as it is they need an expert, a professional, someone who's used to working against the odds. They need someone who's been around, who knows the game backwards. That was me. They were going to use me to get the second aircraft simply because by then they knew perfectly well that someone like Glazey wouldn't stand a chance of getting anywhere near the second fighter, not once the security was tightened. So where do we go from there?'

Landford struck a match and lit a cigarette, let the match burn itself out, watching the dying flickers of flame with an intense concentration. 'I'm beginning to wonder,' he said thoughtfully, 'let's think about Glazey, and the fact that they killed the girl — were definitely going to kill you.'

'Exactly,' Driscoll said, 'there's only one answer. If Glazey didn't have anything to do with the disintegration of the first aircraft it's odds on that was an accident. You might say that someone else could have fixed the first aircraft besides Glazey. But that still leaves the second one, for which they wouldn't dare use the same person. Regardless of the fact that they'd have to have a professional, so they'd still need me. But they didn't. Barnett was just going to prove that quite conclusively. An' that isn't all. By killing Janine they kill the last person who could ever prove they were interested in the aircraft at all. Who could prove it now? The only ones who ever could were Janine, that guy Williamson who was stabbed, and Glazey, if he ever knew. So they're all three dead, and I don't know for certain they wanted me for the KB–12, although it's fifty quid to a seagull's beak that they did. So they quietly fade away. Why?'

Landford frowned. 'I don't like it, but there's only one logical answer.'

'Yeah, an' it says they don't need to touch the second one because they didn't touch the first. If the second one comes through the tests that broke up the first they can start worrying. Until then they can let the test pilots and designers worry for them.'

Landford sat down on the bed, ignoring the body that lay diagonally across it. He smoked slowly and thoughtfully, his head between his hands.

Driscoll said nothing. In his mind he was examining every angle, turning over every little fact to see where it fitted. Whichever way he looked at it, it seemed watertight. Idly he looked down at Janine, thinking he had wondered as he left her flat that night just how long she'd last. He thought life was pretty funny like that.

Landford stirred, stood up. He walked round the bed, crushed his cigarette in the little ashtray on the bedside table.

'It's the only answer.' He looked straight at Driscoll. 'You know, Johnny, I tailed you this afternoon because I didn't quite trust you. I think I'd like you to know that, now there's no doubt about where you stand.' He grinned. 'There's nothing changes one's opinion quite so fast as seeing someone you don't quite trust just about to be shot by someone else who you know damn well is on the other side. I'm glad I got here in time.'

'An' I'm glad you didn't trust me, Willy, otherwise you wouldn't have tailed me and then...' He shrugged his shoulders, pointed at the gun Barnett had dropped.

Landford turned away. His voice was brisk and businesslike again. 'We might as well check through his clothes. Then we can search the flat.' He broke off, as if suddenly remembering something he had overlooked, glanced at his watch. 'Hell, I've got an appointment at four. It's three-fifty now.'

'You keep your appointment. I'll check the flat over.' Driscoll said.

Landford grinned. 'But you've got an appointment, too Johnny. With the Colonel. He wants to see you very urgently about something or other. I don't know what it's about. Would you like to go through his clothes while I check in?'

'Sure.'

Landford picked up the telephone, dialled a Euston number.

Driscoll kneeled down beside Barnett, went carefully through his pockets. There was no tailor's mark on the suit, nothing in the pockets except a slim billfold, cigarettes and matches, a bunch of keys and some small change. The billfold held eighteen pound notes, one ten shilling note. Nothing else at all.

Driscoll straightened up, watched Landford. He thought the little man was very good. Beneath the calm, peaceful exterior there was a quick, cold brain, an ability to take instantaneous action when it was necessary. And he was a very good shot. Even at six yards range it was good shooting to hit a man three times, not miss him once. Especially with a heavy gun like a Luger. He wondered whether anyone except the experts realised that, thought probably not. Most people had been brought up on gangster films where cops hit tiny targets like a man's hand at twenty yards. Driscoll only knew two people who could do that — and then with a target revolver, certainly not with an automatic.

He noticed that Landford was not speaking at all, was listening to the voice at the other end with a stiffness in his whole bearing that was alien to him.

At last Landford said, 'Yes, Driscoll's with me. A spot of bother but it's worked out all right... right away... within ten minutes. Have the stuff ready for me, will you?' He replaced the receiver.

Driscoll looked at him curiously. Landford was obviously excited, yet he was making no effort to speak. He stood quite still for ten seconds or so, then he turned to Driscoll with a beaming smile gradually spreading over his face.

'Johnny, something's broken. They've got a character at Notting Lane who claims he's a contact man for them. He mentioned something about an aeroplane, and apparently he's willing to talk. They're holding him for us to get there.'

Driscoll said, 'This could be the break we've waited for. Let's go.'

'On our way. Browne's digging out all he can on this boy. He'll have the stuff ready for us. We can call in for it then go straight to Notting Lane. Anything on him?' He indicated Barnett with a casual wave of his hand.

'Just this.' Driscoll held out the stuff he had collected.

Landford picked out the keys, looked at them curiously, 'Maybe these will help. I doubt it. These boys are getting smart. Never any laundry marks, never any address. I'll get Browne to bring the Special Branch in to guard this place until we have a chance to go over it.' He tossed the keys back to Driscoll.

They walked out through the living room. As they came to the outer door of the flat Driscoll saw it was slightly open. He remembered that he had closed it behind him, heard the Yale lock click shut.

Landford saw him looking at it. He dug him in the ribs, said, 'Remember I told you I had a way with locks? Have you oiled yours, by the way?' He grinned at Driscoll, looking very pleased with life.

Driscoll smiled. 'Not yet, Willy. I'll leave it for you to do. Since you have a way with them.'

He thought the news from Browne had had a livening effect on Landford, made him almost frisky. He smiled, following the little man down the stairs, watching him open the outer door, following him across the road and into a big open Jaguar that was parked fifty yards down the street.

As Landford let in the clutch and jolted him back in his seat he thought that he had been right when he felt that things were beginning to get interesting.

18

As they drove fast through streets bright with afternoon sun Driscoll glanced at Landford from time to time. The little man was humming, lips moving tunelessly as he concentrated on the road. Driscoll, without being at all conscious of them, watched the people on the pavements.

A traffic light held them up momentarily at Oxford Circus, behind a big open tourer filled with gaily dressed, laughing girls. Tattered shreds of laughter, spilling back from the tourer as it moved away, jerked Driscoll back to the present, turning his mind from the detailed analysis of events which was shaping itself in his brain.

Landford pulled up outside the furniture store, turned to Driscoll and said, 'You stay here, Johnny. I'll see what Browne has for us.'

He opened his door, swung out of the car. Before he had started to cross the pavement Driscoll saw Browne appear at the side entrance, walk rapidly toward them.

Landford stopped, waited for Browne to reach the car. Driscoll noticed that Browne was carrying a piece of paper, a large sheet folded twice over.

Browne said, 'It's not much, Willy, but what there is is all here. The Inspector at Notting Lane knows you're coming. The boyo's yours until you're ready to let Special Branch have him.'

Landford took the folded sheet from the Colonel, stuffed it in his jacket pocket. 'Right, we're on our way.' He walked quickly round the front of the car, opened the door and slid in behind the wheel.

Browne leaned over Driscoll's side of the car. He said, clipping his syllables even shorter than usual, 'This may be the one big break we've been waiting for. You two simply must crack him. But I was forgetting — you don't speak the language, do you, Driscoll?'

Driscoll said slowly, 'No. It's one of the few European languages I know nothing about at all. I'm afraid Willy's on his own for that.'

Browne frowned. 'That's a pity. I always think two interrogators get better results.'

'All right,' Landford said, 'we can still do it that way. Johnny can start on him in English. If that fails I'll do my best with his own language. I think he'll be able to understand me.'

'Don't be so infernally coy, Willy,' Browne said lightly. He turned to Driscoll. 'He speaks it very well indeed. Better than most of the natives.' He stepped back, waved a hand as Landford pressed the accelerator and the Jaguar shot away.

Landford took his right hand from the steering wheel, flicked casually round a milk-tanker, brushed past a traffic island. He rummaged in his pocket, pulled out the paper Browne had given to him, and passed it across to Driscoll. 'You might read that out as we go along. It will save a little time.'

'Sure.' Driscoll unfolded the sheet, glanced up as Landford squeezed between a truck and a bus at fifty, missing both by inches. Driscoll looked down at the paper again. He thought it would be easier on the nerves if he didn't follow Landford's progress. 'There's not much Willy. I'll read it straight out.'

'Go ahead.'

'The man's name is Kubin. They have a Kubin listed as an official at the Embassy. A junior official. The description seems to tally with this chap, and Browne thinks the name is right. Age about thirty-five, address in his own country not known. He's been noticed once or twice leaving the Embassy or returning to it, always in the company of someone else. Never been seen at any of the receptions or parties there, which is apparently in keeping with his status. The presumption seems to be that he would have been employed only as a courier or contact man, for taking someone who was strange to London to a designated rendezvous with someone who didn't want to be seen near the Embassy. That's all, except that he's believed to speak very little English.'

'Very few of them do,' Landford said as he pulled up with a harsh squeal of brakes outside the police station.

They got out of the car, walked up the stone steps and into the station. Landford walked quickly up to the sergeant at the desk, produced a card. The sergeant escorted them through the charge room to the inspector's office. He tapped at a frosted glass door engraved: *Detective Inspector J. W. Frost*, then held the door open for them to go in.

Frost rose from behind his desk to greet them. He was tall, slightly built, with iron grey hair and eyebrows. He was wearing a plain brown suit, baggy at the pockets, and a hard white collar. He looked tired.

Landford produced his card again, introduced Driscoll.

Frost said, 'Right, gentlemen, I expect you'd like to go right in.'

'One moment.' Landford said.

Driscoll thought his voice was a little sharp.

'You'd better tell us exactly what's happened, give us the background on it.'

Landford sat on one of the chairs by the desk to hear the Inspector's report. The Inspector sat down, took up an old pipe from his desk, lit it carefully.

Driscoll looked at Landford out of the corner of his eye. He thought he was definitely on edge, excited. He saw him strumming with his fingers on the desk.

'Not much to it, sir,' Inspector Frost explained, 'one of the sergeants brought him in. Said he'd fainted on the street. Apparently thought two men were trying to kill him. The sergeant didn't spot any suspicious looking men, but decided to accept this man's word.'

'All right,' Landford said, impatiently. 'So the sergeant brought him in. Was the man able to describe the two who were tailing him?'

'Not really. Said they were large and not very smartly dressed, but quite neat just the same. Might almost have been plain clothes men, by the sound of it.' He chuckled appreciatively, struck another match, tamped the tobacco down in the pipe with the match box. 'Soon as they brought him here I had him searched and put in a cell. Wondered if I ought to call a doctor for him, but he seemed to have got over his fainting fit. He's still pale and shivering though.'

'What has he said so far?' Landford asked. 'Did you

find anything when you searched him?'

'Not a thing on him except a photograph. I'll let you have that in a minute. He hasn't said much either. Just kept asking us to protect him. But he did say something to the sergeant about having information valuable to the Air Force. Naturally, I didn't question him. Thought it was better to leave that for the experts.'

Driscoll looked up quickly, wondering if Landford had detected the faintly sarcastic tone of the Inspector's last remark.

But Landford was standing up, anxious to get on with the questioning. 'The photograph, Inspector? And I take it you've got him in a cell with a hidden microphone?'

The Inspector looked shocked. 'Oh no, sir. That isn't normal at stations you know. Not normal at all. Dare say I could get a cell rigged with one, but it would take a little time. Not normal procedure you know.'

Landford snarled, 'I don't care a tuppenny damn about normal procedure.' He made a few more remarks about normal procedure, using a nice variety of short, pithy words. Then he said, 'Get one rigged as quickly as possible in another cell. Let me know when it's done and we'll transfer him. What about the photograph?'

The Inspector passed across a small snapshot. It showed a girl dressed in peasant costume, and holding a little boy by the hand. It was a good, clear snap. Driscoll looked at it as Landford held it out to him. The Inspector squeezed past them, and they followed him back through the charge room, picking up the sergeant on the way. They went through a door on the far side of the charge room, found their way barred by a heavy grille. The sergeant opened it with his key, and they walked on down a short, concrete-floored corridor, with cells on each side.

They stopped at the last cell on the right. The sergeant pushed his key into the lock, turned it, swung the heavy door outwards.

Landford waved Driscoll into the cell, said to the Inspector, 'Please leave us completely alone. We'll let you know if there's anything we need.'

The heavy door swung shut behind them. Driscoll looked at the man sitting hunched on the bunk. He was of medium height and build, with dark hair and a haggard, pallid face. He looked from one to the other of them, his eyes wide and helpless as a trapped animal's. The cell was barely furnished with a plain wooden bunk, wooden head rest, a chair, and the usual bucket.

Landford crossed the cell, stood leaning against the wall without speaking a word. Driscoll pulled the chair up close to the bunk, offered Kubin a cigarette, lit it for him. Then, very quietly and slowly, using very simple words, he began to talk to him.

He confirmed that his name was Kubin, that he worked at the Embassy. Only when Driscoll probed a little further, asking Kubin where he had been going, why he had given himself up to the police, did Kubin suddenly seem to recoil and draw back into himself. It was not, Driscoll felt sure, that he did not want to answer. Rather it seemed as if there were some block in his mind that made it impossible for him to speak.

'Who were you going to meet?' Driscoll asked, and again and again, 'Who were you going to meet?' Then, in a flash of intuition that Kubin's fear might be connected with the person he was going to meet: 'Were you afraid of him, this man? Is that why you went to the policeman?'

Kubin nodded several times, said as if he were a child talking to himself, 'Yes. Afraid of Nicholas and all of them. Please, they would kill me.'

He looked directly at Driscoll with round, vacant eyes, suddenly turned away and pillowed his head in his hands.

Driscoll looked across at Landford. Landford shrugged, motioned slightly with his hand for Driscoll to continue.

'They can't kill you now. You must understand you're safe now. This Nicholas. You were going to meet him, and you were afraid of him. He must be an important man then?'

'Yes. Important. He is chief of all secret police here. Nicholas.' He shuddered.

'But he can't touch you now,' Driscoll said, softly and insistently. 'He can't touch you here. What did he look like?'

'I never saw him. Always would arrive after us. Never allowed to look at him. Always must face away.' He spoke tonelessly, his head still buried in his hands, the voice muffled by his fingers. 'He was going to kill me. I know. They did not tell me but I know. Today they were going to take me away. They suspect everybody. I know today they kill me…' His voice tailed away into silence.

'All right,' Driscoll said gently. 'But they can't kill you now. And the information for the Air Force? Tell us about the aeroplane. You know about an aeroplane, don't you?'

Kubin jerked upright, his eyes quite blank. He looked

at Driscoll for a second, looked away again. His expression was quite uncomprehending.

Driscoll sighed, reached out his hand to Landford, said, 'Photograph please, Willy.'

Landford handed it to him without speaking. Driscoll held the photograph up where Kubin could see it, offered him another cigarette. Kubin accepted it, took a light from Driscoll's lighter. Driscoll moved the photograph gently to and fro, watched Kubin's eyes following it. He began to question Kubin again, slowly drew from him, piece by little piece, the details concerning the girl and the little boy in the photograph.

The girl's name was Ladia. She came from a family who had been in trouble with the authorities, Kubin had never married her, but had lived with her over a period of nearly three years as man and wife. The little boy, Vitu, was their son. Kubin had done a good job in concealing his relationship with her. He was quite sure no one knew about it, or suspected the fact that the money he sent to his mother was sent on by her to Ladia. It was quite obvious that Ladia and the little boy were the most important people in Kubin's life. Possibly, Driscoll thought, they were the only real thing. Even now in his frightened misery, Kubin was proud because they would not suffer, because he had managed to conceal that one secret from the prying of officialdom.

Driscoll could detect the increase in strength of Kubin's voice as he talked about them, where they lived, how he had not seen them for years. He thought that he would have little trouble now in finding out everything Kubin knew. But when the questioning started again, Kubin relapsed, the same vacancy returning to his eyes, the same slumping dejection bending his head forward.

Landford walked to the door, motioned to Driscoll to come outside. The cell was equipped with the usual bell push to summon the gaoler, and the sergeant let them out.

Landford told him to wait, walked Driscoll along the corridor away from the cell. He said, very quietly, 'He's pretty badly scared. We can't afford to waste the time on him that would get results.'

Driscoll said, 'You're right. I've seen them like this before. They want to talk, but they just can't get it past the barrier in their minds. You going to try him in his own language?'

'Yes. I'm going to do more than that. I'm going to shock him, try to break through that way. You saw how he reacted when you started on the photograph? I think if I shock him enough he'll break down, and it will pour out.'

Driscoll stood quietly for a moment. He was thinking of other people he'd seen in the past. Sometimes a sudden shock would work. Sometimes not. He said, 'It's worth trying, Willy. How are you going to play it?'

Landford looked up at him. His eyes were very hard. 'I'm going to tell him unless he breaks down and tells us everything he knows I'm going to see that the Embassy get this photograph, together with the information on where to look for them. Then I'm going to tell him that we'll turn him over to them, and see that the word gets to them that he's told us everything he knows. He'll know exactly what all that implies.'

'It's pretty rough.' Driscoll said.

A quick smile flitted across Landford's face, then it

was as hard and set as ever. 'Yes, pretty rough, Johnny, but then it's a pretty rough game.'

'You're telling me'. Driscoll grinned. 'Let's hope it works.'

They went back into the cell, had the sergeant leave the door ajar behind them. Kubin was sitting just as they had left him, his head still leaning on his hands. Driscoll walked across to the far wall, turned and stood under the long, shallow, barred window.

Landford began talking to Kubin in his own language. In contrast to the gentle way in which Driscoll had talked there was savagery in his voice, so that the harsh Slavonic sounds cut roughly through the quiet of the cell.

Kubin jerked at the sound of the voice, cowered away from it as though it were impacting physically on him. He swung his head despairingly round to look at Driscoll as Landford pointed to him. The terror in his eyes was clear and wild. He pressed back against the tiled wall of the cell, his shoulders wriggling against it as though he sought to burrow into the hard, cold tiles.

Landford stopped. The cell was quiet again, the only sound the deep irregular panting of Kubin's breath. His gaze was riveted on Landford's face. Driscoll, looking at Landford, was amazed at the cold malevolence that the little man was conveying.

Landford spoke again. This time he spoke slower, softer. Kubin's whole attention was still drawn to him, Kubin's eyes following his every little movement. Then abruptly he stopped. He turned away from Kubin, signalled to Driscoll.

Driscoll walked past Kubin, swung the door of the cell open, stood in the open doorway. Landford started to leave the cell, turned as if on a sudden impulse, held out the photograph which he had been displaying in his left hand the whole time he talked. Kubin stared at it dully, slowly stretched his hand out and took it.

Landford backed to the open door of the cell. He spoke again, softly and encouragingly this time. Driscoll saw Kubin's head come up, something that might have been hope gleam in his eyes. Landford paused, then rapped out a short phrase that ended on a questioning intonation. Kubin nodded. Landford stepped back through the door, swung it closed. The sergeant turned the key in the lock.

As they walked up the corridor Driscoll saw that Landford's face was beaded with sweat. He thought it was hardly surprising.

'He was certainly shocked, Willy. You think it'll work?' Driscoll asked.

Landford shrugged.

'I think so, Johnny. I think he was really scared when I told him I'd see they found out exactly where the woman and the boy could be found. Let him have a few minutes to think it over and calm down. Right now he can only think of the threat. It'll take a few minutes for his consciousness to understand that the threat's only valid if he doesn't open his mind to us. As soon as his conscious mind picks that up, it's odds on that the subconscious barrier will disintegrate. He'll realise he can talk, and he'll want to. Then he won't be able to get at the bell fast enough.'

'Willy, you amaze me. A gunman and a psychologist too.' He took out a packet of cigarettes, offered them to Landford.

Landford took one, smiled a little sheepishly, 'You won't find it in the psychology textbooks but I've seen it work. I've told him he's got exactly ten minutes before I call the Embassy to collect him. I think that will be lots of time.'

The sergeant let them out through the grille, rattled his keys menacingly across the observation panel of the cell on the left nearest the grille. The drunken singing subsided for a moment, and a stream of the purest cockney obscenity echoed through the block.

The sergeant grinned at them, said, 'Old Perce. Regular he is, every time he lands a winner.' He slammed the grille shut, followed them into the charge room.

Driscoll and Landford sat on the long bench facing the wall clock, smoked in silence.

19

Landford stirred, wriggled on the hard, wooden bench. 'They don't make these things too comfortable, Johnny. I think I'll let Browne know what's happening.'

Driscoll nodded, shifted his position slightly, watched Landford disappear through the far door. He would phone in private from the Inspector's office. Driscoll thought about the Inspector, wondered whether he realised his disapproval of peculiar civilians assuming the run of his station was quite obvious. Probably, he decided, the Inspector was the kind of man who didn't particularly care whether it was obvious or not. He knew British police methods were the best in the world and he didn't see any reason to conceal his knowledge. Especially from peculiar civilians.

Driscoll thought that was half the trouble. People, even the police, didn't realise that it wasn't just a game any more, with both sides keeping certain unwritten rules even if they broke the official ones. It was a viciously serious business now, with no pretensions to respectability, no need to justify the means so long as the end was attained. It was the kind of business a democracy could never hope to enter successfully, unless it pushed responsibility on to people like Landford and himself. And even then, it crippled them by insisting that they played to the rules. Of course, they never did. And of course, everyone knew that. But they went outside the recognised rules as individuals, not as representatives of the State. And if they slipped up they answered for it as individuals, without protection from the State.

Driscoll thought the odds were balanced pretty heavily against them. The amazing thing was how much success had been achieved even against the odds. But the really big successes had always been individual, the direct result of someone deliberately breaking the rules, sticking their neck out to achieve results. He grinned to himself as he remembered the times he'd done it in the past.

The far door opened, and Landford came through it. He walked slowly across to Driscoll, said quietly, 'Browne's pleased. I've fixed it to transfer Kubin somewhere more convenient than here if it doesn't work. Somewhere we can take our time over him, and the Embassy won't be able to trace him. Officially he'll be on the dangerously ill list at one of the hospitals, unable to see anyone on doctor's orders.'

He sat down beside Driscoll again, lit another cigarette.

Driscoll smiled. He knew exactly what Landford had in mind. At the same time he was doubtful whether they would break Kubin down if he didn't break in the next few minutes. A man who wanted to hold something back would talk, in the end. It might take a very long time, but in the end he would talk. A man who wanted to talk but couldn't — who had some impenetrable block in his mind that made it impossible for him to talk — was a much tougher proposition.

Driscoll checked his watch against the big wall clock.

Nine minutes had gone. The last minute stretched out into an infinity of time, the seconds spilling loudly and with exaggerated slowness from the circling hand of the wall clock.

They waited a full thirty seconds past the ten minutes, and then Landford stood up. 'I don't like it, Johnny. It looks like he's gone bad on us. I thought he'd have rung before five minutes were up.'

'Yeah, so did I,' Driscoll said. 'Going to take a look?'

'I think so,' Landford said slowly. 'He won't know we're watching if we just use the peephole without opening the communication panel.'

Driscoll walked over to the door, beckoned to the sergeant, followed him to the grille.

The sergeant swung it open for them, gave Landford the cell key, then locked the grille behind them. They walked slowly down the corridor, placing their feet softly, making as little noise as dead leaves falling.

The communication panel was between four and five feet up from the bottom of the door. In the very centre of it a small metal disc pivoted on a top pin to reveal a peephole.

Landford pushed the disc round and up, looked through the hole. He turned, whispered to Driscoll, 'I can't see him', then looked through the hole again. He muttered to himself, released the catch on the panel, swung it out to give them a full view of the cell.

They stared in through the aperture, saw Kubin. Landford backed away, inserted the key in the lock, swung the door open. They looked down at Kubin.

He was lying near the door, his body twisted and contorted, still and unbreathing. He lay huddled over his right leg, his face pressing into the cold concrete of the floor. His right arm was under him, his left stretched out, fingers curved into talons, as though in death he had scrabbled despairingly at the door of the cell.

Landford jabbed viciously at the alarm in the wall, below the little framed notice that told prisoners of their right to appeal.

Driscoll heard the bell ringing in the distance. He bent over Kubin, sniffed the faint but definite odour he had expected.

Landford released the alarm button, knelt down on the other side.

Carefully and gently they turned Kubin over, looked at his face. It was drawn in agony, as though death had come hideously if swiftly. Landford bent further, sniffed just above Kubin's mouth. He looked up at Driscoll.

Driscoll nodded slowly. 'Yeah, the old lullaby drops. The old last resort capsule. Open his mouth up, Willy.'

Landford inserted the fingers of his right hand into Kubin's mouth, forced the jaws apart. He whipped a handkerchief from his pocket, poked the index finger of his left hand into it, pushed the finger deep into Kubin's mouth, rubbing gently round the back teeth on each side of the mouth. Then he pulled the finger out, spread the handkerchief out so that the part that had been in contact with Kubin's teeth was exposed.

On the wet surface of the handkerchief they saw two or three little globules of half-melted gelatine. The odour of hydrocyanic acid was a little stronger than it had been. They heard the rattle of the grille, the sound of heavy footsteps hurrying towards the cell.

Driscoll said, 'Must have had it in his mouth all the

time.'

Landford let Kubin's head drop back on the floor as he stood up. It thumped on the concrete with a dull, flat sound, rested there face upwards, the mouth lolling obscenely half-open.

Driscoll stood up, followed Landford out of the cell.

Landford stood in front of the cell door, facing the desk sergeant. He said, softly, 'Who searched this man, sergeant?'

Driscoll thought his voice was as softly vicious as a viper's hiss.

The sergeant, peering wide-eyed past Landford at Kubin's huddled body, said, 'I did. What's happened to him? Is he dead?'

Landford said, coldly, 'No, trying to dig his way out. Naturally, you looked in his mouth? Did you?'

'Yes, sir. Of course I did.'

'That's fine. And what did you notice about his false teeth?'

'False teeth?' The sergeant hesitated, looked quickly from Landford to Driscoll. 'Well, I don't know that I...'

Landford cut in on him, softly venomous, 'So you didn't notice anything. Did you even notice whether he had false teeth at all? Well, *had he*?'

The sergeant wriggled uncomfortably, looked away from Landford, twitching his shoulders as though his uniform jacket were suddenly too small for him, too tight on his back. 'Well, I wouldn't like to say exactly. I didn't really notice, as you might say.'

Driscoll noticed beads of sweat on the sergeant's forehead, that he was going very red in the face.

Landford said, still softly but very unpleasantly, 'This

man was vital to us. He had information that was literally priceless. We were told he'd been searched. And all the time he was carrying a capsule of prussic acid in his mouth, probably somewhere near his back teeth. All he had to do was bite it and he was dead. When we put the pressure on him he bit it. You can see the result for yourself.'

He stepped aside, let the sergeant look past him into the cell. The sergeant muttered something, stopped as Landford looked at him, looked away.

Landford said distantly, 'Send the Inspector in. I'm not going to waste my time cursing you, but for God's sake search a man's mouth properly next time. For your information he had no false teeth. If you didn't even notice that how the hell could you notice whether he had anything concealed in his mouth?'

The sergeant swallowed, nodded, turned away and walked quickly down the corridor, obviously very glad to get out of range of Landford.

The little man turned to Driscoll, said tonelessly, 'It's our fault too. We shouldn't have relied on those people searching him properly. It isn't fair to blame them too much. They aren't trained to deal with things like this.' He sounded very tired and disappointed.

Driscoll nodded. 'It's not much use worrying about it now. Maybe it doesn't matter too much anyway. After all, it looks pretty much as though they're not trying for the aircraft. Anyway, we got a name out of it. This bird Nicholas must have something. You saw how scared that fellow was of him?'

'Nicholas,' Landford murmured. 'Yes, very scared indeed. They get like that you know. Any man will if you subject him to pressure for long enough. Then they break. But the only time we hear of it is when they have a chance to get away, like Kubin did. And that only comes when they're serving in another country, and when they're trusted out on their own. You can bet your boots someone at the Embassy's going to be in trouble over Kubin.' He broke off as the Inspector approached.

The Inspector stopped in front of Landford, looked quickly past him into the cell. 'I'm sorry,' he said. 'I'm very sorry. But you know we didn't really want to keep him here in the first place. It was your people insisted we kept him here until you arrived. I told Colonel Browne I'd be happier if we just passed him on right away but he…'

'All right,' Landford said. 'All right, all right, it's done and it can't be helped. Will you arrange for photographs and a post mortem?'

'Yes, I'll do that. Would you like the PM right away?'

Landford smiled, a weary, cynical smile. 'No, there's no need to rush it. We know how he died. It's just a formality.'

'What about his clothes? You'll want those for examination?' The Inspector asked.

'No. We'll arrange for someone in Special Branch to look them over.' He looked at Driscoll. 'Nearly forgot the photograph. We'd better take that.'

They went into the cell, could find no trace of the print. They searched the cell thoroughly, looked carefully through Kubin's clothes. They didn't find it.

Driscoll stood up slowly. 'He was very scared, Willy. What would you think he'd do?'

'You mean he ate it?'

'Why not? Obviously he believed you when you said you were going to contact the Embassy. So when he found he just *couldn't* talk he decided the only way out was to bite the capsule. He must have figured that without the photograph they'd have a hell of a time tracing the woman and the boy. He probably thought if he could get rid of the photograph you wouldn't even bother to mention it. After all, there'd be no point once he was dead.' He looked down at Kubin. 'Poor little beggar, he had a lot of guts in some ways. I can admire someone who's as determined as that.'

Landford said, 'You're probably right, Johnny. Anyway, the post mortem will tell us for sure. Shall we go?'

They said curt goodbyes to the Inspector, went out through the charge room where the big sergeant bent busily over the desk as they passed, ostentatiously too busy to see them.

Outside, Landford said, 'I'll have to go back to the section. Browne's going to raise hell about this one.'

Driscoll grinned. 'Cheer up, I don't think he'd have given us very much anyway. You want me to come along an' tell him what a job you did on Barnett?'

'No, there's no need for you to come. Maybe you'd like to write a few things down on paper, sum up the arguments. After all,' he smiled whimsically, 'if I'm going to catch hell I'd like to feel you were suffering too.'

'And I will. All right, where do I contact you?'

'At the section. It's just past five. Could you have something by seven do you think?'

'I could try,' Driscoll said.

'OK, I'll expect you. Will you be in your flat, if we

need to contact you in a hurry?' He paused, lit a cigarette, went on, 'As a matter of fact we probably will need to, I know what Browne's like when he gets hold of something like this. Could you stick by your telephone and let me know where to find you if you leave the flat?'

'Sure, I'll do that. Don't bother to run me back, I'll get a taxi.'

'Right,' Landford said. They walked down the steps. As they got to the pavement a taxi came past. Driscoll hailed it.

He climbed in, told the driver the address of his flat. As it pulled away he saw Landford walk across to the Jaguar.

20

Driscoll leaned back in the cool interior of the taxi, lit a cigarette. He stared idly out of the side window, barely conscious of the press of people on the pavements, his mind busy with the details of the afternoon's events.

He thought that he had been very lucky with Landford. If the little man had arrived a few seconds later it would have been too late. And again, if Landford had not fired immediately and accurately, he would now be with Janine and Barnett in the flat, as dead as they were. He was quite certain now that Landford was very good indeed, a very dangerous person to cross. He smiled, twisted round in his seat to look carefully at the road behind the taxi.

Satisfied that Landford's Jaguar was nowhere in sight, he leaned forward and slid back the glass partition to speak to the driver. The driver nodded to his instructions, turned right at the next intersection.

As the taxi headed south toward Janine's flat Driscoll went over very carefully everything Barnett had said. The words he had used were indelibly printed on his mind. He lit another cigarette from his old one, crushed out the old butt. He thought that everything fitted, that Barnett's confidence could have only one explanation.

He wondered whether the Special Branch had got to Janine's flat yet. On the whole he considered it unlikely.

Colonel Browne and Landford had been too occupied with the Kubin incident to have called them in right away. But there was just a chance that Browne had notified them immediately. In that case Driscoll was going to run into trouble. He decided that it was a risk he must take, that he had to be sure about the receipt.

He recognised familiar streets, realised that the taxi was approaching the square in which the flat was situated. He stopped the driver near the bright scarlet of a telephone box. Inside the box he thought for a moment, then put three pennies in the slot, dialled Marian's number.

As soon as he heard her answer Driscoll said, 'Marian, Driscoll here. I was hoping you'd got back. I haven't got much time at the moment, but I'll be along to see you in about an hour. Will that be all right?'

'Right,' Marian said. He thought her voice was very attractive over the telephone, clear and well-toned. She went on, 'I got quite a lot of stuff. Do you know where to come?'

'That I do,' Driscoll murmured. 'Be good.'

He pressed down the receiver bar, held it for thirty seconds then released it. He put in three more pennies, dialled Janine's number. The sound of the telephone ringing in Janine's flat was a harsh buzz in his ears. He received an instant, sickening impression of a fat blue fly, disturbed by the vibration of the telephone, lifting momentarily from the red hole in Janine's temple, dropping back again with an eager dipping of its proboscis. He shivered, listened to the ringing for another minute, then replaced the receiver.

As he walked quickly along the hot pavement to the

flat, Driscoll thought it was almost a certainty the Special Branch were not there yet. If they had been they would have answered the telephone, tried to keep him talking while the call was traced.

Once inside the house he went up the stairs quickly and lightly. On the last flight he took great pains to ensure that he made no sound. At the door of the flat he paused, listened carefully for voices or movement. He heard nothing. He took Barnett's keys from his pocket, found one that looked as if it would fit the lock. The key turned easily and he swung the door open.

He walked quickly through the flat, satisfied himself that it was empty. In the bedroom he located Janine's handbag, snapped it open. The bag contained the usual feminine accessories, some loose change. No receipt. He opened her wardrobe, her dressing table, searched them quickly and thoroughly. No receipt.

He went through Barnett's clothes again, checking them with minute thoroughness. Then he searched the flat. He moved quickly and methodically, examining all the places an expert would examine, finding nothing of any use, and no receipt.

There was one item of minor interest in the kitchen. In a wall cabinet, where several bottles of liquor were stored, he found a small screw-topped aluminium container. No label. He screwed open the top, shook out two or three small, white tablets. He frowned, pressed one of the tablets on his tongue, rubbing it gently backwards and forwards. He recognised the slightly bitter taste immediately, knew from experience that the taste would disappear when the tablet was dissolved in something like whisky. He thought that if Winterley had been given one or two of the tablets he would have had a nasty hangover the next day. The tablets were extremely efficient sleep producers, but they left a violent reaction the following morning.

He walked slowly back into the bedroom, gave a final check to one or two possible places, but without any real hope of finding anything. He was sure now that the receipt was nowhere in the flat. He glanced at his watch, saw that he had been searching for nearly forty minutes. He had taken a big chance but he felt that it had been worth it.

He looked down at Janine. The blood had stopped welling in the little hole, and the pallor beneath the golden brown of her skin was heavier and more distinct. He lifted her hand, felt no trace of stiffness in the body yet. He turned away to look at Barnett, then back to Janine. Even in death her body had a loveliness that was breathtaking.

Suddenly he heard the voice of the bartender at the Mandolin again. *'Very cold?'* it said. *'No.'* And again. *'Very cold? No.'* Driscoll shook his head, murmured, 'Very cold? Yes.' Then he went out of the flat.

On the landing below he tried one of Barnett's keys in the lock of the door, was not at all surprised when it fitted. There was no recording apparatus in Janine's flat, but the microphone in the wall shaft meant there had to be one somewhere. The flat below was the obvious answer.

The flat was exactly the same shape as Janine's. The main room had no furniture except for a heavy, mahogany sideboard which stood right underneath a small, grilled ventilator that let into the airshaft. Driscoll peered into the two inch space between the sideboard and the wall, saw the thin cable emerge from the wall directly beneath the ventilator, lead into the back of the sideboard. He used a handkerchief to swing open the door of the sideboard, looked inside.

The tape recorder was big, square, new looking in green crackle-glazed metal. Most of the tape was on the right hand spool, very little on the left. He shrouded his finger in the handkerchief, flicked down the rewind switch. When the rewinding was almost complete he stopped it and pressed the play button.

At once he heard his own voice, disturbingly loud in the quiet of the room. He reached forward, adjusted the volume until his voice and Janine's were quieter. He knelt close to the amplifier, hearing the sounds from the past. There were the vibrant and caressing tones that had been Janine's, and his own deeper sounds. The whole of his meeting with Janine was there from the time he came into the flat until they moved out into the small lobby.

And there the recording faded and stopped, the microphone unable to pick up their conversation in the lobby. The silence lasted a minute or so. Driscoll grinned, thinking that it had been quite a full minute. Then, faintly but definitely, there was the sound of the door closing, followed by the small sounds as Janine came back into the flat. After that nothing.

He speeded up the replaying tape, let it run swiftly through the spools, ready to stop if he heard any deviation from the steady hum. He ran through the whole tape, was quite sure there was no other conversation or sound on it. Then he rewound it to approximately the same place it had been when he came in, switched the machine off.

He stood quite still for a few moments, running through in his mind the conversation between himself and Janine. He thought that taken together with the receipt it would be fairly good evidence. He shrugged, took a cigarette out, paused in the act of lighting it as he heard heavy regular footsteps on the stairs. There were two sets of steps.

The footsteps passed the landing, went on up the stairs to Janine's flat. He heard nothing else for several minutes, then came the noise of a door closing. He thought it had taken them rather a long time to find a key that fitted. He crossed to the window, looked down on the square. Thirty yards along to the left from the entrance of the house a small dark green car was parked by the kerb. No other cars were parked anywhere near. Driscoll could see in through the rear window of the car, was fairly sure it was empty. He took several minutes to look carefully round the square, inspecting each person who was walking anywhere near the flat. At length he was satisfied they had not left anyone to watch the entrance. He noticed that he could hear very little movement from the flat above, presumed that the thick carpets were muffling the noise.

He inspected the rest of the flat quickly, saw that it contained no furniture at all other than the mahogany sideboard, no place where the receipt could have been hidden. Then he moved out of the flat, shutting the door quietly behind him, and going down the stairs fast and without noise.

Outside the house he turned right, walking quickly. He took alternate turnings to left and right until he was quite sure he was not being followed. He made his way gradually to Gloucester Road station, walked in past the magazine stall to the telephone booths on the left past the ticket office.

He walked to the end booth, making sure the next one along was empty. Then he dialled Davidson's number. Immediately he heard a voice that he recognised as Davidson's secretary, Ann.

'This is Driscoll. Is the old man in?'

'I'm sorry. He went half an hour ago. I don't quite know where he is. Incidentally, Mr Driscoll, someone's trying to get in touch with you. At least, someone's been enquiring about you.'

'You interest me. Just what enquiries were made?'

'Well, I don't really think I can pass that on. Not without the old man's approval. You know how he is about things.'

'Oh sure,' Driscoll said. 'Just tell me this. Were the enquiries to do with any of the information on my confidential dossier?'

'Why yes,' the girl replied. She sounded rather puzzled, Driscoll thought. She went on, 'Then you know about it?'

'Yeah,' Driscoll said. 'Just routine. Did the old man give the information?'

'Yes. It was someone from Special Branch who was asking.'

'OK. Thanks a lot Ann. When the old man comes back tell him I'll be in touch some time.' He paused, spoke very carefully. 'I don't quite know when it will be. Tell him not to worry if he doesn't hear from me for a day or so. Goodbye.'

He put the receiver down, remained in the booth while he lit a cigarette. He thought about things for a moment, decided that the game was really on now. Things were beginning to happen. He thought that the next few hours might be very interesting.

He came out through the station entrance, walked the few steps to the right to pick up a taxi. Near Earl's Court he changed into another, was cautious enough to have the driver drop him round the corner from Marian's flat. Only when he was quite certain he was not being followed did he walk in through the entrance and take the lift to Marian's floor.

21

The lift stopped with a soft hiss at the fourth floor. Driscoll turned to the attendant, 'Which way for 4D?'

The attendant looked at him. He was an old man, tired looking, with a face like a thousand lost battles. He said, 'Nice girl, ain't she?'

'Yeah. Which way?'

The old man slid back the outer door, jerked his thumb down the corridor to the right. 'She don't get many callers. Know her well?'

Driscoll said, 'Maybe. An' why are you worried?'

The man stepped back into the lift. Behind the dullness of his eyes there was a wary caution. 'No offence,' he said. 'No offence at all. Just that she's a nice girl. You know how it is.'

Driscoll said softly, 'Yeah.'

He watched the door slide suddenly shut, saw the indicator register the downward passage of the lift. He turned, shrugging his shoulders, walked along past a door lettered 4C, stopped at the last door. The letters 4D were neatly painted in black on the light brown door. Below them a card, *Miss Marian Courtney.* Below that a chromium bell-push.

He pressed the bell, heard the sound of toned chimes behind the door. He took out a cigarette, lit it, blew smoke in two fine streams through his nostrils. The door opened.

'Late again. Really, Johnny, you're always late.' She smiled, held the door open for him to come in.

Driscoll paused for a moment, looked her up and down. She was wearing three quarter length jeans, tight round the calf, in white duck. A loose outside sweater in blue plaid cotton, rope soled espadrilles with narrow straps of matching blue, and toenails lacquered in bright red. The skin round her temples was very faintly damp, her eyes puckered slightly as though she had been staring into the sun.

Driscoll said, 'For the beach, magnificent. In fact pretty good anywhere.' His eyes were frankly appraising, admiring without any effort to conceal it. He thought she looked very good indeed.

Marian smiled again. 'I was on the balcony. It faces southwest over the river. The late afternoon sun is the best of all don't you think?'

'Oh yes,' Driscoll murmured. 'Definitely the best.'

He followed her through a casually furnished lounge, out through glass doors on to a wide balcony. It held two cane reclining chairs with foot rests and oversize cushions, a low table with a composition top between them. On the table a silver ice bucket, a bottle of Scotch and an empty glass. A tall, misted glass already sat on the solid flat armrest of the far chair.

Marian walked round to the chair, sat down. She swung her feet up on it, leaning lazily back, picked up her glass. 'Have a seat, Johnny, and a drink. You like Scotch, don't you?'

'Yeah, I do.'

He poured himself a drink, added a cube of ice, reached under the table for the soda syphon. He played the soda on the ice cube, watching it turn over and over in the jet. He thought that Marian was putting on a very good show of sophistication. He wondered just how far it would stretch.

He tinkled the cube around in his glass, relaxed on the other chair. The whisky tasted very good, cold and sharp in the thickness of his mouth. He looked out of the corner of his eye at Marian, saw she was leaning back with her arms above her head, her eyes closed. Her breasts were swelling curves beneath the blue plaid, her hair a vivid flame against the soft cream of her arms.

'So you like the sun?' Driscoll asked.

'No.' Her voice was soft and throaty. 'Not very much. I thought perhaps I'd try to get a little browner. I don't quite know why.' She turned her head slowly, opened her eyes and looked at him.

'Is that so?' Driscoll's voice was casual and disinterested. He leaned toward her, then slumped back into the chair again, said, 'OK, I get it. Now tell me all about Winterley.'

He closed his eyes, feeling the pleasant warmth of sunshine on his eyelids.

Marian looked at him, wondered if the interested appraisal in his eyes had been genuine, felt vaguely disturbed.

'I managed to get quite friendly with one of Winterley's colleagues. Incidentally that Roebuck is a good pub. And very popular with the all the airfield people.'

'Yeah, I know. What was his name?'

'Masterson. He's one of the design people there. He and Winterley used to go around together occasionally, generally with a couple of girls.' She paused, pushed the tip of her tongue through her lips, moistened her upper lip with it. 'Now, Winterley,' she went on softly, 'there was quite a boy. He must have had something. He managed very well for girls.'

'Girls. That's what I want.'

'All right. In the past six months there were four. Jean, Hilda, and two Bettys. Might have been slightly confusing that but I should think Winterley was careful not to get them mixed. He seems to have been the sort of person who would have managed things like that pretty well.'

She leaned forward, poured whisky into her glass, added ice and soda.

'And that's all?' Driscoll asked.

'All I could find out, I think it was definitely all. I rather think Winterley was the type who would have made no secret at all of his girl friends. The other way in fact. He strikes me as the sort of person who would have been quite proud of his girls. You know, a kiss and tell sort of person. I don't very much like the idea of kiss and tell, do you?'

Driscoll grinned. 'It all depends.'

'On what?'

'Who you've kissed, how much you tell. You've got details of these girls of course?'

'Yes, quite a lot. Everything's in writing ready for you.'

'All right, that's fine. Shall we have a look through it?'

Marian sat up, put her glass down on the table. 'It's inside, in the lounge.'

She stood up, walked past Driscoll through the wide doors. He caught the whispering smell of her perfume as she passed, thought it was a very attractive perfume, quiet and calm, yet with a hint of excitement in it, an undertone of suggestive warmth. The right sort of scent for a girl like Marian.

He stood up, stretched lazily, followed her into the lounge. She was bending over a table in the far corner, the white jeans tight against the smooth velvet of her legs. She turned, holding some sheets of paper in her hand, began to walk toward him. Halfway across the room she stepped into the broad shaft of slanting sunlight that poured in through the wide doors.

Driscoll said softly, 'Stop right there.'

She stopped, looking right at him, the papers loosely held in her dangling left hand. She was quite still and motionless, her smoke-blue eyes wide and calm, a smile curving the red of her lips. The sunlight painted her in glowing colours against the dark background of shadow, tinting her skin with white gold, flicking shafts of fire through the vivid gleam of her hair.

Driscoll walked softly up to her, stretched out his hands and placed them on her shoulders. Through the thin stuff of the sweater he could feel the warmth of her smooth skin. Her eyes were wide open, looking right into his. Gently he pulled her forward moving her slowly toward him, bent down to brush his lips against hers. She shuddered delicately, a small rippling shudder that ran swiftly along the length of her spine. Then as Driscoll lifted his head away she moved hard into him, flinging her arms round his neck, her eyes closed and her mouth soft and warm against his.

And suddenly the ice had gone, there was only a blazing warmth as she pressed tight against him and felt the hard strength of his arms around her. She moved against him, her mouth eagerly straining and her body hard against his, hungry and demanding.

Driscoll lifted away from her, saw the glow of her hair in front of his eyes, smelt the warm perfume rising from her. He thought that Marian was one of those things that happen very seldom, the kind of things that mean a great deal if they are handled right. Then he felt his head dragged down to hers again, sensed the storm of passion that was rising in her, broke abruptly away.

'I think you're pretty good, Marian. An' I think we're going to have a lot of fun. I've thought it since I first met you.' His voice was very quiet with an undertone of gentleness that was very unusual in him.

Marian turned slowly, her eyes very warm and alive. 'I'm glad you feel like that.' She laughed quietly, a little nervously, held out the sheets of paper she had crumpled as she flung her arms around his neck. 'Better take these.'

'Thanks.' He took the papers from her, scanned through them quickly. He walked across to the windowsill next to the wide doors, where a telephone sat. 'Mind if I use this?'

Marian shook her head slowly, watched him intently while he dialled. She thought that Driscoll was a very strange person. She had never suspected the existence of that gentle, sentimental streak beneath the surface hardness. She remembered that it had flickered for a moment when he was talking to her at Number 87, but she had dismissed it then as an act. Now she was sure it was no act, that it was genuinely there. She wondered, flicking a small tongue quickly round her lips, whether beyond it lay another stratum of ruthlessness. Whether, once he was really aroused, the gentleness would disappear altogether. She decided that it would, that in any case it would be very interesting to attempt the discovery.

Driscoll heard Landford's voice on the telephone, said, 'Willy, Driscoll here.' He listened while Landford spoke, then said, 'Yeah, I'm sorry about that. I got tied up in some personal business.' He grinned at Marian.

Landford went on, 'I think you'd better come right away, Johnny.' His tone was rather impersonal, Driscoll thought, a little cold. 'Something unexpected has happened. It's fairly serious.'

'Right Willy. Fifteen minutes.' Driscoll heard the murmur of Landford's goodbye, put the receiver down. He turned to Marian. 'I'll have to go.'

Marian said, 'Something to do with this?'

'Right. Something serious has happened. I don't know what yet. I'll ring you later.' He smiled at her. 'Maybe I'll drop round for another drink?'

'That would be nice.' Marian said carefully. She walked with him to the door, holding his arm quite naturally with an ease that had a thousand years of inheritance behind it. At the door she waited for him to kiss her with a calm assurance that Driscoll found amusing.

He bent forward, brushed her lips with his own again, said, 'Never mind the sun, you don't really need to be browner.' He smiled, opened the door, went through it with a casual, 'See you soon.'

Marian walked back to the balcony, poured herself

another drink. She drank it slowly and thoughtfully, quite unconscious of the warmth of sun on her skin. She realised that she had fallen pretty hard for Driscoll, felt fairly sure he was the same way about her. She wished she could rid herself of the small stab of fear that needled her with the suspicion that she might be wrong, that Driscoll was making a play for her for some reason other than that. She finished her drink, walked into the lounge and through to the bedroom to change.

She thought that he would definitely come again that night. Something was telling her that it would be much safer if she did not dress specially for him, that he would notice it immediately. She decided, calmly and coldly, that she would not, that she would wear something attractive but not really special.

She turned to her wardrobe with that decision firmly made, immediately took out the hostess gown she had put on for him once before when he had cancelled the appointment at the flat, and which she had been keeping for a really special occasion.

22

Fellows stood in the tall angled windows of the flight control tower, looked out across the concrete and grass of the airfield. The green was tinged with yellow in the oblique rays of the evening sun, and the runway seemed almost mirror like as it reflected the beams.

He turned his head anxiously to left and right, watching for the first distant speck that would be the fighter returning. He thought grimly, as he stood there with an unlit cigarette in his mouth, that the last two days had been a nightmare.

A nightmare in which he had hardly left the control tower, so that he could be in constant touch with the progress of the tests. It was absurd, he thought, quite unreasonable to expect anything else than worry and strain until the fighter had gone safely beyond the hours that the first model had flown before it crashed.

The worry was there with him constantly as he sat in the tower shivering and straining with every awful stress that was being inflicted on the airframe as he listened to the calm voice of Bellamy report the plane's progress.

They had done just over ten hours of flying in the two days, and now the aircraft was only a little off the total of the first model, say five hours or so.

In his mind Fellows thought that really she was already beyond it. Only he and Bellamy knew just what stresses had been imposed on the aircraft in the past two days. Every flight had been a deliberate attempt to impose a breaking strain, every flight the equivalent of two or three normal flights in terms of stress and strain on the airframe. Really, Fellows thought, the fighter had already flown the equivalent of about ten hours more than the first model. Just one more day he promised himself, just one more day of total breaking-strain flying, and he would be quite sure that the fighter had no design flaw, was as perfect as it had always seemed to be.

He stiffened suddenly as he caught sight of the aircraft, a black spot in the distance. Rapidly it approached, seeming to sprout wings as the distance decreased and the shape began to appear.

He heard Bellamy's voice on the radio-telephone saying, 'Four miles finals low run and break.'

And then the controller answering, 'Clear low run and break. No aircraft in circuit.'

The next instant the fighter flashed along the runway at about three-fifty knots, its turbines making the air hideous with their echoing scream. Halfway along the runway the fighter lifted into a hard climbing turn to port.

Fellows heard the noise of the turbines die away as Bellamy reduced power, watched the white trails stream from the swept-back wingtips as he dragged the fighter round in a tight turn.

Then the fighter was turning on base leg, the undercarriage suddenly visible beneath the polished silver body. It was turning on final approach, gracefully dipping its port wing, catching the rays of the sun and reflecting them in mirrored flashes.

Fellows watched it touch the runway some fifty yards

from the downwind end, heard over the five hundred yards of separating grass the first harsh scream of the rubber, then the repeated diminishing squeals of the brakes. He watched the fighter turn off at the end of the runway, then he walked slowly out of the control building and to his office.

He sat behind his desk, staring at the wall, waiting with an anxiety that lengthened the seconds into minutes, the minutes dragging on in the slow wait for Bellamy to come in with the after-flight report.

He heard Bellamy's voice outside, watched him come into the room, sit down slowly and deliberately, light a cigarette. He found the slowness of Bellamy's movements an intense source of annoyance, and yet strangely comforting too. It was difficult to imagine anything happening to an aircraft that Bellamy was flying.

At last, unable to restrain himself any longer, he said, 'For God's sake, Gordon come on. Is she all right?'

Bellamy broke the matchstick between powerful fingers, smiled at him.

'Easy, Bill,' he said, his voice calm and placid as an old bramble enclosed pool, 'she's fine. Little more rough than usual at point nine eight, but it was pretty warm up there today. That probably did it. Apart from that, fine. Happy now?'

'Sorry I jumped, Gordon. That's the way it's getting me. I shall be bloody glad when tomorrow's over.'

'So shall I.' Bellamy smiled. 'Pulling this high G all the time is a bit tough. You think tomorrow will see us safely through?'

'No doubt of it. We'll pass the flying hours of the

other one, and you and I know that even if they're much the same on paper this one has had a much tougher life than the other. I'd say it was equivalent to about another thirty hours of normal flying. You tired?'

'A little.' Bellamy stood up, stretched. 'Think I'll push on home. I've left the pad with the fitters. Everything normal, no need for you to worry about it at all.'

He came over to the desk, leaned on it. 'Why not go out this evening?' he asked softly. 'Go out and get drunk Bill, or pick a woman up or something. Get away from all this for a while.' He waved his arm round the office, indicating the charts, the aircraft models, the untidy, heaped textbooks. 'You'll crack up if you don't you know,' he finished gently.

Fellows pushed his lips into a weak imitation of a smile. 'Never mind me Gordon. You go home and get to bed. First take-off six thirty.'

Bellamy grinned. 'Six thirty. So long, Bill.' He paused after opening the door. 'And get away for a bit will you?'

'Sure,' Fellows said. 'I will later. So long.'

He watched the door shut behind Bellamy, heard the slow, deliberate footsteps in the corridor. He lit another cigarette, thinking that the smoke was quite tasteless, that he really must get round to giving up smoking some time. He picked up the telephone, asked the operator for an outside line. When he got through to the outside exchange he asked for a trunk call to a Euston number, held the receiver slightly away from his ear as the connections were made.

He heard Colonel Browne's voice, identified himself with the code word he had been given.

'Ah yes, how are you, Fellows?' Browne said. 'Good

news?'

'Pretty good. We're up to within five hours of the total of the other one. One more day will see us past it. As a matter of fact we've really passed it anyway.'

Browne said, 'How?'

'Well, the testing we've done in the past two days hasn't been normal at all,' Fellows said, 'to start with we've flown about five times as much as usual. And the flying has been much tougher. We've imposed really severe strains on the aircraft, so that each hour has been equivalent to several hours of normal flying. She's stood everything we've done. I think she's going to be all right, though of course no one can really say definitely yet.'

'So tomorrow is the crucial day?'

'Well, no more so than today or yesterday, but crucial just the same.'

'All right,' Browne said. 'I'll be sending someone down tonight to check on the security arrangements. You needn't have any worries about that side of it. And good luck tomorrow. Let me know tomorrow night, will you? And of course, you won't mention the fact that someone is coming down.'

'Of course not.' Fellows said. 'Goodbye.'

He put the receiver down, crushed out his cigarette in the ashtray, lit another. It was just as tasteless as the last. He decided to make one last inspection of the fighter himself before it was wheeled into the hangar and the security people took over for the night.

He stood up, placed his cigarette on the edge of the ashtray as he climbed into a pair of light overalls. Then, without a backward glance, he hurried out of the office.

The cigarette burned slowly away until it fell back on

the wood of the desk. There it burned away to a small cylinder of ash scorching a deep burn in the desktop. There were many burns like that on Fellows' desk.

23

Browne put the telephone back on its rest, turned to Driscoll, 'That was Fellows. Chief designer at the works. He thinks tomorrow may be the crucial day. If she comes through that she'll be all right. I hope to God he's right. Where was I anyway?'

Driscoll looked across the room at Landford, then down at the untidy heap of Clifton's body. He wished that Landford would turn the body over again, hide the leering grimace of Clifton's death mask.

'You'd got as far as telling Clifton that Kubin had been brought in,' Driscoll answered, 'how shaken he looked when he heard it.'

'Ah yes. He did indeed,' Browne said, 'I expected better than that of Clifton. But really, when you think just what a shock it must have been, you can understand it. Anyway, he was badly shaken. Of course, he covered it very well as soon as the initial shock had passed. Still, I knew he was scared. So when Landford phoned to tell me he thought Kubin would crack I took a chance — you may have noticed my replies were a little strange, Willy.'

Landford frowned. 'I can't really remember — wait a moment though. There was one thing I noticed. I said that I *thought* Kubin would crack. And you said, *He has? That's good.* I remember now, because I put you right straight away. But of course Clifton wouldn't have heard that.'

'No,' Browne said. 'He didn't. He only heard my reply. It shook him badly. Badly enough so that he didn't notice me when I slid the drawer of the desk open and made sure the gun was handy. I had an idea even then he'd try to shoot his way out.'

'You weren't wrong,' Driscoll murmured. He looked at Clifton's gun, harshly black against the light brown of the carpet, lying about a yard from the body where it had come to rest after dropping from Clifton's dead hand.

Browne smiled. 'I am rarely wrong, Johnny,' he said softly. 'And that's really why I took the chance on bluffing Clifton. I knew I was right. The way I saw it time was getting short. Willy had already told me that Kubin couldn't identify Nicholas. I thought if I could rattle Clifton enough there was a good chance of him letting the cat out of the bag. On the other hand, there was always the chance he'd start shooting. Either way it would clear the air a little. You see, when I put the telephone down I turned to Clifton and told him point blank that Kubin had talked. And that he was implicated. That did it. Do you see?'

Driscoll said slowly, 'To a point. But Clifton must have known quite well that Kubin couldn't identify him. Especially if he was Nicholas. He'd have known that Kubin had never seen him, exactly as Kubin told us.'

Browne smiled. It was a mere ghost of a smile that flicked across his face and disappeared, leaving it serious again.

'Yes, Johnny, but not the way I played it. We know that Kubin was driven to us by fear. But I told Clifton he'd come in quite voluntarily as a logical step in a course of action he'd been planning for some time. In other words that he was a deliberate traitor who'd been working steadily to the point where he could come to us with information he knew would be valuable. And the most valuable information we could possibly have would be the identities of their big men over here. *Now* look at it. Clifton never suspected Kubin would come to us, or he'd never have been let out of the Embassy today, but if Kubin could conceal that, then he could also conceal the fact that for a long time he'd been gathering information. How about that?' Browne concluded.

'It's good,' Driscoll said. 'It's definitely good.' He looked at Browne, thinking Landford had been very right when he'd said that Browne had a fine intellect, that his brain worked twice as fast as anyone else's. 'And it worked. Clifton swallowed it. So then he pulled the gun on you?'

'Yes. He did it very well too. As a matter of fact he was nearly too fast for me. As it was he got one shot off.'

He pointed a finger at the junction of the ceiling and the wall above his desk. Looking up, Driscoll could just see the small round hole.

Browne finished, 'Though I think he was dead before he fired it. Purely reflex.'

Driscoll nodded, 'How long have you suspected him?'

'That's just the point,' Landford said slowly. 'It's not a happy thought, Johnny, but it looks as though Clifton's been with them for a long time. You remember I told you we'd noticed some irregularity in Glazey's screening? It was that started the enquiries about Clifton, because he'd let that report through. I'm afraid we found pretty conclusive proof he was in with them. We're only starting to crosscheck the people he's cleared. And the whole hellish part is that he's been doing it for at least two years, because that's when Glazey was screened. God only knows how much damage he's done since then.' His tone was bitter, his eyes savage in a hard, resentful face.

Browne broke in on Landford, 'Maybe not too much, Willy. Don't forget that now we know, we can check everything he's done, maybe uncover a lot more. But I've got a hunch he hasn't done too much. I think he was holding himself back for something really big. Maybe something like wrecking the production plans for this fighter. I've got nothing to go on. It's just a hunch, one of those things you feel. There's one thing sure. If they did have any plans for sabotaging the fighter they're pretty well wrecked now. Apart from the way you and Johnny have things weighed off, and incidentally I agree with you, they really haven't much chance of doing anything now. Not with Barnett and Clifton written off.'

Landford said softly, 'Haven't you forgotten something?'

'Have I?' Browne said.

'Nicholas,' Landford said. He spoke viciously, almost spitting the word. 'Nicholas. What about him? We don't know Clifton was Nicholas.'

Browne said, 'On his own? Or at least with half his organisation out of business. I don't think so, Willy. And I haven't forgotten it. Didn't you hear me talking to Fellows?'

'I was thinking of other things,' Landford said loftily. He grinned at Driscoll.

'Ah yes,' Browne murmured. 'Well, I told Fellows I'd send someone down to check on the security arrangements. That's you, Willy. I'm not taking any chances with someone I don't know. You're going down there to check the arrangements personally. What's more you're going to sleep with the fighter. At least, not sleep. But spend the night in the hangar, stay with it every moment until it's wheeled out to fly tomorrow. There'll be other security personnel of course, but I want you there just to make sure nothing happens. You should have a very uncomfortable night.' He smiled.

Landford said, 'All right, when do I leave?'

Browne glanced at his watch. 'It's a little after seven now. They'll be inspecting the aircraft doing the pre-flight checks for tomorrow until about ten-thirty. You can drive there in a couple of hours I reckon so you'll need to leave by eight-fifteen at the latest really. I want you actually there when the engineers finish. Right?'

'Right. Will I be able to contact you here?'

'Yes.' Browne gave a little, tired smile. 'I'll be uncomfortable too, Willy, if it's any consolation.'

'That will help.' Landford smiled, looked down at Clifton's body. 'Shall we move this?' He flicked Clifton's jacket with a small shoe.

'No. I'm getting Special Branch in,' Browne said, 'they can search his flat. I think they're probably getting very tired of us today. They seem to have done nothing but go round clearing up the bodies we leave. Incidentally, who's got Barnett's keys?'

'I have.' Driscoll took the keys from his pocket, gave them to Browne, said carefully, 'Sorry, I forgot all about them when the Kubin thing came up. I was excited about that, couldn't think of anything else.'

Landford said, 'We all were. They got into that girl's

flat all right without them apparently. At least, they haven't called yet.'

'And I don't suppose they will for a long time yet,' Browne said, 'it takes them a very long time to search a place. Mind you, they do a thorough job. But definitely slow.'

Browne grinned as he tossed Barnett's keys in the air, let them fall on the desk, then suddenly stiffened and said, 'Willy, chuck in Clifton's keys too, will you?'

'Of course. Why didn't we think of that sooner?' Landford said as he threw another bunch of keys on the desk.

Then he and Driscoll bent over the desk while Browne compared them with Barnett's keys. On Clifton's key ring there were two keys that were exactly the same as two of Barnett's. Driscoll saw that they were the keys that opened Janine's flat and the flat beneath.

He saw more than that. He realised, suddenly, exactly where the receipt would be found. He said, 'That certainly ties it in.'

'Yes,' Browne said. 'Do you happen to know which particular keys of Barnett's these are?' He looked at Driscoll, an expression of mild interest on his face. But his eyes were very bright and hard.

Driscoll said, 'No. But there's a Yale lock on that flat. It could be that.' He thought his voice was just right, that it gave away nothing at all.

'All right,' Browne said. 'Another little pigeon for the Special Branch. Really, they'll be getting very acid with us if we keep on like this.' He chuckled. 'I don't think they're very keen on us anyway.' He looked at Driscoll. 'Did Willy tell you I wanted to see you this afternoon?'

'Yes. I'd forgotten it.'

Browne was smiling. 'I won't mention any names, but it appears someone handled one of the Special Branch very roughly the other night. Of course they don't actually know who it was, but they're not very pleased. I'm quite sure it wasn't you, was it, Johnny?'

Driscoll laughed. 'I think you're very often right.'

'All right,' Browne said, 'so that's my duty done. How good a tail was he anyway?'

'Lousy, but I think he'll be much better in future. You put him on to me of course?'

'Yes I did,' Browne said, 'I'm rather surprised you didn't spot him earlier than you did.'

Driscoll yawned, covered his mouth with his hand, said through his fingers, 'Earlier I wasn't bothered particularly. In any case it's fairly easy when there are people around. It's when the streets are empty it gets difficult. Anything you want me to do?'

'No. Perhaps you'd better stick around at your flat in case I need you. You know how fast things are liable to move — if they do move.'

'OK, I'll stick around the flat,' Driscoll said, 'I'll find it quite pleasant sitting there with a drink an' thinking about Willy in a nice concrete-floored hangar.'

Landford grinned, showing his teeth. 'It may be your turn next time. Be good Johnny.'

'So long,' Driscoll said.

He smiled at the Colonel, turned and walked past the sprawled inertness of Clifton's body, the ghastly grin on Clifton's face burning itself indelibly in his mind. He walked through the outer office, shut the outer door and looked carefully at the lock, went slowly down the stairs.

As he left the side entrance of the building he saw two men in plain suits, both of them wearing dark trilby hats, walk toward the entrance. He felt the keenness of their scrutiny as they passed him, recognised them immediately as Special Branch. He thought they would soon be on their way straight back out of the office, bound for Clifton's flat. He looked round for a taxi thinking that this was where time counted, that he did not have any too much of it left.

He was lucky enough to pick up a taxi within a minute. The worst of the rush hour traffic had eased now, and the driver made good time. Ten minutes after leaving the section, Driscoll was climbing out of the cab at the entrance to his block of flats.

He fumbled for change for the driver, found he had none. He passed over a ten-shilling note, said, 'Keep the change.'

The tip was sufficient for the driver to acknowledge it. 'Thanks, guv. Looks like rain don't it?' Then he let in the clutch and moved away.

Driscoll stood still on the pavement for a moment, looking up at the darkening sky, at the first few black clouds that were starting to edge across it. He thought the weather was turning bad, that they were in for a storm. He smiled to himself, thinking perhaps there was something a little symbolic in that.

24

Driscoll shut the door of his flat behind him with a bang. He walked across to the sideboard, poured himself a long whisky. He drank it straight off without adding water, poured another equally large and carried it over to an armchair by the empty fireplace. He lit a cigarette, sat there quite still smoking and occasionally sipping the whisky.

The smoke from his cigarette spiralled in lazy wreaths to the ceiling where it hung in a gently undulating pall. He looked through the layered smoke at the ceiling as he thought hard about the things that had happened. He sought for the break, the little half-remembered thing that could tell him what to do if only he could interpret it.

Mistily, through the vague dimness of smoke, Barnett's face, bullet shattered and wrecked, drifted across the ceiling. It slid imperceptibly into the twisted features of Kubin. And Kubin, with a few minute alterations in the twisting tendrils of smoke, gave way to the dead leer of Clifton. Driscoll looked at Clifton's face again, before the smoke changed once more, feeling sure that the receipt he had signed would be found at Clifton's place. Feeling sure, too, that by now the Special Branch had found and played back the recording in Janine's flat. Or rather in the flat beneath Janine's. And pretty soon they would find the receipt. Then it would not be very good. Not when it became one man against the whole massive organisation they could call in.

Driscoll grimaced, stood up. He carried his empty glass over to the sideboard, then irritably slammed it down and turned away. He walked across to the mantelpiece and slid back the picture that concealed the neat little wall safe. He juggled the dials into the right combination, swung open the door of the safe and lifted everything out on to the table. Then he closed the safe again, and twisted the dials round to reset the lock.

There was very little on the table. Two guns. A Mauser 7.65, and a small black .25 automatic. Spare clips of shells for both guns. A wad of pound notes, much of it still in packets of a hundred. And a passport in the name of Dainton, with current visas for a good many countries. The passport described Dainton as a journalist. Strangely enough, his photograph was a very good likeness of Driscoll.

He left the Mauser on the table, slipped the little automatic into a shoulder holster under his left armpit. Four packets of a hundred pound notes formed a bulk in his hip pocket. The other notes went into his wallet, and the wallet and the passport back into the inside pocket of his jacket. He paused, his hand still at the top of the pocket, as Clifton's remembered face suddenly danced before him again.

This time it was not dead but living. The mouth was moving, the lips forming words. In Driscoll's brain the little cam flicked over, obedient to the stimulus of the memory of Clifton's words that morning at the Section: *Money and the old place. Not much money. A very small amount of money.* And the old place.

He frowned, walked over to the sideboard and poured another long whisky. He drank it in one long swallow, feeling the raw sting of it in his throat and the urge of his fast moving brain. He stood quite still for nearly a minute while the little pieces dropped into place. Then he replaced the glass gently on the sideboard, walked across to the telephone.

When the number answered Driscoll said, 'Put me through to passenger reservations.' He waited for the clerk's voice, then said, 'My name's Dainton. Do you have any berths on the night train for Brussels? First if possible.' He waited again while the clerk went off to enquire, heard the affirmative answer then said, 'All right, one first sleeper, all the way through to Brussels. I'll be along to pick it up about half an hour before train time, about one o'clock this morning, all right?' He listened again, then put the telephone down.

He walked across to the window, saw that the sky was dark with scurrying rain clouds. From his bedroom he fetched a belted fawn raincoat, picked up the cold weight of the Mauser, hefted it for a moment in his hand, then slipped it into the pocket of the raincoat. He looked at his watch, saw it was just after eight. He smiled mirthlessly, looked carefully round the room to see he had not overlooked anything, then went through the door and down the stairs.

Outside the house he paused on the rain spotted pavement, looking up and down to see whether anyone was taking undue interest in him. He was not really expecting to be tailed yet. Nevertheless he took the usual precautions on the way to the old place.

The old place. Otherwise Luigi's. Otherwise the Prospect Restaurant, proprietor Alfred Hocking.

The old place where Clifton and he and some others — most of whom were dead now — had played cards all night in the old days, drinking vast quantities of Scotch and eating huge grilled steaks at a time when neither steaks nor Scotch were at all easy to acquire. Legally to acquire anyway. The place where they had insisted on calling Alfred Hocking, *Luigi*, in spite of all his protests and arguments that his change of name and nationality were legal and valid. Luigi's, the old place, where the answer might lie.

As he walked the last few hundred yards the rain suddenly increased, changing from heavy, occasional spots to a continuous, lashing downpour. Driscoll stuck his hands deep in his pockets, feeling the smooth mortality of the Mauser, hunching his big shoulders forward as the rain drove into his face.

He screwed up his eyes as he looked ahead into the rain, seeing electric lights in a misty blur, brushing past a few early whores who ducked hastily into doorways to preserve their cheap finery from the cloudburst.

At last, after he had walked three hundred yards north from Oxford Street, he turned into the bright, recessed doorway of the Prospect Restaurant, pushed open the glass topped door, passed through into the dry world inside.

He breathed in the old smells, the familiar compound of minestrone, spaghetti bolognaise, Gorgonzola and steaming café espresso. He looked round the room, shaking little bright drops of rain from his coat. On the right, a row of tables ranged down the wall. Nearly all of them were occupied, mostly by men.

His gaze flicked over the tables and the people, noticing the covert interest of those present, the careful hostility with which they regarded a stranger.

Driscoll felt the tangible coldness in the atmosphere as a dozen pairs of eyes inspected him from behind half-closed lids, he grinned at the room and turned to the bar-like counter.

Mr Alfred Hocking put down the glass he was wiping and walked slowly down the counter toward him. A brief light of recognition flickered in his eyes. He smiled, putting his hand over the bar to shake Driscoll's, saying nothing as he observed the slight shake of Driscoll's head. He turned slowly, walked down the counter toward the end flap, Driscoll pacing him.

Conversation began again in the restaurant, as men who had not looked at all at the meeting suddenly began to talk again to the men sitting with them. The cold atmosphere became carefully warm again, the watchful eyes relaxing until the door should open and another stranger enter.

Driscoll followed Hocking into a back room, took a seat opposite a small, old-fashioned desk. Hocking squeezed his vast bulk behind it, wiped small beads of sweat from his forehead with a quick sweep of a massive forearm. He pushed a bottle across the table to Driscoll, frowned slightly as Driscoll shook his head.

'Long time, Johnny.' Hocking said. 'Four, maybe five years.' His voice was a startling falsetto, a pencil on slate squeak that was quite incongruous in a man of his size.

Driscoll carefully brushed rain from his face with a handkerchief. He looked right at Hocking, smiled. 'Five years, to be exact. You haven't changed a bit, Luigi.'

'Ha,' Hocking squeaked. 'Still this Luigi business, eh? All the time Luigi. And me naturalised fifteen years.' He chuckled, heaving enormous shoulders. His eyes, deep set in folds of chalk-white flesh, had the brilliance and watchfulness of a snake's. 'Who you work with now, Johnny?'

'Various people. You know how it is, Luigi.' He grinned. 'You know one of them. Mike Clifton.'

'Mike? Mike you say. Yeah, I know Mike. I ain't seen him maybe as long as I ain't seen you. Maybe five years?' The eyes were very cautious under the hooding fat.

'Maybe you're a lying bastard,' Driscoll said casually.

He eased himself in his seat, opened the raincoat. He felt in his hip pocket, closed his fingers on one of the packets of notes, pulled it out. He held the packet of notes on the table for a moment, then pushed it into the right pocket of his open raincoat, kept his hand there.

He tilted back his chair, said lazily, 'You know why I know you're lying? Because Mike left something here with you, not long ago either. Something I want to pick up.'

Hocking giggled, his cheeks shaking. 'Always a card, Johnny. But you in the money now, eh? Good. I like people to be in money. Always good, money, eh?'

'Yeah. When you got it.' He looked straight at Hocking. 'An' when you're willing to pass some of it on.' He took the money out of his pocket, tossed it casually on the table. 'A century, Luigi,' he said softly.

Hocking looked at him. He said slowly, 'Lot of money, Johnny. But Mike's a lot of friend, eh? Friend to me. You know, one or two little things? He always fix it.

Keep your money, Johnny. It don't buy that.' The eyes were hard and bright.

Driscoll grinned, 'So you *have* got something. How the hell d'you think I knew? Mike wanted me to have whatever you've got. So stop clowning and get it.'

'You think I clown?' He shook the massive head, twisting the skin of his neck into deep crevasses. 'No good, Johnny, I don't believe you.'

'No? Maybe I can persuade you to change your mind.' Driscoll pulled his hand out of his pocket, the Mauser very solid and menacing in his big hand. 'Listen, Luigi,' he went on softly, 'an' listen good. If I have to I'll blow bits of you through the wall, but I'm gettin' what Clifton left. An' you know goddam well I don't fool with people. You've got just thirty seconds to think about it.' His voice was soft, and a little sneer was twisting his lips.

Hocking moistened his lips. He thought Driscoll hadn't changed at all. That he was quite capable of doing exactly what he threatened. He said, 'Wait Johnny. You know I just want to look out for Mike, is all. Just look out for Mike. How I know about you, eh? How I know Mike want you to have this. Why don't he come himself?'

Driscoll said softly, 'Because he's dead. Maybe there's a way I can prove I'm with him. In the first place he told me it was here. In the second — you know the name Williamson? Or Smythe, or Grattan. Or maybe Penny. You've heard of Penny, haven't you?'

Hocking smiled, pushed thick black hair back from his white, faintly moist brow. 'OK, Johnny. That's the word. Mike said about Penny. You know what there is?'

'Just a small packet, maybe?'

'Right.' He heaved himself out of the chair, squeezed

past the desk. 'You wait here, Johnny, eh? I get.'

'OK, Luigi, but get the packet, nothing else. Otherwise…'

He left it dangling in the air, smiled at Hocking. It was a very nasty smile, not at all friendly enough to dispel the menace from the Mauser he was still holding in his right hand.

Hocking nodded, went out through the door. He was gone only a minute. When he came back he put the packet on the table in front of Driscoll.

It was a small packet, about four inches by two, very slim. It was wrapped in brown paper, sealed with brown stickers.

Driscoll broke the stickers, opened the brown paper. Inside there were eight clear contact-prints, eight negatives. Driscoll looked at the first print, saw the complex of infinitely fine lines that were the blueprint tracings of the KB–12. He looked up, saw Luigi peering at the prints, said coldly, 'You seen these?'

'Me? No, I ain't seen them. Not on your life, Johnny. I don't mess in other people's business.' He smiled placatingly, his eyes fixed on the packet of money on the table.

Driscoll grinned. He said, 'Take it an' scram.' He held the prints face down while Hocking picked up the money with a fat paw, went hastily out of the room.

He laid the prints out on the table, made sure there was a negative for each of them. He examined them carefully, thinking Williamson had been a very good photographer. The lines of the blueprints were perfectly reproduced in miniature. They had a clarity which Driscoll was sure would allow them to be blown up to the size of the actual blueprints. He looked at the pictures for a long while, nodding with satisfaction as he saw the detail in one or two of them, finally gathered them up and stowed them carefully in his wallet.

He belted his raincoat together, walked out through the restaurant, paused at the counter. 'Luigi,' he said softly, 'you look pretty good. Like to stay that way?'

Hocking nodded slightly, his eyes very wary.

'All right. Just forget I ever came here tonight. Understand?'

'Sure, Johnny, that'll be right. You rely on me.'

Driscoll said, 'Yeah. I'll rely on you. An' you rely on me coming back if you don't. So long.'

He turned away, pushed open the door and stepped through it into the rain outside.

Hocking stood at the counter, automatically polishing an already polished glass with a towel. He was wondering just what had happened to Clifton, whom he had liked. And what Driscoll — whom he didn't like nearly as much — was going to do about it. He wondered if he had been right to give the package to Driscoll.

Then the thought of the money reassured him. A hundred pounds said he had done the right thing. That and the big gun in Driscoll's large fist. The gun that he knew he might see again if he ever told anyone Driscoll had been there that night. He knew enough about Driscoll to make himself a promise that he never would. It was one promise he definitely intended to keep.

25

As Driscoll rang the bell at Marian's flat it was just ten minutes past nine. He waited for her to open the door, using the time to take his raincoat off.

The door swung open. He looked at her silently for a moment, appreciating the glowing beauty of her hair, the smooth outline of her figure in a tailored hostess gown of dark green silk.

'Hello, Johnny, I was expecting you to come.'

'That gown's really something.'

She smiled, walked back into the lounge. He hung his raincoat in the short passage between the front door and the lounge, followed her as she walked, thinking that the supple ripple of her body was like the sleekness of a stalking panther.

She bent over a small table, poured coffee into a fine china cup, added sugar but no milk.

'You see,' she said, handing him the cup, 'I know you don't take milk. Davidson told me that.' She offered him a cigarette from a figured ebony box, held a lighter for him, went on, 'As a matter of fact, he told me quite a lot about you.'

Driscoll inhaled, smiled at her. 'Such as?'

'Such as you being a little dangerous to women.'

He laughed, the laugh turning to a cough as the smoke caught at his throat. 'I didn't know they called it danger these days. Incidentally, is that how you dress for danger?' He grinned.

'That's not very kind, Johnny.' She smiled, parting red lips to show white, even teeth. 'How do you like it anyway?'

'Any old way at all,' Driscoll said softly.

He put his empty cup down, slowly reached out and drew her toward him. She came slowly, not resisting at all, her eyes laughing and bright. He held her very close, bent and kissed her, felt her lips part beneath his, her body warm and soft against him.

Then he took his arms from around her, put one of his hands on each of her shoulders, said quietly, 'Listen, Marian, there may be a lot of funny things happen tonight. I don't know quite what they'll be yet, but I'm sure they're going to happen. I just want you to remember that. Will you?'

Marian opened her eyes very wide. They were very blue, very clear, very troubled. She said slowly, 'Johnny, I think you're in trouble.' She looked at him without speaking for a few seconds then went on, 'You are in trouble aren't you?' Her voice was very soft and anxious.

Driscoll smiled. 'I'm always in trouble.' He took his hands from her shoulders, turned away. 'Sometimes things get a little confused. Maybe the ball doesn't run the way it should. It's just one of those things, you have to play along the way it is. Incidentally, I need to make a phone call. May I?'

'Certainly. It's over there, Johnny.'

Driscoll shook his head. 'Not that one. Now look, I don't want you to get any wrong ideas. I'd just rather you didn't hear. I think everything will be much better if it's that way. Can you understand?'

'It wouldn't be much use my lying would it? I can't.' She said, tonelessly. 'But you can use the telephone in the bedroom if you like. Through there.'

Driscoll walked across to the bedroom door. He opened it, turned toward her. 'There's some writing I want to do. Would you mind if I do it there?'

'Of course not.' She looked at him, her eyes questioning and appealing.

'Take it easy,' Driscoll said, 'go and make some fresh coffee. Really hot. I could use some good hot coffee.'

She nodded, bent to pick up the tray. He watched her carry it through the door into the kitchen. Then he went into the bedroom.

It was a smaller room than the lounge, very feminine, but the feminine effect was achieved without dolls. Driscoll was glad. He hated dolls. He walked over to the bed, sat down on the candy-striped bedspread, picked up the telephone. He dialled, heard the ringing tone, waited two minutes. No reply.

He shrugged, dialled for the operator and asked for a Haslemere number. Again the ringing. Again, after two minutes, no reply. He put the receiver slowly back on the rest, thinking it had to be that way tonight. He looked at his wristwatch, saw it was twenty-seven past nine. He thought that time was running out on him fast now.

He took out the passport, opened it, removed a sheet of very thin paper he had folded between pages six and seven. It was a quarto sheet, folded over twice. He smoothed out the folds, doubled the sheet, rested it on the bedside table and began to write. After ten minutes he had covered one side in his ungraceful, sprawling writing. He read through what he had written, turned the sheet over and wrote ten or eleven lines on the other side.

He heard Marian moving about in the lounge, the distant metallic thud as she put the tray down on the table. He replaced the cap on his pen, folded the sheet of paper again, placed it carefully between pages six and seven of the passport. He looked round, saw her handbag on the table, pulled it over and opened it. He checked that it held her compact, lipstick, all the usual little accessories. Then he placed the passport inside it.

Before he'd shut the bag he heard the ringing of the bell, loud and clear in the flat. He quickly snapped the bag shut, left it on the table. Then he moved very softly over to the door, listening against it as Marian went out to the front door of the flat.

He moved, opening the bedroom door and quietly shutting it behind him, fast and silently across the lounge, through the self-shutting kitchen door into the darkness of the kitchen.

He held the kitchen door open slightly against the powerful spring, leaving the minutest crack through which he could watch the room. He heard the muffled sound of voices, quiet voices, in the space between the lounge and the front door. Then the lounge door opened, and two men came quietly into the room. They were fairly tall men, both wearing plain fawn raincoats and dark trilby hats, both carrying Webley & Scott .38 automatics in their right hands.

He watched them go toward the bedroom door, stand facing it but to each side of it, two yards apart. Marian was standing against the wall, not looking at them, her face dull and lifeless.

The man on the left said, clearly and distinctly, 'Come on out, Driscoll, we want to ask you a few questions. Special Branch.'

Driscoll grinned wolfishly in the darkness of the kitchen. He thought they had already checked his raincoat, seen the Mauser there. He eased the small automatic out of the shoulder holster, noiselessly pushed the door open, said, 'I shoot if you move. Don't try it.'

His voice cut like a whiplash across the silence of the room, a voice edged with the coldness of death that froze them into silence.

'I have another gun,' Driscoll said, 'the girl can see it. Tell them, Marian. An' don't either of you move.'

Marian looked at him, gulped with a peculiar small movement in her throat, said in a little voice, 'He's got a small black automatic.'

Driscoll, in the same icy voice, said, 'She's not wrong. Let them fall to the carpet. An' don't try anything smart. You don't get paid enough.' He watched the two guns thud to the carpet, said, 'That was good. Hands well out to the side an' turn nice an' easy.'

They turned, holding their arms well away from their sides, looked at the gun he was holding. Driscoll smiled at them, baring the gums from his teeth unpleasantly. 'Smart boys,' he said. 'So what few questions do you want to ask me?'

Marian said quietly, 'It's true, Johnny. They are Special Branch. They showed me their cards.'

Driscoll laughed. He said, 'Sure they're Special Branch. They're just itching to tell me I won't get away with this. Aren't you boys?'

The man who had spoken through the bedroom door said, 'It's not going to do you any good, Driscoll. We'll get you all right.'

'In a pig's eye you will,' Driscoll said. 'I've played this game before. Keep those arms wide out. You got my Mauser?' He looked intently at the man on the left.

The man said, 'No. That was pretty smart, Driscoll. But it still won't buy you anything but a rope.'

Marian said, 'Listen, Johnny, this is crazy. Why are you doing this. Why?' Her eyes were puzzled, filled with a hurt bewilderment.

'He doesn't know why,' the man on the left said. 'And he doesn't know what he'll do next either. He's got no passport and anyway the exits will be watched. He knows he's got as much chance as a celluloid doll in hell. Why don't you wake up, Driscoll, and come in with us. You might stand a chance.'

'Don't waste your breath. You may not have much more of it,' Driscoll said as he motioned to Marian, 'kick those guns over, and you two, move over to your left, into the corner.'

His eyes were very cold and watchful. The two men knew quite well it was hopeless to start anything. They knew all about Driscoll and his reputation. They moved.

Marian kicked the guns over to Driscoll, watched him bend down and pick them up, one at a time, never letting his eyes or the muzzle of his gun waver from the two men. He dropped the guns into his left-hand pocket, the weight of them dragging down on the left side of his jacket.

'OK, boys, this is your lucky day. In the bedroom. And you, Marian.'

He followed them into the bedroom, took the key out of the lock, fitted it into the outside of the door with his left hand.

Then he said, 'You won't grudge me a small start. An' if you want to live don't be the first ones to catch up with me.'

He grinned at them, backed slowly through the door. For a moment before he pulled it shut he looked straight at Marian, thought she was very lovely. Her smoke-blue eyes were looking straight at his. He smiled at her, a little sadly. Then he pulled the door shut, turned the key in the lock.

He went swiftly out of the flat, picking up his raincoat on the way, feeling the Mauser still in the pocket. He ran down the three flights of stairs, went out of the back entrance to the flats, shrugging on his raincoat as he went.

Outside the rain was falling steadily, the street very dark. He ran along to the first corner, turned right, took the next turning on the left, then right again. After a minute or so he slowed to a walk, followed the street down through a tree-surrounded square until he came out on the river embankment.

He crossed the road, looked swiftly up and down to make sure he was unobserved, dropped the two Webley automatics in the river. Then he began to walk down toward Westminster Bridge, looking for a taxi.

He thought that it was a good thing London was a big place. A good thing it was a dark night, with rain that reduced visibility even further. For just one fleeting instant he wondered whether London would be big enough, the darkness and rain thick enough, to hide him once the heat was on.

26

He paid off the taxi halfway up Wardour Street, stood on the pavement for a moment, his hands bunched deep in his raincoat pockets, looking at the shops on the other side through a fine drizzle.

He turned, walked quickly along towards Coventry Street, suddenly ducked into a small alley on his left. He went past the smell of cooking oil, past dustbins overflowing with sodden refuse, turned right and then left again into Lisle Street.

He walked fast along the street, on the right-hand pavement, was only fifty yards from the end when he saw a policeman turning the corner. On his right was the blank back wall of the Empire cinema. The policeman was walking toward him, would pass him in an area which was well lighted. Driscoll thought it was unlikely the general alarm was out yet, but he took no chances.

He crossed the road, heading straight for one of the doorways on the other side. He saw a woman in one of them, standing just inside the pool of light thrown by a street lamp. He went right up to her, seeing the policeman almost opposite him.

She was smartly dressed, young in years, and with a face that had a surface cosmetic prettiness, the staleness of flat beer underneath. She murmured the conventional phrases. He listened, seeing the policeman walk past on the other side, shook his head and hurried on. He grinned as he caught the soft hiss of a very nasty word following him.

He cut down on the right, crossed the bright garishness of Coventry Street with its perambulating girls and cheap hamburger restaurants, cut through on the left again to William IV Street and turned into the side entrance of the all night Post Office. He brushed the fine rainspots from his coat, walked up to the counter and bought a stamped envelope, carried it over to a writing booth in the corner.

He unscrewed his fountain pen, addressed the envelope. Then he took the negatives from his wallet, slipped them inside. Finally, he wrote a brief message on a telegraph form, slipped that into the envelope too. He ran his lips along the flap, tasting the bitterness of the gum, conscious of a fleeting, absurd memory of Marian. Then he pressed the flap down, carried the envelope across and pushed it between the brass jaws of a post box.

He walked across to the row of glass-fronted telephone cubicles, waited until one of them was free. He stepped inside, wrinkling his nose at the smell of stale tobacco, dialled a Gerrard number. He heard the voice at the other end, said, 'Brad?'

The cockney voice said, 'Naw, I'll get 'im. 'Oo is it?'

'Tell him, Johnny, an old friend.'

'Right guv, 'ang on.'

Driscoll heard the echoing flatness of feet on concrete, then silence, then feet again, growing louder as they approached.

Then someone said, 'Johnny who?'

Driscoll grinned into the mouthpiece. He said,

'Johnny nothing, not tonight anyway. Recognise the voice?'

'Yeah. You hot?'

'I don't know,' Driscoll said slowly. 'That's one of the things. The other was a car. Nothing flashy, say a small family saloon of some kind. An' definitely nothing with the wrong plates if you get me. Fix?'

'Yeah. It'll cost, Johnny.'

'All right, so it costs. I can go up to two hundred, Brad. No more. Less if possible.'

'All right. When you want it?'

Driscoll looked at his watch. He said, 'It's a quarter after ten. Have it waiting for me opposite the main entrance to St Pancras at eleven. If I'm not there by eleven-thirty I won't be needing it. And find out just how hot I am, will you? How far it's gone.'

'OK, Johnny, I'll bring it.' There was the click of the receiver as Brad put his phone down.

Driscoll came out of the kiosk, lit a cigarette. The Mauser was heavy in his raincoat pocket. He kept his right hand in his pocket, disguising the lumped outline of the gun.

He came out of the main entrance of the post office, turned right towards Trafalgar Square. A hundred and fifty yards along he came to the cab rank in the centre of the road, walked across and climbed into the first. He told the driver to take him to Euston Station, then countermanded it, said, 'No, drop me the top end of Tottenham Court Road.'

He looked at his watch, saw it was twenty-five past ten. He thought the general alarm would have gone out by now. Say another half-hour for all the constables on the beats to be alerted. But he couldn't rely on that. Some of them had probably been warned by patrol cars already. He decided that as soon as he left the taxi he had better start assuming that they all knew, that they were *all* looking for him. He thought it would be much safer to assume that.

He leaned back, lit another cigarette, watched the smoke hang foggily in the humid air of the taxi. Past Cambridge Circus, up the Tottenham Court Road, with sudden fleeting blares of music from the dance hall, padding coloured boys on the rainy pavements, their dress as loud as the music. He relaxed, enjoying the taste of his cigarette, smoking with his left hand while the right caressed the hard comfort of the Mauser. Looking ahead he could see the rain impacting on the driver's windscreen, thought that an English summer was one of the things which made the race so tough. Then the taxi was sliding into the kerb, the driver leaning over to read the fare.

He watched the taxi turn round in the broad roadway, looked carefully up and down. Then he began to walk slowly down the street in the direction he had come, paused at the next corner, standing carefully in the shadow of a bus shelter.

He crossed the road walking quickly, went straight on up the narrower street toward Browne's place. When he came to the furniture store his pace did not slacken, but as he walked he glanced up, saw that the light in the end office was on, the curtains drawn. The rest of it seemed to be in darkness.

He continued another fifty yards, crossed over, doubled back in his tracks, heading for the furniture store again. He walked lightly and easily, placing his feet softly on the pavement like a cat. As he came nearer he took great care to ensure that his feet were making no noise at all, save for the soft squish of rubber on the wet pavement. He reached the side entrance, turned into it. On his left the small brass plate: *Tasmanian Import Export Co. Ltd.* gleamed dully in reflected light from a streetlamp. Driscoll pushed on into the small lobby with the stairs showing dimly in front of him. He thought that of all the places in London, they were least likely to look for him here.

He went up the stairs without the slightest noise, moving on the balls of his feet. Three or four times he stopped, listened intently with his breath held and the beat of his heart heavy in his chest. He heard no noise at all except for the low soughing of the rain outside. He was quite sure there was no one except himself on the staircase.

He came to the small landing at the top of the stairs, risked a momentary flame from his lighter. The door leading to the offices was brown and solid before him. The brass company plate and the little round brass lock were slow yellow flashes in the darkness. He moved softly up to the door, put his ear against it and listened. He could hear no sound inside.

He flicked his lighter into flame again, looked carefully at the lock. He began to work on the lock, taking infinite pains to make no sound at all. After five minutes he felt the tumblers click inside, pressed gently on the door as he held the celluloid strip in position. It opened slowly under the touch of his hand and he slipped through into a room dark and empty, the only light a clear bright narrow strip under the door of Browne's office.

Driscoll held the door half open while he removed the celluloid, then shut it softly letting the bolt of the lock ease slowly home. He put the celluloid back in his pocket, touched the cold sleekness of the Mauser. He shook his head, left the Mauser where it was, took the small automatic from the holster beneath his left armpit. He thought that if he had to use a gun the Mauser would make too much noise. On the other hand it was more likely he would have to use the small gun, since Browne was more likely to try to draw against the small gun than the Mauser. Driscoll shrugged. He thought there was a small balance in favour of the automatic.

He moved with extreme caution over to the door, taking fully a minute to cross the room. He felt for the handle with his left hand, listening for the slightest noise in the other room. He heard a faint scratching that might have been a pen, suddenly turned the knob and flung the door open with a nudge of his right shoulder, stepped into the room with the gun steady in his right hand.

He saw Browne behind the desk, saw the pen clatter from his fingers, knew instinctively as he saw the expression on his face that Browne was not going to take it.

Driscoll said sharply, 'Don't try...' broke off as Browne dropped his hand to the right, going for the gun in the drawer of the desk.

Driscoll squeezed on the trigger of the automatic, saw Browne shudder, squeezed again as Browne's hand started coming up with the gun, he fired twice more as Browne tried to aim the gun at him. Then Browne was slumping sideways, the gun dropping from nerveless fingers, rolling out of the chair and on to the floor, his feet catching the chair as he fell and dragging it over with a bump.

Driscoll was quite motionless at the door, the smell of smoke acrid and powerful in his nostrils. He held the gun very steadily, the muzzle still pointing at the sprawled stillness on the floor.

After ten seconds or so he moved slowly and with caution over to the body, looking down at it with the gun still ready. He had very little faith in the killing power of a .25 automatic.

He pushed out his foot, heaved the body over on to its back. Then he shoved the gun back into its holster, seeing at once it was no longer necessary. One of the slugs — he thought probably the last — had caught Browne squarely between the eyes, bored on into his brain. Already the film of death was spreading over the eyes, fogging their brightness.

Driscoll walked over to the desk, tried the left-hand drawer. It rolled open, and he took out the folded blueprints of the KB–12, the big sheet that Browne had been given by Maclaren. He pored over the opened sheet, examining each portion of it. At last, satisfied, he folded it again, put it back in the drawer.

He looked at what Browne had been writing, saw that he had been doing a report on Glazey and Clifton. He read the first few sentences, left it and walked across to the body. He searched Browne's clothes quickly and expertly, found the receipt he had signed in the wallet. He thought that the Special Branch must have turned it up in Clifton's flat, realised its importance and brought it straight in. He turned it over in his hand, remembering the golden loveliness of Janine, then tucked it away in his pocket.

Then, without another glance at the body, he went out of the office, making sure that the outer door was shut behind him. He went down the stairs as noiselessly as he had come up, paused for a moment just outside the doorway to listen for any sound of activity in the street. There was nothing. He grinned, thinking that he had been right to use the .25. It made very little noise, and obviously no one had heard it.

He came out of the building, deciding to walk through the side streets to St Pancras. His watch showed the time as a little before eleven. He thought grimly that when Browne's body was discovered the heat would really come on. Even London would not be big enough then. But with any luck he would be well clear of London before that.

He came out on the Euston Road, turned right, hurrying past the chattering groups round the coffee-stalls. Almost opposite St Pancras he saw a large American sedan at the kerb, behind it a small black saloon. He walked past the saloon, saw that the driving seat was empty, that a man was sitting in the seat beside it. He turned, walked straight back to the car, jerked open the door and swung into the driving seat.

Brad said, 'On time, Johnny. She's tanked up and ready to go.'

Driscoll fumbled for a cigarette, lit it. He said, 'You're sure she's not hot?

'Sure,' Brad said laconically. 'Can't say the same about you, Johnny. There's a general out for you. You're very tropical indeed. It takes two hundred.'

'Yeah,' Driscoll said. 'I had a feeling it might.' He jerked forward, reached into his hip pocket and pulled out the notes. He passed two packets to Brad, tossed the other bundle carelessly into the cubbyhole by the instrument panel.

Brad held the two packets, riffled casually through them. 'You know how it is,' he said. His tone was almost, but not quite, apologetic.

'Oh sure. I know how it is. So long, Brad.'

'So long, Johnny.' Brad pushed his door open, stepped out of the car. He walked round the bonnet, did not look round as he moved away down the pavement.

Driscoll thumbed the starter, put the car in gear. The sooner he got out of London the better it would be.

27

Driscoll looked ahead through a windscreen that was drying now that the rain had eased. In the weak headlights of the small car he saw the sign of the pub swinging in the wind, just caught the word *Roebuck* as the headlights flicked on past it.

He continued until he found a turning on the right, pulled into it, drove along a narrow lane until he came to a wide gateway leading into a field. He went slightly past it, stopped and reversed the car, turning her off the lane into the gateway.

He stretched forward, turned the dashboard light on. His watch told him that it was just after one thirty. The drive, coming the longer way round on quiet country roads, had taken him just over two and a half hours. He lit a cigarette, got out his wallet.

In the weak light of the dashboard he took out the photographs, tucked them into the inside pocket of his raincoat. Then he spread out the plan of the airfield that Landford had passed to him with the other papers on Winterley, looked at it closely.

He saw that there were three large hangars, and that the KB–12 was in the one on the extreme right. It was the smallest of the three, if the plan was correct. He thought that he was now about three miles from the hangars, on the other side of the airfield's runway. He looked carefully at the disposition of the airfield buildings, came to the conclusion that they would be guarded by security patrols, and that Landford and possibly another guard would be actually in the hangar with the fighter.

A small smile twisted his lips as he thought of Landford. He wondered what Landford would say now, if he knew that Driscoll was so close, was using the airfield plan that had been given to him for a very different purpose.

Driscoll thought he had better start to move cross-country and through the airfield perimeter, then lie up close to the hangar buildings. He thought that it would be quite dark about two hundred yards from the hangars, out on the grass between the flying control building and the runway.

He put the plan back in his wallet, checked the Mauser again, turned the dashboard light out and climbed stiffly from behind the driving seat. He was extremely thankful that it had stopped raining, though he realised as soon as his feet touched the ground that he was still going to get extremely wet. He swore softly, thinking that he was not very fond of the country at the best of times, was definitely hostile to it when it was wet and soggy.

He moved off up the lane, walking slowly and easily. Three quarters of a pale white moon shone thinly through a veil of fast-moving cloud. Occasionally it found a gap in the veil, pushed bright exploratory beams through to the ground, giving a surprising amount of illumination. Driscoll, swinging easily over the single strand of barbed wire that kept cattle off the airfield, thought he would have to watch for that, be ready to duck the instant the cloud parted.

He went on across the thick wet grass, swearing softly and monotonously as the chill of it penetrated through wet trouser-legs to his ankles. Already his feet were soaking, his shoes heavy with clinging mud.

Eventually the moonlight flicked through a passing gap of cloud showing him the runway two hundred yards or so ahead of him, a broad silver river in the slanting moonbeams.

He stopped, kneeling down on the wet ground until the cloud filled in the gap and darkness came again. He moved faster then, crossing the runway at a quick walk, going steadily toward the hangar buildings that he could see faintly now, looming black bulks against a dark grey background. When he judged he was two hundred yards from them he sunk down to the ground, lying flat on his stomach in the grass, realising that he would be very uncomfortable but accepting it as inevitable.

He looked at his watch, was surprised to see it had taken him well over an hour to cover the two to three miles. He settled himself to wait, the slow minutes ticking away as he stirred damply in the cold grass.

He could see lights in the end hangar, and also in the centre one. He could hear a continuous low roar which seemed to be coming from the centre hangar. It was a sound like the slow suck-back of waves on a pebbly beach, low pitched and sullen. He remembered that the plan had shown a high-speed wind tunnel in the centre hangar, concluded that now the rearmament drive was well launched, the tunnel probably operated all night.

Gradually, as his senses became attuned to the sounds and the sights half seen in the distance, he identified movement beyond the hangars in the main body of the works. There were further sounds, too. The occasional heavy boom of a drop forge for example, and very lightly and faintly the insistent chatter of riveting guns.

He noticed a regularly recurring light that circled the looming hangars at a speed too great for walking. He decided that it was a mobile patrol, timed the circuits. He found that they varied between eight and nine minutes, grinned to himself as he thought that they would be playing the old game. A nice lighted patrol that everyone could see. But behind that, another patrol, no lights on at all, probably mounted on cycles. The patrol that would pick up the man who timed the circuits, began to move immediately the light had passed. It worked sometimes. But not with people like Driscoll.

The minutes dragged on until the hands of his watch pointed to four o'clock. In the east the first faint greyness high in the sky proclaimed the fast approaching dawn. He moved then, slowly at first to get the stiffness from his muscles, then quicker as he approached the black height of the flying control building. He hugged the shadow of its walls, pressing closely to the roughness of sandstone, watching for the circling lights of the patrol.

At last he saw them, caught the blurred outline of an open Land Rover as it went by quite slowly and noiselessly. He looked at his watch, seeing the second hand faintly as it swept round. Exactly ninety seconds after the first vehicle a second went past at the same speed. No lights, moving very quietly.

Driscoll gave it thirty seconds more, moved quickly across the perimeter track and into the hulking shadow of the end hangar. He went along the wall, stopping often to look and listen, turned the corner, went past the coldness of giant steel doors. He turned the next corner, decided that if there was a door open it would be on this side of the hangar, the side facing the main works. He tried several, found them all locked. Then, looking up, he saw the faint brilliance of windows set high in the wall, and that one of them was open.

He ducked behind some strips of aluminium sheeting, waited for the two patrols to pass. Then very quickly he hoisted himself on the roof of the offices that lined the foot of the hangar, looked round for a way up to the open window. He stood right beneath it, thought it was about ten feet up, just out of reach for a jump. He felt very naked on the roof, realised that the patrols would be round again in four minutes.

Then, further along the roof, he saw a plank, hurried across to it. It was a plain wooden plank, five feet long, about six inches wide, two inches thick. The wood was wet and dirty.

He carried it back to the spot beneath the open window, leaned it at an angle against the wall. He thought he could run on to the plank, get enough extra height into his jump to reach the bottom edge of the window quite easily. But if he missed, if he slithered down from the window without gripping, they would get him. There was only a minute left, not nearly enough for two attempts.

He backed to the edge of the roof, took a deep breath and ran forward on to the plank, jumping off his left foot as it hit near the top. He found his face opposite the window, desperately grabbed with his arms, felt his fingers scrape on something, clench tight, then an awful searing jerk in his elbows and shoulders as the weight of his body dropped on to his arms. He held, dangling from the windowsill, staying as still as he could while he gathered strength to drag himself up.

He breathed deeply again, felt the power of his arm muscles as he dragged himself up into the narrow gap between the swing-down window and the concrete sill. Then his head and shoulders were through the gap, looking down at a narrow steel gangway about three feet below him round the wall of the hangar. He swung his legs through, let them silently down on to the reassuring solidity of the steel, crouched on the gangway. Outside he heard the soft swish of tyres, louder on the wet concrete than the quiet engine of the Land Rover, grinned as he thought he had just been in time.

He poked his head cautiously over the edge of the gangway, saw the fighter standing alone in the centre of a large space in the end half of the hangar. At the other end several aircraft were parked, but Driscoll barely noticed them. He had eyes only for Landford, who seemed hunched and restless from the cold as he paced by the side of the KB–12.

Driscoll looked round the hangar, saw that the gangway went right round the walls, that there were steps down at each of the corners. He walked, crouching low, away from the end where Landford was guarding the fighter, came to the stairs at the corner, went down them very carefully and silently. As he left the foot of the stairs he ducked swiftly behind one of the parked aircraft, began to work his way in little darts toward the end where Landford was.

The last aircraft gave him cover to within thirty yards

of Landford. Driscoll took out the Mauser, decided quickly he would go along the wall as far as possible, but slowly, ready to start shooting the instant Landford saw him.

He slipped out from behind the nose of a Meteor, smiled as he saw that Landford was facing away from him stretching his neck and shoulders as he paced beside the gleaming fuselage of the KB–12.

He went very slowly and quietly along the wall, then struck off diagonally toward Landford, only fifteen yards from him. He was absolutely sure Landford was alone in the hangar, that this was the moment he had been waiting for.

He was ten yards from Landford when the little man heard him, suddenly turned. His face was very white under the glow of the strong roof lamps. His hand began to move toward his left armpit, then checked as he realised Driscoll's fingers were tightening on the trigger of the Mauser.

Driscoll said softly, 'Clever, Willy. You'd never have made it.' He moved a little closer, until he was only ten or eleven feet from Landford.

Landford let his hand fall slowly to his side. He said, with an infinite menace in the slow, almost whispering, tone of his voice, 'You murdering swine, Driscoll. I'll get you for Browne if it's the last thing I do.'

'So you know already?' Driscoll said. His voice was soft too, but with a caressing softness that was very unpleasant to hear. 'You heard right, Willy. I killed Browne. An' guess who's next?'

Landford began to say something, changed his mind and shrugged. He looked straight at Driscoll, his eyes glowing and bitter in a savage, hating face.

Driscoll laughed quietly, viciously. 'All right little man, so where do you want it? High up or low down. You name it.'

Landford stood very still, his hands down by his sides. He said coldly, 'Make the most of it, Driscoll. You've got the gun.' His voice was steady, completely without any trace of fear.

Driscoll smiled. He said banteringly, 'An' you're getting the tombstone. Just one thing bothering me. The name to go on it. How about that?'

He paused, the whisper of his voice dying into the remote distance of the hangar, leaving a deep stillness.

'What name? Willy Landford?' Driscoll continued, then paused again, grinned savagely at the little man, went on, 'Willy Landford? Or the real name? What about *Nicholas?*'

28

Driscoll walked a little closer to Landford, until he was six feet from him. He thought Landford was definitely good. Apart from the first flash of surprise when he saw Driscoll he had given no indication of being shaken.

'You've always been a trouble boy. This is trouble you won't get out of, Driscoll.'

Driscoll grinned. 'Act your age, Willy. You're cooked. At first I was playing a hunch, but I don't have to now. I know everything. I know you're Nicholas. I know Browne was in with you. I know you wrecked the first fighter. I know you killed Kubin, an' even how you did it. Sure I'm a trouble boy. That's why Davidson put me into things in the first place. He knew I'd start something, and he hoped it would be the right thing. An' it was Willy, it was.'

Landford said, quite softly and calmly, 'I think you must be insane. It's the only possible explanation.'

'Not the only explanation. Not if we assume you're Nicholas. Grant that one little fact and there's a much better explanation. Like to hear it?'

'One must humour the insane,' Landford said carefully. 'Especially when they've committed murder and are holding a gun. I'd be most interested in your explanation. Also amused, I expect.'

'I don't think so.' Driscoll said. 'I don't expect you to be amused at all. Remember, for the moment I'm assuming you're Nicholas, just to see how it fits. All right, you're Nicholas. You're the head of their overseas people in this country. But also, you've a fairly important position in the British organisation. Very useful to you. So you hear about the fighter and you get interested. You arrange for photographs to be taken, and you collect a lot of information about the plane. Pretty soon your people back there decide it's a menace, and they give you the word to fix it. With me?'

'Physically only.' Landford said drily.

'All right. You get the technical know-how from Rakiev. You have the boy who took the photographs knocked off, so there's no lead back from him. You have Barnett get hold of people who might be useful. One of them was me. I feel rather flattered about that ,Willy.'

He broke off, grinned at Landford.

'Finally, You're ready to roll,' Driscoll continued, 'but you must have more details of the routine for the test flights. Of course, you could have got it yourself without too much risk, but you were too careful to take the slightest chance of any lead back to you in your capacity as a British security expert. So you used Janine. She did her job, and after that she was no further use. In fact she might even be a menace because she knew too much. The same applied to Barnett. Still amusing?'

'Perhaps to you. You're holding the gun.'

'Yeah, an' incidentally I'm very good with it. Let's not inch forward any more, Willy. Otherwise the nice, clean floor might get dirtied.'

Driscoll saw the edging forward of Landford's feet

cease, went on conversationally, 'So now we come to Glazey. He put the first fighter out, using whatever contrivance you'd supplied for the purpose. But he was cleared after interrogation. Yeah, an' who cleared him Landford?'

'I did. Plus a security man who was present right through of course. But don't worry about that.'

'No, I won't. Because I'll bet he was a security man you and Browne had specially selected. One of the tame stooges you've been working into our security organisation. But anyway, Glazey was cleared. So the fighter was gone without a trace of sabotage. Now it gets really interesting because I come into it.'

'This is the part I've been waiting for,' Landford said as he smiled nastily, a mere wrinkling of his mouth.

'I'd already been approached by Barnett,' Driscoll continued, 'after I agreed to go in with Davidson I decided I'd tap the opposition too. It seemed the obvious thing to do. Of course that suited you very well. Maybe I was playing both ends, maybe only one. Whichever way, you'd know exactly where I stood, because whatever instructions I got from Barnett would come ultimately from you. So you arranged for me to meet Janine at the Mandolin, an' you instructed her to pay me five hundred in cash an' get a receipt.'

Landford shrugged, shook his head slowly.

'That part goes fine, then comes the big pay-off,' Driscoll continued, 'you see how you can tie everything together, you tell Barnett to be in Janine's flat, instruct him exactly what to say. He obeys you, then he gets the surprise of his life. Just when he's getting set to give it to me you arrive. Nice timing. Much too nice. An' what a shock Barnett must have got when the script suddenly went crazy. Right then, Willy, you were sitting on top of it. You only had to wait for me to suggest the only explanation that fitted the facts — that the first fighter had been wrecked by accident not by sabotage. I did just that. It was the obvious explanation. Then the phone call an' suddenly you were in trouble. A second before it was fine, all the leads destroyed, anyone who knew anything dead. Then bang, Kubin turns himself in an' you're in big trouble.'

'Kubin?' Landford said. 'Oh yes of course, I killed Kubin didn't I. Do tell me how I killed him?'

Driscoll dropped his voice a little. He was grim now, not conversational at all. 'You had to act fast, Willy. You took a big chance and it worked. You killed Kubin before he could say anything incriminating. Then it became necessary to kill Clifton too. I was scheduled for it later, but I'm a very suspicious person, Willy. I don't kill too easily. Before you and Browne could get your boys after me I'd skipped. But Clifton you had to get, and you got him through Browne. You see, Willy, Clifton had suspected you for some time, but he didn't suspect Browne. That's where your little set-up was so good.'

'Yes it was, very good indeed,' Landford murmured sarcastically.

'But not good enough,' Driscoll said. 'Too subtle. Too many little unexplained points. By the way, that was a nice little touch with Clifton's keys. Very convincing. Except, of course, that you'd naturally have keys to Janine's flat — and it was easy enough to put them on Mike Clifton's ring before I got to the section. So there we are. Fellows tells us tonight is the important night, that if the fighter comes through tomorrow it'll be OK. Right, so you come down here to supervise the security arrangements, stay all night in the hangar to ensure that no one gets at the aircraft and then in the morning comes the second crash. That settles it. The KB–12 goes on the scrapheap. There's no one left alive to question that. Except, of course, poor old Driscoll. If he *is* still alive. It's much more likely he's been knocked off during the night. Quite legally of course. Resisting arrest or something like that. That's the outline, Willy. Give me more time an' I'll fill in the rest. But how do you like it so far?'

Landford said slowly, 'If I were Nicholas it might be quite convincing. If I were Nicholas. And of course if you could prove it. What about that part? That's where your little theory comes apart. There's only one bit of proof anywhere. It's a receipt signed by you and found in Clifton's flat. A receipt made out to a traitor, found in a traitor's flat, and signed by you. Don't make me laugh, Driscoll. The only proof that exists will hang *you*, no one else.' His voice was cold and sneering. He was completely unruffled and at ease.

'Nuts to you, Willy. An' nuts to the receipt. I keep telling you you're too subtle. You know why I signed that receipt? To give someone a chance to start a play. To let someone think he had something on me because that might encourage them to think I was no trouble to handle. You don't think I'd be sucker enough to sign a receipt like that otherwise? Really, Willy, you disappoint me.'

'Proof. Not talk, proof.' Landford said coldly.

'Proof?' Driscoll said slowly. 'You know, it's a little difficult, Willy. Lots of indications, but not much proof.

That's why I'm going to kill you rather than take you in. By the way, we haven't yet settled where you want it. Any preferences?' He grinned nastily at Landford.

Landford shrugged. 'I'm still waiting for your non-existent proof.'

'Correct. All right, here are a few little indications. Just to help us along. You remember when you shot Barnett? That cannon of yours made a lot of noise. No one in the street heard it because I checked on that. But how about people in the room below, Willy? They would certainly have heard it. That never occurred to you. Let's say you didn't worry about it in the heat of the moment. Or was it you knew quite well there was no one in the flat below, because it was you had installed Janine in that building?'

'You're wasting your time, Driscoll, I'd never been in that building before in my life.'

'Ah. That's very interesting. But let's skip it for now. How about my urgent appointment with the Colonel? That wasn't so urgent at all, was it? But of course you had an important appointment at four, and you wanted me out of the flat without a chance to prowl round. Then you telephoned the section to put Browne in the picture, an' you suddenly got the bad news about Kubin. By the time he gave himself up to the police, I'd judge Kubin's appointment was also about four o'clock, wouldn't you?'

Landford said, impatiently, 'I can't understand why you're playing around Driscoll. You have the gun. And obviously you have no proof. I can assure you I'm not going to entertain you by pleading for mercy. Surely you're not hoping for that?'

'No. Not that, Willy. I'll give you that much. I think

you're very tough indeed. But I want you to hear what put me on to you. I think you'll appreciate it.'

He looked carefully at Landford, noticed with an acute feeling of uneasiness that the little man was still unshaken, still calm.

Driscoll wondered how calm he'd be when he heard what was to come. He smiled, began to talk again.

29

'There's one thing you've got to remember, Willy,' Driscoll went on. 'I've been around for a long while. One of the reasons is that I don't miss the little things. The mistakes you an' Browne made were little mistakes. But you made them, and I picked them up. Two of them I can understand. When you made those you thought you had me over a barrel because you held the receipt I'd given Janine, and the recording of my conversation with her. For the rest — well, you an' Browne must have been pretty shaken when Kubin turned himself in. You had to act fast. Naturally you made mistakes, but you thought I wouldn't be alive long enough to do anything about them. That was a very dangerous assumption.'

Landford said, 'My, but we think a great deal of ourselves, don't we?' His voice was sneering, but quite calm and unconcerned.

'Yeah, we do. You'll see why later. But let's think about the first two mistakes. Barnett made those — or at least he brought them to my notice. He was too convincing with his details, Willy. For example he mentioned exactly where the money would be found. Not just in my flat, but in the safe. How did he know that? I'd told Janine I was putting the money in a safe-deposit box. That's a very different thing.'

Landford said, 'So he guessed. Quite a natural

assumption. Or perhaps he'd had someone search your flat.'

'How right you are. But the someone was you. I told you I'd been around a long time, Willy. One of the things I always do before leaving a place I'm living in, is to fix things so that if anyone searches it he leaves traces. After you'd been to my flat I knew you'd found the safe behind the picture. But I also know that no one else had. As soon as Barnett mentioned the safe I got suspicious. Then there was the receipt. Barnett said it would be found in her bag. But it wasn't in her bag. It wasn't in Barnett's clothes anywhere, and it wasn't in the flat or the one below. So Barnett must have known a third party would be bringing it along to plant in Janine's bag. It could have been Clifton, or you, or someone we've never even heard of. But out of all those people, Willy, you're the only one who could have told Barnett I had a safe in my flat. From then on I was wise.'

Landford said coldly, 'You mentioned proof. So far you're producing suppositions, Driscoll. No proof at all.'

Driscoll glanced at his watch. It was just six minutes before four-thirty. He began to talk again, but quietly, listening for the sounds of movement anywhere in the hangar.

'I've still got a little way to go, Willy, then I'll show you the proof. But I'll just mention one or two other things in passing. First there was Janine's telephone number in Winterley's notebook. That was silly. If she handled Winterley — and I'm fairly sure she did — he'd never have been allowed to take her telephone number with him. It's a safe bet that if she got him to talk he was drunk, or drugged, or both. She'd have been able to go through his clothes pretty thoroughly. You're not going to tell me she or Barnett would have missed that number? Besides, if Winterley remembered Janine, he'd have got in touch with her. He'd have considered her quite a scalp. I know he didn't, that he never mentioned her to anyone.'

'So what?' Landford retorted. 'If he'd talked he'd have been scared. He wouldn't have dared mention her for fear a security leak would be traced back to him. He was well educated about security, all those test pilots are.'

Landford's voice was still calm, but Driscoll thought he could detect the beginning of a crack in it.

'Right,' Driscoll said. 'Which makes it double damn sure he wouldn't have talked unless he was drunk or drugged. So there's the first piece of proof. A handwriting expert will be able to tell Winterley didn't write that number. How many people had access to the book beside yourself?'

'Again, so what?' Landford said, 'why would I want to draw attention to Janine. It doesn't fit.'

'But that was just what you did want. You were too smart to hope that without any lead people would assume it was an accident. Not when they knew Rakiev had been here, and the plans had been photographed. So you played the old double bluff. You provided a lead, then turned it into a bad lead. You made it look as if they were intending to go for the aircraft and then didn't need to. When you shot Barnett I supplied the theory for you. It seemed the only one to fit the facts. It was only later I realised it had a hole in it big enough to drive a bus through. An' because you wanted that theory, because it was the one you were hoping I'd produce, I don't suppose you've seen the flaw even yet.'

'No,' Landford said. 'I haven't, because there isn't one. That theory is still valid and good.'

'On a hog's razorback it is.' Driscoll was still speaking quietly, still listening intently for movement. 'Listen, when Janine gave me the five hundred, the aircraft had already been gone nearly forty hours. They knew that all right. But next day, when Barnett's getting set to give it to me, he makes a big spiel about it not being necessary to use me any more. Apparently he doesn't see anything incongruous in that. But, of course, he's got no way of knowing that I already know the aircraft's gone. He doesn't know I'm working for Davidson. And he's acting under instructions. See where it's leading?'

'Nowhere.' Landford was still very calm.

'Be patient for a moment. Whoever was instructing Barnett knew the aircraft was gone when Janine gave me the money and I signed the receipt. If it went accidentally, so they'd never need me — why give me the money? If it didn't, why was Barnett instructed to say what he did next day?'

Landford said, 'I really wouldn't know.'

'Wouldn't you? How about this, The person giving the instructions must have had two objects. One, to get a receipt from me. The other, to make me associate Barnett's remarks with the aircraft, convince me the crash was an accident. But what's the use of a receipt, unless to put pressure on me later? An' even then, what's the use of it unless I'm in a very fragile position, like someone who's working for both sides. And if my opinion on the crash is going to be worth something I've got to be alive to give it. So where does that leave you, Willy?'

'It's not proof.'

'When Janine got me to sign the receipt you were the only one who knew I was working for Davidson. But, even more important, you were the one who came along in time to make sure I stayed alive. And only the man who'd given Barnett the instructions would have been able to do that. Still feeling good?'

Landford looked straight at Driscoll. He said softly, 'All right, it's a flaw. But still not proof. Not proof at all.' He smiled, seemed to be quite at ease.

Driscoll glanced at his watch again. It was a minute to four-thirty. He raised his voice, spoke a little more loudly.

'That's the basis of it, Willy. That's what put me on to you. Only little things, an' I don't doubt that you could wriggle out of them if that's all I had. But there's more. Up to that point you had time to be clever. From there on in you were rushed. As soon as Browne heard about Kubin and passed the word on to you, you both made mistakes. One of them was not to shoot me in Janine's flat while you had the chance.'

'Kubin,' Landford murmured. 'This should be good.'

'It is. Let's start it with a question. Why did we go back to the section first, not straight to the police station? Not for those bits of information Browne had on that paper. He could easily have phoned them through to the station. We went for two reasons. First, so he could let you know I didn't understand the language, so you could say what you liked to Kubin. Second, to slip you the paper. And the capsule inside it. You could have handed the paper to me right away, but you stuffed it into your pocket. Yeah, an' as we're going along you fumble around in your pocket, detach the capsule, pull the paper out. It's warming up now, don't you think?'

Landford said, 'Browne could have told me on the phone you didn't speak the language.'

'Nuts. He didn't know. He knew nothing about my qualifications. When Maclaren was talking about the fighter Browne had to ask me whether I knew anything about aircraft. If he didn't know that, why should he know whether I could speak the language? The point is that when you phoned him he'd just heard about Kubin. By the time we got round to the section he'd got the capsule ready. An' he'd telephoned Davidson to ask about my languages. I can prove that part, Willy. Maybe the call didn't come from him, but from Special Branch. One of his stooges perhaps. But it was made and answered, an' that's how Browne was able to say to me that he'd forgotten I didn't speak it. Forgotten, huh? Until ten minutes before, he had no idea whether I spoke it or not.'

Landford said, 'I suppose you've forgotten you were with me all the time I talked to Kubin. Maybe your proof's a photograph of me stuffing a capsule down Kubin's neck.'

'No, not a photo of *that*.' He accented the last word slightly, went on, 'You took a desperate chance. You let me conduct the first part of the interrogation, while you kept your mouth shut. You never said one word. Kubin didn't hear your voice at all. Then you gave me the stuff about throwing a scare into him. You'd taken the trouble to find out from the Inspector the cell wasn't wired. Why? It didn't strike *me* to ask. Kubin was on his own, and you had no reason to think he'd talk to himself. But you had to be quite sure there'd be no record of what you said to

Kubin. Or what he'd say when he heard your voice and realised who you were. An' boy, was he scared when you started. Scared right away, as soon as you spoke, before you had any chance to say anything really threatening. Your voice alone did it, and when you told him what you were going to do unless he killed himself, that tied it up neatly. By that time you knew all the details of the girl and the little boy. So you offered him a swap. His death against their safety. He took it.'

'And the capsule I'm supposed to have brought with me? I suppose I put it in his mouth. Don't forget you were there all the time.'

Driscoll smiled. It was not a nice smile. 'Easy. You passed it to him with the photograph. That was part of the bargain. He got the photograph to destroy. Quick thinking, and it worked. You convinced the police it was their fault. You didn't convince me, but you couldn't know that. In any case you thought you had me where you wanted me. You thought you could have me picked up at leisure and shot. Resisting arrest, escaping, something like that. It looked good. But from then on it was tougher, because I knew. And I knew you'd be after me. So then I took advantage of another of your mistakes. You were dumb to knock off Williamson. You thought that lead died when Clifton went, but it didn't.'

'Clifton. A traitor. It can be proved by papers at the section and the receipt at the flat.' He smiled calmly at Driscoll.

Driscoll felt a twinge of anxiety. Landford was too calm, too assured. He shrugged, went on, 'I'm quite sure you and Browne have fixed some papers implicating Clifton, just as I'm sure you put the receipt in his flat after

Browne shot him. But you overlooked the fact that Clifton was very clever. He'd been suspicious of you for a long time. How long I wouldn't know, certainly since Williamson — the guy who actually broke into the factory to get the photographs — was knocked off. I don't know this for a fact, but I imagine Williamson had left certain instructions in the event of his being murdered. I suppose your dumb bunnies didn't even give him a chance to mention it an' save his life. Did they?'

'I wouldn't know,' Landford said quietly. He smiled, looking at Driscoll without the slightest trace of fear or discomposure.

Driscoll felt very uneasy. He shrugged, thinking that the photographs would clinch it. Very faintly, in the distance, he heard movement. He grinned, glanced quickly at his watch. The time was four-thirty-five.

Driscoll said, loudly, 'All right, Willy, here it is. Williamson didn't trust your organisation. He was an old pro, a guy who was used to double-crossing and being double-crossed. So he took insurance. He took some more photographs. On his death they went to Clifton. Clifton tipped me off about them, just in case, but I rather think he also mentioned them to Browne. He couldn't have suspected Browne was in with you. So when Kubin came in Clifton had to go. An' here's why.'

He dug into his left pocket, taking great care that the Mauser was still covering Landford, pulled out the packet of prints and tossed them at Landford's feet.

Landford picked them up, looked at them.

As he was going through them Driscoll said, 'The first two are the blueprints of the fighter. The next two show you going into the house where Janine had her flat, coming out again later. The next two are Barnett doing the same thing, and the last two are Kubin. An' you say you've never been to Janine's flat until the day you shot Barnett. How does it look now, pal?'

Landford said quietly, 'So I went to the house. Nothing in that. These could have been taken different days.'

Driscoll shook his head. 'No,' he said softly. 'Not the ones of you an' Kubin anyway. Look at the briefcases you an' Kubin have as you go in. You're carrying one with a single centre lock, no strap. Kubin's has two straps, two locks where the straps join the case. Now look at the photographs as you come out, you'll see you've got Kubin's case, he's got yours. There's the proof you little bastard, and it's good. It's good enough for me not to worry about shooting you. I'm going to let you swing instead. I'll even come along an' watch if they'll let me. Mike was a pal of mine.'

Landford looked at Driscoll. In his cheeks two bright red spots flamed, and his eyes were bitter and hostile. He opened his mouth, but not very wide. And not to speak, but to snigger. It was an unpleasant, dry sound. Driscoll, watching him in amazement, thought he must have lost his sanity.

Landford cut short his snigger, said suddenly, 'You know, it's quite true. But you're too late. There must be other copies of these, so I'm finished. But so are you Driscoll, and so's the fighter. By the time anyone gets round to taking action on those photos it'll have gone. You're really very good,' his voice suddenly hardened, became steely. 'But not good enough. Just one thing you forgot, Driscoll. You forgot the security man from here, who helped me with Glazey. He also helped me guard the aircraft last night. And he's right behind you now.' He smiled, continued to hold his hands loosely by his sides.

Driscoll said, 'I don't fall so easily, Willy. Now I'm taking you…'

His voice died away to nothing as behind him another voice cut in.

Hard and dry it said, 'Turn your head, Driscoll. Not your body or you'll get it. Let the gun drop before you start to turn.'

Driscoll's brain worked with ice-cold quickness and precision. Instantly he realised why Landford had remained unconcerned. He realised the sound he had heard was the security man creeping up on him, not what he had taken it to be. He had made the big mistake, he thought, allowed Landford to play him on while the other man got into position. He was opening his fingers to let the gun drop when he decided to turn round firing. There was just one chance in a hundred the man might miss.

Then the voice cut in on him again, cold and menacing, 'The gun. Now, or it'll be too late.'

Driscoll keyed himself, stiffened unconsciously as his body prepared for the impact of a slug. Then, even as he started to turn, every light in the hangar went out.

30

As the lights went out the hangar was plunged into instant, absolute darkness. With a quickness that was purely instinct, far too fast for a conscious act of mind, Driscoll dropped. He thudded down on the concrete, began to roll even as the vivid orange flash from a gun stabbed through the blackness.

He heard the whine of a slug, felt the concrete vibrate as the bullet jarred it near him. He continued rolling, until he judged he was the other side of the fighter. As he went the gun flashed again, and again there was that slight vibration as the bullet hit the concrete and ricocheted off, screaming into the cavernous darkness of the hanger.

He stopped rolling, lay very still on his stomach, with the Mauser in front of him in his right hand. He strained his ears for the slightest sound of movement, heard a confused murmur of voices in the distance. Very gently he pushed his left hand into the pocket of his coat, brought it out holding a spare clip of shells. He lay still again for a moment, then tossed the clip with his left hand, hearing the clatter as it bounced along the concrete.

Instantly there was a flash from the gun, then another. Driscoll lined the Mauser on the first flash, pulled the trigger twice in rapid succession as the second flash gave him a brief indication of the right direction. He heard a definite, flat thwack as the bullet impacted on something soft, followed a moment later by a clatter as the man's gun dropped to the floor, and then the noise of a man falling crumpled to the hard concrete.

Driscoll rolled again, wondering if Landford had a gun. Wondering why, if he had, he had not fired at the flashes of the Mauser. Then, as suddenly as they had gone off, the lights flashed on again, and he saw Landford thirty yards away from him, moving quietly toward the side wall.

Driscoll scrambled into a kneeling position, raised his gun to look along the sights for a careful shot. Over to his right he could see the inert mass of the man who had fired at him, thought grimly as Landford's figure appeared against the blade of his foresight that if the first hit had been lucky this one would be intentional.

He saw Landford lift his hand, a gun in it pointing toward him. And he saw something else. He saw Davidson and three others at the far end of the hangar, stepping out from the wall and coming toward Landford in a long diagonal.

He let the Mauser's aim drop lower, thinking it would be much more interesting if they could get Landford alive.

Landford saw Davidson and the others, began to run across the hangar.

Driscoll snapped two shots at him, firing low for his legs. Then he saw that Landford was going for the steps that led up to the balcony round the hangar.

He scrambled to his feet, started after him. He was still fifteen yards from the steps when Landford reached the top.

Davidson and the others were forty yards away, coming up fast.

Driscoll saw Landford turn, look and aim at him. The gun in his hand suddenly smoked, and Driscoll jumped toward the shelter of the wall as a slug kicked bright red sparks from the concrete only inches away from him.

He heard the clatter of Landford's feet on the balcony, then he started up the steel stairs, saw Landford half way along the gallery as he reached the top. Driscoll ran, his feet kicking up a clatter that echoed the clatter of Landford's.

At the end of the gallery Landford did not attempt to go down the stairs. Driscoll saw that a member of Davidson's party had detached himself, was running to cover that staircase.

Landford looked quickly round, sighted another deliberate shot at Driscoll.

Driscoll saw the flash of the gun, kept going as a slug hit a cross-girder a foot above his head. Then Landford turned, swung open a steel door that faced on to the gallery, went through it out of the hangar. Driscoll raced up to it and through it, only just prevented himself falling sideways to the ground as he found himself on a narrow steel catwalk rising steeply to a door in the side of the adjoining hangar.

Driscoll clutched at the single steel rail, saw Landford negotiate the last few feet of the angled catwalk. Then the little man pushed open the door of the other hangar and instantly the noise of the wind-tunnel was a deep rumbling roar like summer thunder. Driscoll gripped the rail tightly with his left hand to steady himself for a shot as Landford went through the door. He squeezed the trigger carefully, saw Landford stagger against the side of the door as he went through.

With elation bursting through him Driscoll knew that he had hit him, probably in the leg. But a slug from a Mauser made a mess, even in a leg. It was the beginning of the end he thought.

Then he was going up the catwalk, crouching as he neared the top in case Landford was waiting for him just inside the door.

He went through the door cautiously, saw immediately that Landford had gone straight on. He went after him round a balcony that was much higher above the ground than the one he'd come from in the aircraft hangar. He saw Landford stop, realised that the little man could go no further, that the gallery ended abruptly in a steel buttress that reached out from the wall to support the end transom of a heavy crane.

Landford turned, saw him, lifted his gun and fired three shots in quick succession.

Driscoll pressed back against the side grateful for the slight protection of a girder that projected four inches from the wall. Two of the slugs whined past him, the third bouncing with a dull clang from the girder.

Driscoll saw that Landford was swaying, realised that he had certainly been hit in the leg. But his shooting was still accurate. He edged round the girder, saw Landford drag himself on to the rail of the balcony and swing up to one of the cross-girders. Instantly he saw that the little man was taking a last desperate chance.

A few feet out from the rail a double chain hung down from a pulley near the roof. A heavy weight and hook was six feet beneath the pulley at the end of one of the chains.

Landford was going to grab the chain that reached to

the roof of the wind-tunnel beneath, go down it hand over hand, with the hook and weight tight against the pulley to hold the chain still.

Driscoll leaned on the railing, lifting the gun for a steady-sighted shot, cursed as Landford ducked behind one of the girders, hastily dropped as a slug shrieked past him to impact on the wall.

Then he saw the little man swing out from the girder, grab for the chain with his right hand and miss.

Landford shrieked as he began to fall, but before he had dropped more than a yard his wildly flailing right hand had struck the other chain, gripped it just above the weight.

Afterwards Driscoll thought that what happened then could only have taken a second. But at the time every tiny detail was an epoch in itself, the whole a ghastly charade played in slow motion.

He saw the chain start to move through the pulley. Landford's weight was dragging it down, faster and faster as the weighted end dropped toward the roof of the enclosed interior of the wind-tunnel forty feet below.

The noise of the chain was quite inaudible, lost in the heavy roar of enormous airscrews at the end of the tunnel. Yet even above that roar, Driscoll heard the thin high-pitched wail of Landford's scream as he hurtled down toward the roof of the tunnel.

He saw Landford let go of the chain but hit the roof at the same time as the pulley's weight tore on past him ripping a large hole in the roof, the roar suddenly louder and more menacing as air was sucked into the tunnel. Landford was immediately sucked through the gaping hole, his body accelerating as it fell into the six hundred mile an hour wind that ripped through the tunnel.

The horrified engineers, watching the test model in the tunnel, saw Landford's body flash past them in a blur of flailing arms and legs, heard it detonate against the far wall as the colossal wind propelled it like a shell from a gun.

One of them jerked back the lever and cut power from the turning airscrews. The roar died down to a whisper and a soft whirring as the airscrews slowed down.

Driscoll leaned on the railing. He looked down at the hole Landford's body and the pulley weight had torn in the roof of the tunnel. Even over the roar of the airscrews he had heard the explosive impact of the body against the far wall.

He heard the clatter of feet along the gangway, looked up and saw Davidson coming toward him. He turned away feeling queasy, needed some breakfast.

31

'When,' Driscoll said. He raised the glass into which Davidson had been splashing soda, took a deep and satisfying swallow. Then he lit a cigarette, grinned across the room at Davidson and the two other men who had come with him.

It was half an hour after Landford's death, and they were sitting comfortably in the directors' room while Fellows and a working party searched through the fighter.

Driscoll went on, 'You really cut it fine. I wasn't too worried while I thought Landford was on his own. But when I heard the other boy I was saying some very choice things about you.'

Davidson smiled. 'I tried to make it exactly four-twenty when we got into the hangar. But we had to move very carefully. As a matter of fact we heard most of your talk with Landford. But we didn't see the other chap approaching until it was too late to do anything but turn off the lights and hope you'd get by.'

'I'm glad you heard my talk with Landford. Saves me telling it all again.'

'But not,' Davidson murmured, 'making a full report in writing. Still, that can wait. So it was Clifton gave you the proof?'

'It was.' Driscoll finished his drink, set the glass down. 'Poor old Mike. He was very clever. He actually told me where to find it in front of Landford. Mentioned how little he was paid, said that if he were to die there'd only be a small amount of money. He stressed that — a very small amount. An' he followed right on by mentioning a place he and I used a lot in the old days. A place Landford wouldn't know anything about. When I saw that Clifton was dead, it suddenly clicked into place. I saw he'd been tipping me what to do if he was knocked off. Obviously he knew quite well that there was a very good chance of that. See how he did it?'

'No,' Davidson said.

'The very small amount of money. Think of a very small amount of money an' then think of one of Williamson's aliases. Got it?'

Davidson paused, 'Penny. Neat.'

'Yeah, Clifton was that good. Of course, as soon as I picked up the photographs I saw where it all fitted in. That gave me the proof I needed. But even without them I'd have played a hunch about Landford, come down here an' bust in on him.'

'I think you would, Johnny,' Davidson said. 'I seem to remember reminding you how you've always endeared yourself to those in high places by playing hunches and busting in on people.'

Driscoll grinned. 'But I play the right hunches. Like the one about Marian. I had to gamble on that. When I found I couldn't contact you I knew I'd have to use her to get a message to you. I couldn't risk coming myself. In addition to the alarm that was out for me there was always the chance that I wouldn't find you. Then I'd have been too late to stop the fighter getting airborne this morning.'

'I still don't quite see why you played it the way you did.' Davidson said. 'Booking a berth to Brussels for example. What about that?'

'That was before I saw the photographs. At that time I had no *proof* Landford was Nicholas, however much I suspected it. So the way I played it gave me the biggest possible chance of catching Landford red-handed. Remember, things didn't look too good at the time. The money I'd taken and the receipt I'd given were evidence. They could have made things pretty hot for me.'

'All right, go on.' Davidson said.

'I saw it this way. If I couldn't prove my case without it, then I *had* to get Landford with the aircraft, prove he had interfered with it. But there was a snag. There was an alarm out for me. I might be picked up any time by his lot. An' I knew I wouldn't live too long if I was. So I had to try an' convince them I was scared and skipping out. I knew they'd trace that call for a berth back to me, an' by that time I figured I'd be out of London and up here. The train didn't leave until half-past one in the morning. That meant I was covered until then. They'd figure I was hiding out. When I didn't show at the train they'd start to worry. But even then they might think I was still trying to get out, but had been scared off by spotting them watching for me. Whichever way, it gave me time. As it happened I didn't need it, but I had no way of telling it then.'

'But what about Marian. Why did you go out of your way to make her suspicious of you?' Davidson asked. 'By that time you had the proof.'

'Yes, but look at it this way. I knew that sooner or later Special Branch would be after me. An' I knew who'd have issued the instructions. Browne. How could I tell exactly who he'd send? Don't forget, Browne and Landford had years to get their own boys into this game. So I did what I could to protect Marian. I had to figure out a way to make her suspicious of me. That would protect her when they arrived. Otherwise, if they were people who were working in with Browne and Landford, they'd have knocked her off right away if they thought she was batting for me. I had to make it obvious that she wasn't. An' the easy way to do that was to make her suspect I was on the wrong side of the fence. She fell for it beautifully.'

'But she came out of it too.'

'I banked that she would,' Driscoll said. 'I figured that as soon as I left her flat the boys would chase me. So I wrote that note to you an' put it in her bag in my passport. In the passport because I thought if she saw that she'd realise at once I wasn't trying to skip. So then she'd read the note and know she had to get it to you, that she'd better move quickly before they came back. Without the passport to prove I wasn't trying to skip out of the country I don't think it would have worked. Incidentally, I posted the negatives of the photographs to you. You'll find them in your office in the mail. Landford had the prints.'

Davidson said patiently, 'But you still took a big chance. She might not have gone to the bag for hours, and then I wouldn't have been in time.'

'No?' Driscoll said softly. 'I knew she *would* go to the bag. She cared for me just a little. An' I'd let her down with a big bump. So what does she do as soon as she's alone? She sniffles. In her bedroom, they always do. What does she need when she sniffles? A handkerchief — and it's in her bag. Later on, she'd want fresh make-up to remove the traces. Again, in her bag. An' a woman like Marian doesn't sniffle in front of people. So I was pretty damn' sure she'd open the bag an' see the passport when she was alone an' there wasn't anyone there to see the note. Though she's probably not adult enough ever to admit that's what she did.' He stubbed his cigarette, smiled at Davidson.

'All right, Johnny. Another drink?' Davidson asked.

Just as he said it, Fellows came into the room. He was holding a small metal cylinder, about eight inches long and an inch across.

Fellows held it up. 'Pressure bomb,' he said briefly. 'Don't quite know how it works yet, but probably there's a plunger connected to the aneroid. When the aneroid registers a pressure about the same as the air pressure at the height we do our tests the plunger lets acid through to cause the explosion. We found it at the place where the radome joins the main fuselage. I don't know how much explosive is inside, but it wouldn't take much at that particular point to blow the nose off. Then the air would do the rest. A six hundred mile an hour wind does some pretty amazing things.'

'Just ask Landford.' Driscoll added drily.

Fellows turned to leave the room, muttered in annoyance, 'Damned man, can't use the tunnel until we've cleaned the mess up... it's a confounded nuisance.'

At the door Fellows turned again and looked directly at Driscoll. 'Thanks, Driscoll. We're going into production right away with the KB–12.' Then he disappeared quickly through the door.

Driscoll grinned. 'A single-minded gentleman. You know Landford worked things out very cleverly really. Did you have any ideas about Browne and him?'

'No,' Davidson shrugged, 'but I had a feeling something was wrong somewhere. Little leakages I could never trace. What I did have an idea about was you. I knew if I put you in among them something would break. All I had to do was sit tight and hope it was the right thing. You ready for the next part of the job?'

'Which is?'

Davidson smiled. He picked up his raincoat from the chair where he had left it, moved toward the door. 'Someone's got to clean up the mess, start work on the people Landford and Browne have planted on the inside. Like it?'

'It depends. How about that bonus?' Driscoll asked.

'How about that five hundred pounds?'

Driscoll grinned. 'My legitimate expenses… I had to buy a car an' dump it.'

'I've had it brought in,' Davidson murmured. 'It's waiting for you outside right now. As a matter of fact I've left someone in charge of it for you.'

'We'll still talk about that bonus, right?'

'Six o'clock tonight in my office. When we start work on the clearing up.' Davidson smiled sweetly, opened the door and went out.

Driscoll walked over to the window. He saw the small saloon outside the main entrance to the building. He stood there while Davidson came out of the entrance and crossed to the side of the car. He bent over, spoke to someone through the open window. Driscoll saw a head of hair that was a live, glowing red. Then Davidson walked away with a wave of his hand.

Driscoll grinned, stood a little back from the window, watched Marian's face tilt up toward it. He crossed the room to the table where the whisky stood. He lifted the bottle, took out the cork, suddenly changed his mind and replaced it. He put the bottle back on the table.

He started to walk to the door, turned back half way, went back to the table. He picked the bottle up, tucked it into the pocket of his raincoat. Then he walked quickly down the stairs, out of the main entrance and across the paving to the car. It was fully light now, and a fine summer morning.

He swung back the driver's door, slid in behind the wheel.

'Johnny, I'm so glad. Really I am.'

He looked at her, saw the smoke-blue eyes were wide and soft. 'I want the answer to one question, Marian. The honest answer.'

'Yes?'

'What did you want when you went to the bag? Handkerchief or lipstick?'

'Handkerchief. Why — how did you know?'

Driscoll grinned. 'That's all right. You've grown up. Now you're even better than Patti.' He leaned across, kissed her gently. 'Back to town?'

Marian said, 'Yes, darling.'

She snuggled back in her seat, watching him as he turned the car to exit through the main entrance of the airfield works.

He headed along rural roads into the early sun before joining the main road going to London, the sun swinging round behind them.

The road was quiet. He drove fast, pushing the little car as much as he could.

After ten minutes or so Marian spoke, 'Johnny?'

'Yes?'

'What was that Chinese proverb again? The English version?'

Driscoll smiled, glanced at her, *'Don't take your shoes off before you come to the river*. Why?'

'Oh, I just wondered.' She leaned back in her seat, suddenly lifted her legs and put two small stockinged feet on the dashboard.

Driscoll eased into neutral, pulled the car over to a stop. He turned to her, 'But no river. There must be a river.'

'Yes,' Marian said. 'My flat looks out on the river. Would that do?'

Driscoll pursed his lips, nodded slowly. 'It might. We could always try.'

'Why not?' Marian murmured.

She watched him start up again, saw him press his foot hard to the floorboard. She snuggled up close to him. She thought she really must thank Davidson for telling her what to say when Driscoll asked her what she'd gone to her bag for. Very soon she was asleep, her head rocking against his left arm.

Driscoll looked down at the fiery mass of her hair, slipped his left arm round her shoulders. He thought she was quite a girl. He grinned as he decided that Davidson had certainly warned her what to say if he asked her why she went to her bag. He looked down again at the rounded slimness of her legs, the small perfectly shaped feet. He thought it didn't matter at all.

He came over the top of a low rise, saw the main road stretching straight and empty before him, bright with morning sunlight from behind them. He pressed his foot hard down on the accelerator, driving as fast as the car would go to London, and Marian's flat.

For the first time in many years he had a bottle of whisky with him and forgot all about it.

Dr Strangelove Or: How I Learned To Stop Worrying And Love The Bomb
Peter George

It is the height of the Cold War and the two power-blocs stand on the brink of war. On a routine patrol, US bombers receive a coded message. Doomsday has arrived; the fight for democracy, freedom and bodily fluids has just gone nuclear…

Peter George's novelisation of Stanley Kubrick's classic film, *Dr Strangelove* is a hilarious and provocative satire of the madness of Mutually Assured Destruction. Featuring impotent generals, a sieg-heiling scientist and one very Big Board — this is how the world ends, not with a whimper, but enough megatonnage to make you abandon monogamy.

Having written the novel *Red Alert — Two Hours to Doom*, that the film Dr Strangelove was so precisely based on, Peter George then worked extensively on the development of the film's screenplay with Stanley Kubrick. Together they finessed the script into the blackest of comedies ever to hit a cinema screen.

Peter George's *Dr Strangelove* novel has now been republished in a newly updated edition with an introduction by the writer's son, David George.

Also included in this edition is the first ever publication of the 7000 word vignette: *Character of Strangelove*, written by Peter George during the time he was working on the screenplay. He describes the comical back-story of an earlier version of the film's Dr Strangelove and his rise to the peaks of political and strategic influence at the heart of the US Government.

The publication of this piece for the very first time has caused great interest among Dr Strangelove academics, experts and aficionados. Read it and find out why.

Character of Strangelove is available only in this edition of *Dr Strangelove Or: How I Learned To Stop Worrying And Love The Bomb* published by Candy Jar Books.

ISBN: 978-0-9931191-4-9

Come Blonde, Came Murder
Peter George

Pacific City is beautiful. All the travel folders say so, and they should know. We have the swellest climate, beaches, movie studios and nightspots. The brochures tell you all about them, as they do about our transportation system, resident celebrities, moonlight, mimosa and eucalyptus trees. We have everything and of one quality only: The best.

We have other things. A City Administration that rides in custom-bodied Cadillacs. A Police Department that likes easy answers. And assorted gangsters, hoods, whores, junkies and blackmailers. We have modern, streamlined, commercialised sin, of one quality only: The best.

For information on the things beneath the surface of the travel folders you come to people like me. Steve Bryant. Private Investigator. I'll be glad to be of service — at fifty dollars per, plus expenses.

Mornings I may be in the apartment, or I may be in the office next door. But if you're a client, don't be formal. Crash right in and you'll be sure of a welcome. Naturally, you won't have come in time, but maybe it's never too soon.

Just one more little thing. Any morning except Monday. Since the Milroy case I'm allergic to Monday mornings. That one started on a Monday — a fine warm morning just like today...

© Copyright 1952 Peter George

First published 1952, T.V. Boardman, London.
Boardman Bloodhound No. 42

Hong Kong Kill
Peter George

She was tall for a Chinese. Slim, of course, with the lithe, greyhound slimness Chinese women have as their own. She is very beautiful, Brandon told himself. This woman I have come ten thousand miles to kill.

Tony Brandon, off to Hong Kong in connection with the Yellowknife Organization, had been told that a Chinese courier captured in Chicago had been induced to give the name of the head of that organisation.

Furthermore, the body of Brandon's fellow agent, Henry Lanham, had been discovered in a state which indicated he must have been persuaded to talk. How much had he said and what was the mysterious object Lanham had sent to London before his death?

Brandon's task was two-fold: get the head of Yellowknife, and patch up the hole left by Lanham's death. To achieve this end Brandon was joined in Hong Kong by CIA field agent Johnny Lundstrom. Together they would take on the deadly organisation.

This precarious mission was made more complicated and intriguing because the name whispered by the captured Chinese was *Lily Wang* — arrogant, beautiful, clever and very, very dangerous. Carrying out this job in the glamorous and colourful bustle of Hong Kong brings not only danger to life and limb but an unexpected emotional conflict to this experienced agent.

With Yellowknife on their backs and the 1956 Kowloon riots blocking their progress, Brandon and Lundstrom are in serious danger of not being in time — or too dead — to complete their deadly mission…

© Copyright 1958 Peter George

First published 1958, T.V. Boardman, London.
British Bloodhound No. 210

LETHBRIDGE STEWART: THE SHOWSTOPPERS
Jonathan Cooper: Indroduction by David George

"The Brigadier is such an integral part of Doctor Who mythos, it seems right and proper he now has his own series."
Doctor Who Magazine

There's a new TV show about to hit the airwaves, but Colonel Lethbridge-Stewart won't be tuning in. With the future of the Fifth Operational Corps in doubt he's got enough to worry about, but a plea from an old friend soon finds Lethbridge-Stewart and Anne Travers embroiled in a plot far more fantastical than anything on the small screen.

Can charismatic star Aubrey Mondegreene really be in two places at the same time? And is luckless journalist Harold Chorley really so desperate that he'll buy into a story about Nazi conspiracies from a tramp wearing a tin foil hat?

There's something very rotten at the heart of weekend television, and it isn't all due to shoddy scripts and bad special effects.

A series of novels from the classic era of Doctor Who, starring Colonel Lethbridge-Stewart and Anne Travers based on the characters and concepts created by Mervyn Haisman and Henry Lincoln.

ISBN: 978-0-9935192-1-5

Gangsters
Philip Martin

John Kline has served three years for manslaughter. Now, back on the streets of Birmingham, he is a hunted man. The man he killed was in the mob. And his brothers want revenge…

Philip Martin's Gangsters features the characters of the cult 70s BBC series Gangsters.
What Get Carter was for Newcastle,
The Long Good Friday for London,
Gangsters was for Birmingham.

Gritty and uncompromising, it won a devoted following for its depiction of a city seething with racial tension and gang violence.

Drugs, vice, corruption, human trafficking… to get clear, to get even, John Kline must unravel the operations of Birmingham's most dangerous criminals, in Philip Martin's Gangsters, an unrelenting journey through the underworld of a changing city.

"Critics called Gangsters amoral, but millions of viewers - black, Asian and white - adored it." The Telegraph

ISBN: 978-0-9954821-2-8

One Woman's War
Eileen Younghusband

"One Woman's War is living breathing history, resonant with warmth and personality." Jed Mercurio

Winston Churchill immortalised the fighter pilots who won the Battle of Britain as "The Few". But behind them was another group - even fewer and mostly women- whose work was too secret to acknowledge.

Eileen Younghusband worked in the Filter Room, calculating the targets of the Luftwaffe's bombing fleets from information supplied by Britain's pioneering Radar network. Barely out of her teens, she and her fellow Filterers were making life or death decisions. Eileen tells the little known story of the Filter Room and describes her own experience of World War Two… living through the Blitz… hunting V2 rocket launchers in Belgium… acting as a "guide" at a liberated concentration camp.

Against this background is a personal story of love and loss, and encounters with a cast of characters - from prostitutes to film starts- thrown together by war.

It reads like a novel. But every word is true.

"I found this book hard to put down and it constantly left me wondering what the next chapter would bring." AEROPLANE MAGAZINE

ISBN: 978-0-9571548-3-4